THRONE
OF
ANGUISH

THRONE

OF

ANGUISH

Bex Gil

This book is dedicated to Cynthia, Maya, Rahah, and all the girls out there whose skin ranges from white to brown to black. You are beautiful, and this book is to remind you that queens come in all shapes, sizes, and colors.

CONTENT WARNINGS

This book contains depictions of violence, rape, human trafficking, depression and suicide.

VENORE
HOUSE STALLIAN
PARDUS
TRIBA
HOUSE SOSONI
HOUSE ROH

N
NW
NE
W
E
SW
SE
S
HOUSE
WULFRIC
RACOUR
CANTON
MAHU
HOUSE
GALAPOS
BUSAHN

CHAPTER ONE

I *wasn't expecting to* get caught. Then again, who does? It was just like any other ordinary mission. Kill the guards, take the supplies and get out. Unfortunately, plans sometimes don't go... as planned. At first, everything had gone as it usually did. We had waited in the forest by the road, having been informed that a shipment of weapons was scheduled to pass, and we had cut down a large limb of an oak tree and dragged it across the trail. The wagon had come as expected with the five guards my scouts had already seen on recon. Our conveniently placed tree branch was blocking their path, and the guards riding next to the wagon dismounted and went to move it. I gave the signal, and we attacked.

I took out the driver with my crossbow and leapt down from the tree that had obscured me from the view of the road. My men handled the others as I raced to the back of the wagon and pulled back the flap.

That's when the plan fell apart.

Six more guards had their swords drawn and crossbows pointed before I could move away.

"It's a trap!" I yelled, knowing that my men would run as soon as the words left my mouth.

I, however, did not have the chance.

Before I could escape, three men on horseback charged out of the other side of the forest towards me. A soldier who had been hiding in the wagon leapt out and hit me with the pommel of his sword. It wasn't enough to knock me out, but my vision clouded as I fell on my knees. The next thing I knew, my face was in the dirt and my arms were pinned behind my back.

"Looks like we caught ourselves a rebel rat," said one of the guards.

I hissed through gritted teeth, "I'm astonished that you'd talk to a lady that way."

The guard who held my arms yanked me up. "Careful how you talk to the Legate, *rat*."

I spat the mud from my mouth. "Legate?"

The guard spun me around to face the Legate.

He looked just like I remembered, tanned skin, dark brown hair slicked back, muscled body rigid as a stone, and emotionless, caramel eyes looking down at me. I had been younger the last time we had met. I was twelve, and he was sixteen, already the perfect example of a disciplined soldier.

He was the son of the Commander, who was brother to the current ruler, a man who had killed my mother and so many others in his uprising. I glared and lifted my chin with as much dignity as one could with dirt smeared across their face. My black clothes were covered in dust and blood, and my dirty braid was falling out, strands of hair protruding like a ruffled rooster's feathers. But I would not grovel at the feet of my enemy. The Legate nodded and the soldiers released my now bound arms, causing an aching tension as my muscles adjusted to the uncomfortable position.

"Valine, I'm quite surprised that you weren't better prepared," he scoffed.

I made a show of looking around. "And yet, Sebastien, it seems that three of your men were killed and none of mine were captured."

Sebastien nodded. "You were the only one we wanted." He took a few steps forward and looked me up and down. "You know, I heard the rumors that you were alive, but I never believed them until now. I see that the rumor of you leading this band of miscreants is also true. You have been very busy."

My fingers worked at the bindings around my wrists. I just had to keep him distracted. "What can I say? Without a kingdom to run, I just have so much time on my hands."

He wiped the sweat from his forehead. "You won't have as much time on your hands to cause trouble from now on."

My hands finally slipped free, and I smiled at him. "I think you'll find the opposite to be true."

I swung my right arm towards his face while the other went for his stomach. The fist to his abdomen landed true, but quicker than I expected the Legate blocked my other punch and gripped my wrists. I stomped my foot onto his, but he didn't even flinch. Stupid steel toed boots.

I cursed and spat in his face. Two other guards appeared, each grabbing an arm and throwing me back against the side of the wagon.

Sebastien stepped back and wiped the saliva from his face. "It's a shame we met again this way."

I bit my cheek to keep from replying and getting myself into even more trouble.

He waved his hand. "Tie her up and throw her in. We leave for Pardus immediately." My face blanched. Pardus was the capital of Racour, and I hadn't been there since the coup, since my mother...

Sebastien ordered as he walked away, "Use chains this time."

I was about to yell something obscene when hands suddenly tied a gag around my mouth. I felt the manacles, hard and cold, snap around my wrists, and I started to panic. I kicked wildly, my feet hitting shins, causing curses to escape my captors lips. I told myself to calm down, but I couldn't help the fear that was welling up inside me. Something hit my head, the pain lasting only a moment before the world went black.

I woke with a start. The gag had disappeared from my mouth, and I slowly sat up. My arms were sore from the restraints, and my head was pounding from what I was sure was a concussion.

"Good morning."

My head whipped to the back of the wagon. Sebastien sat on a small box, long legs awkwardly crossed in the cramped space.

"Morning?" I asked, confused. It had been mid afternoon when the rebels had attacked and everything went so very, very wrong.

"Yes, morning. We had to knock you out. It seems that my men have some very sore shins from a certain noncompliant prisoner."

I shrugged. "Well I don't usually offer hugs and kisses to men who chain me up and kidnap me."

Sebastien narrowed his eyes.

I batted my lashes. "But I might make an exception for you."

He didn't find the quip amusing. "I have other reasons for being here."

I felt the seed of fear start to sprout, but I ripped out its roots. "What reasons are those?"

He leaned back against the canvas covered sides of the wagon. "My father sent me to quell the rebel forces, and my uncle sent me to hunt you down. It seems that I may have achieved both by capturing you."

I glared at him, wishing my eyes could kill. "I'm afraid that you are sadly mistaken if you think the rebels will stop just because I am gone. They were upset with Gabrys and Vukan's rule long before I showed up. I just helped them organize their hatred."

Sebastien's face didn't change. "That's a modest self assessment. The truth is that without you, the rebels will fall into chaos, and they will be easier for the crown to crush. However, there is another reason that my uncle wants you."

I couldn't squash the fear this time, dread crawling through my body like a hundred spiders. "Why?" Luckily, my voice didn't quaver.

His brow furrowed for a fraction of a second, as if he was annoyed, but it quickly smoothed as he shook his head. "I'm afraid you'll just have to find out."

It took me a minute to put it together. "You don't know the reason why he wants me, do you?"

Sebastien began to climb out. "He tells me what I need to know."

With that, he jumped out, leaving me alone. I wasn't sure if Sebastien not knowing why Vukan wanted me was good or bad. Knowing Vukan's character, it was more than likely bad. Very bad.

We traveled for two more days, and I realized that at the pace we were setting that at some point the Legate and his men had to have obtained horses—our speed too quick for walking. This whole prisoner process was infuriating, but what was worse was what lay ahead. I didn't know what to expect when I arrived at Pardus. All I knew was that minute by minute I was coming closer to an unknown future, and that scared me more than I wanted to admit. Anxiety had a way of creating an infinite number of increasingly horrible scenarios.

Would I be tortured? Would I be killed? Would I be sold off as a slave to a far away land? Would I be paraded around the court, the object of ridicule and humiliation? Despite the severity of the situation, I couldn't help but laugh at myself. How was humiliation worse than slavery?

The only thing I could do was plan. I had already tried to escape once when I had gone to urinate in the woods, but the manacles around my wrists had made it pretty hard to run quietly and quickly. I was captured once again, and this time they had put chains on my ankles too, which made any prospect of escape during our travels near impossible. So I sat there thinking, because that's all one really can do when chained both hand and foot, without weapons, and completely and utterly alone.

As I sat looking at the floorboards, my thoughts were interrupted by the wagon flap opening.

I didn't bother looking up. "Go away Sebastien. I'm not in the mood for a conversation."

I was surprised when I saw boots come into view. Sebastien never stood in here. Aside from our first conversation, he always waited outside, holding back the flap of the canvas.

I finally looked up into the face of one of the ugliest men I had ever seen, not that his facial features weren't handsome, as he had a chiseled face, high cheekbones, a strong jaw, and curly, light brown hair. He had the face that made girls swoon. He was gorgeous in every sense of the word, except for one thing. His eyes were dark, blue pits. There was no kindness in them—the cruel coldness in them terrifying.

The man stooped into a crouch, which was unnecessary since he was short enough that his head didn't touch the ceiling. Maybe he was just making room for his ego.

He cocked his head and smiled. "I'm glad you didn't get away earlier."

I said nothing.

His hand brushed my thigh. "It would be such a shame to miss out on such a..." He paused as his eyes roamed. "Beautiful opportunity."

I pushed myself against the wooden side of the wagon, but it only put me a few inches away from him. Ugly Eyes grabbed my chained wrists with one hand and withdrew his knife with the other.

He placed the blade against my throat and straddled my legs. "Don't make a single sound."

I glared at him. "You can't kill me. Vukan wants me alive."

Ugly Eyes moved the knife to my arm. "But he didn't say you had to be uninjured."

I spat in his pretty face.

He cursed and wiped it away with the hand holding my manacles.

His mistake.

I head butted him, which with the earlier hits to my head probably wasn't the best move, and reached both hands towards his knife. I twisted his wrist until he dropped the weapon. He cursed again and punched me in the stomach with his free hand. All the air in my lungs whooshed out, and before I could recover, Ugly Eyes grabbed a fistful of my hair and slammed my head against the side of the wagon.

Why was it always the head?

Spots blurred my vision. I brought up my legs and tried to kick him, but the cramped space made it hard to gain momentum. I was laying on my side now, Ugly Eyes having recovered more quickly than I. He grabbed me by the shoulders and flipped me onto my back, pinning my arms and straddling my torso.

"I'm going to make you pay for that you bi—" He stopped mid sentence when the wagon flap ripped open to reveal the Legate.

I hadn't realized it, but sometime during the scuffle the wagon had stopped.

Sebastien stood outside, a vein bulging from his neck. "What do you think you are doing Hagan?"

Ugly Eyes, or Hagan, as he was apparently called, shrugged nonchalantly. "Just questioning the prisoner."

Sebastien growled, "Get your ass out of this wagon, soldier."

Hagan slid off of me, glaring in my direction as he got out of the wagon. I slowly sat up, my head and heart pounding in tandem.

I stared daggers at Sebastien. "Is this how you encourage your men to treat women?"

Sebastien frowned. "No, it is not. I apologize Valine, Hagan has... issues."

I rolled my eyes. "An issue is waking up late or bad body odor. Rape isn't an issue. It's a crime," I spat.

Sebastien didn't meet my gaze. "He will be taken care of accordingly. Are you okay?"

I was far from it, but I would never admit that to him. "Why would you care? You probably were the one who sent him in here."

"I would never endorse such actions. Even if you are a wanted criminal, you are my prisoner, and there are rules, codes of conduct that should be followed. I will make sure that while you are under my care you shall be treated decently."

I wanted to say some snarky quip, but my head hurt too much to think of one.

"Now if you'll excuse me." He turned to go.

"Wait!" I shouted.

He look back. "What is it?"

I tried my best to shake off the pain. "How long until we arrive?"

His face remained stoic. "Now."

He pulled back the flap so that I could look, and I crawled forward. Our retinue had stopped just outside the main entrance to Pardus.

"Welcome home."

CHAPTER TWO

The city was just as huge and busy as I remembered. Pardus was originally a mountain fortress built by the first High Queen Constella Valoria Polaris, my ancestor. She had traveled with a group of immigrants after their own nation was ravaged by war. The country of their origin was never recounted in historical documents, although some scholars guessed it was from another continent across the Noran Sea.

While still new to the land, a strange disease spread quickly through the newly established villages. During this period, Constella's husband and leader of their people, died. In his place and despite her grief, she took over and helped her people overcome their sickness with the help of the native people—the Ebocians—who were well established with great knowledge of medicine. In return for their aid, Constella vowed to never step foot in Eboc with hostile purposes. She only asked that the Ebocians allow them to keep the land they already settled on. The Ebocians were overly generous, giving the new people a third of their land—from the east coast to a western mountain range that would serve as a border. The two peoples remained close allies and shared knowledge and goods.

However, throughout her time as leader, Constella found that the burden of ruling was quite tiring, so she had a young man whom she trusted, Balastor Wulfric, become the first king under her. The delegation of authority to the five kings seemed a wise choice at the time, but Constella never would have guessed that her system would cause the death of her descendant.

After the creation of the five kings' region, High Queen Constella established the castle that she and her offspring would rule from. It was on the border of two other kingdoms, Eboc and Manchur, but the ever snowy mountains created a protective barrier that was impenetrable. The only way to get to Pardus from other nations was to go around them.

The mountains surrounding the capital city were also the home of ice leopards, huge grey cats that would make a common hound look miniscule in comparison. At some point, the High Queen came into contact with them. The story depicted that the leader of the leopards was so impressed with Constella's integrity and prowess that she chose to stay with her, leaving her own species behind. Following that, each queen had bonded with a leopard since birth.

I wasn't really sure how it worked, but my mother had one. My mother's leopard died alongside her, but not before he had taken a chunk out of Vukan's arm. I hoped he had a scar, so that he wouldn't forget what he had done. Although I suppose that monster did not even know what guilt was.

Through the flap I could see the castle, my breathing quickening as we got closer. How would I face my mother's killers? Well, I supposed I'd face them with as much dignity as I could. Then, I'd kill them.

Unfortunately, my plans for revenge had to wait. There wasn't much I could do with shackled wrists. I hadn't felt this helpless since that moment in the wardrobe and loathed the all too familiar feeling. At least my ankles were unbound. Sebastien was kind enough, if you could call it that, to allow me to walk without rattling chains at my feet. I turned away from the wagon's open tarp and focused on my hands. I stared at the tendons on my knuckles, flexing and unflexing my hand. It always helped me calm down, but it was doing little to settle my nerves at the moment.

I looked up to the wagon's ceiling. *I know we don't talk much anymore, but if you could help me... not die, I'd be very grateful.*

A muffled sound came from behind me, and I whipped around to see the Legate.

Sebastien reached out and grabbed my chains. "There won't be any problems as long as you comply."

I smiled. "I think you'll find I can be quite cooperative when I choose."

The Legate didn't smile back as I climbed out, my feet landing on cobbled ground with a smack. I looked up to see the front of the palace.

It had been seven years since I called this place home, three since I had started gathering dissenters. It looked the same. Same white pillars supporting granite and stone arches. Same tall, narrow windows and stone ledges running the length of the walls. I was brought out of my daze when two guards came to take hold of my arms. I was tempted to kick, to scream, to fight, but I was a princess. I could not let them see me frightened. So, with head high and shoulders back, I walked through the oak doors of my old home and into the house of wolves.

Torches lit the halls we walked down, and I couldn't help but gape. My home had once been a place of beauty and elegance as the Queens appreciated strategic architecture as well as art. There used to be paintings of old battles and tapestries of many colors, but now only portraits of the Wulfrics and the occasional hanging weapon stared back. Small cracks had formed in the wall and cobwebs took up residence in the corners. It seemed that Vukan had been quite neglectful.

The hall echoed in silence as we walked, but my mind screamed, urging them to remember the atrocities that had occurred.

"I see that your father and Uncle have really done a lot with the place. Axes, swords, and pictures of yourselves—quite fitting for a den of narcissistic murderers."

Sebastien didn't react as I hoped he would. In fact, he completely ignored me.

I stuck out my tongue at him.

"I thought princesses were supposed to have manners," he scolded.

I mockingly repeated him, "*I thought princesses were supposed to have manners.*" I knew that it was childish, but I couldn't help myself, felt the need to lash out like a cornered animal.

He gave no reply in return.

I turned my head straight ahead, sparing the occasional glare at the Legate. Eventually we came to another set of tall oak doors.

"Here we go," I muttered to myself.

Two men standing guard opened the doors, and it took all of my self control to remain calm.

One of my favorite places as a child was the throne room. It had a high arching ceiling with seven pillars on each side, and the ceiling was painted with a beautiful mural of fantastical creatures and majestic landscapes. There used to be a throne—carved from a rare white oak—at the end of the hall. Its arms had resembled giant paws of an ice leopard and a hollow leopard's head comprised of silver emerged from the apex of the chair's back, its emerald eyes keeping vigilant watch over the queen, its snarling snout a warning to any who dared harm its mistress.

But that throne was gone, removed and replaced, the King having exchanged it for one of his own.

It wasn't even pretty.

Only a few feet away sat Gabrys and Vukan Wulfric. Although they were brothers, they looked almost nothing alike. Gabrys, the older of the two, was a stocky man with dark brown hair and facial hair. The skin around his brown eyes was wrinkled, as if he smiled too much as a younger man. Sebastien would never have to worry about such things.

Vukan was attractive for his age. He had jet black hair, a clean shaven face, and calculating chocolate brown eyes. He was narrow shouldered, and although he smiled, his eyes remained cold. The only similarities between the two were their eye color and the blood on their hands.

A guard gave me a prod between my shoulders. I continued walking forward until my chains were yanked to a stop at the bottom of the steps.

Sebastien gave a small bow. "Your Majesty, I have returned from my assignment. I have successfully captured the rebel leader and princess."

Unlike Sebastien, I didn't bow, wouldn't bow, for those who did not deserve my respect.

Vukan smiled wider. "Welcome, Princess Valine. It has been a long time since I have seen you. Womanhood suits you." Vukan gave an all too appreciative look at my body.

I gave him an equal assessment. "Indeed, it has been a long time. However, I must say, my throne doesn't suit you."

Surprisingly, Vukan laughed. "My dear Valine, so much like your mother."

I ground my teeth; he had no right to mention my mother.

His laughing ceased. "Oh darling, your poor wrists. Take those off immediately, nephew."

Sebastien hesitated, but proceeded to remove a key from his pocket and unlocked my shackles. I rubbed my wrists. They weren't in too bad of shape, only a little red where my sleeves didn't cover. Gabrys leaned over to whisper in Vukan's ear; it was then that I realized that Gabrys' throne was actually smaller and less adorned than his brother's.

Vukan's obstinate smile remained. "My darling, you must be tired from your long journey. Sebastien will escort you to your rooms. You may bathe and rest, and then you can join us for dinner."

I had to admit, a good bath sounded nice.

"Until then." Sebastien bowed again, and turned to leave the room.

I had no choice but to follow.

As we walked through the angular corridors, I let my eyes wander, taking it all in. It had been several years since I had stepped foot inside the castle, so my memory was a bit foggy. I had to memorize the layout to plan my escape.

One right turn. Straight past five doors. Turn left.

We ended up in a hallway that led to a dead end. There was no window on the wall, which was rather unfortunate. It would have been an easy way to escape.

The Legate cleared his throat, bringing my attention back to him. He was gesturing to the door on the left side. I brushed past him and entered the room, half expecting him to follow me inside.

However, the doors shut with a click. I turned the handle, but it was locked. Sebastien had left without a word.

I looked around and began to study my new living quarters. They were simple but elegant. There was a bedroom and a large sitting area with a fireplace, which were needed in every room in the cold, mountain winters. In front of the hearth was a small couch, table, and a chair, and a door led to a bathing room, natural hot springs allowing the water to be warm year round. I noticed there was only one window in the bathing room, too narrow to fit through. There was also a balcony, the doors to which were also locked. A pity. That was about it. There was no décor. The walls were a pale gray and the only reprieve from the bleak room was an indigo coverlet on the bed and a matching rug and couch by the fire. It was nothing like the rooms I had grown up in. I must have been placed in the guest's corridor.

"I suppose it's a step up from the caves," I said aloud to myself.

Indeed this gloomy room was better than the caves and forest floors that my rebels called home. I at least had a bed instead of a sleeping roll.

The door creaked open and my body tensed, my hands instinctively reaching for my daggers that were no longer there, confiscated by The Legate. I turned around, but it was only a maid. She was a meek looking thing, albeit a pretty girl with mousy brown hair and amber eyes. Her pale skin was dotted with freckles, and she wore a simple brown frock. At first glance she looked harmless, but I knew better than to underestimate anyone here.

The girl gave a small curtsy. "His Majesty has sent me to help you bathe and dress for dinner."

I was about to tell her to get out and tell the Wulfrics they could shove their commands up their ass but thought better of it. If I could get into the girl's confidence, it would be nice to have a set of eyes and ears in the palace. Servants tended to know just about everything that occurred.

I gave her a smile. "I suppose I could use a wash." As I walked into the bathing room I asked, "What's your name?"

The freckled girl padded in after me. "Zenith, My Lady."

I clenched my fists. The Wulfrics had either told her specifically not to address me as royalty, or had at best not informed her of who I was. It was an insult either way.

I began to undress, relaxing my hands as I untied my shirt. "That's a beautiful name. Where are you from?"

The maid went to the bath and started pumping water. "I'm from here, Milady. I grew up in Pardus. My mother is a lady's maid in a lower noblewoman's home."

I slid into the warm water. "And your father?"

Zenith looked at the floor. "He was a soldier."

Was.

"I am sorry for your loss," I offered quietly.

I was unsure how else to respond. I was never good at comforting people. Zenith just shrugged. She didn't seem all that affected by it.

After a period of silence, I asked another question, "If your mother is a lady's maid in a lesser house, then how did you come about working in the palace?"

She shifted uncomfortably. "After the uhh…" She paused to glance at me. "The entire staff was relieved of their duties. His Majesty saw me when my mother's mistress brought me along to the palace and gave me a position here. He… fancies me, I suppose." Zenith smiled sheepishly.

I raised a brow.

She frowned. "I know what you're thinking milady, but he truly cares for me. I'm not some silly girl."

"I didn't mean—"

Zenith pushed on, "I know exactly what you mean. Everyone scolds me for being a naive girl, but I'm not."

Well that went splendidly.

I nodded and began scrubbing my skin and hair. The water quickly dirtied, and it had to be emptied and refilled twice. I was happy to sit in the warm water forever, but all too soon Zenith and another girl returned with a dress in hand. I sighed and reluctantly left the tub. The other girl, who had blonde hair and hazel eyes, handed me a towel, and I quickly dried myself.

Although it was only early autumn, Pardus was already growing colder, and the bathroom tiles sent chills into my feet. I darted into the warm bedroom as soon as I was sufficiently dry. I let them dress me in an ivory gown, the dress clinging to my waist where it was met with an opal overlay and fell to the floor in a shimmering trail. The fur lined sleeves draped off my shoulders, leaving them bare, and the neckline plunged low. I was not fond of it, but there were no other options offered.

After I was clothed, they sat me down behind the armoire and began applying the cosmetics. I loved this part. I sat there while they applied rouge, kohl and face powder, the rabbit fur brushes and clothes tickling my face pleasantly. The blonde girl kept working on my face while Zenith did my hair. She oiled and dried my hair and piled half of it onto my head. She stuck pearl pins into it to keep it in place.

"All done My Lady."

I waved my hand. "Please, Zenith, call me Valine."

Might as well befriend the girl.

She curtsied, and I finally stood and looked into the mirror. "Oh my goodness! You two are amazing!"

The girls straightened, smiles widening and eyes looking brighter.

The compliment did what I intended, cracking open the door to their trust.

It wasn't completely ingenuine though. My face had been polished smooth, my eyes were made larger by eyeshadow and kohl, my lips were smothered in pale pink, and my hair was beautifully styled. My dress was another thing entirely. Since some loyal servants snuck me out of the palace years ago, I hadn't worn anything so extravagant.

I turned and smiled at my maids, hugging them both, and Zenith beamed, seeming to forget our awkward bathroom conversation.

I pulled back. "I'll make sure to sneak you guys some dessert from dinner tonight. You deserve it."

The two servant girls squealed with delight and ran out of the room, and I couldn't help but giggle too. I stopped myself. I couldn't let my guard down. Who knew, maybe they would try to kill me in my sleep.

It wouldn't have been the first time someone attempted such a thing.

Or perhaps Vukan was intending to fatten the pig before the slaughter.

CHAPTER THREE

Two guards waited for me outside my rooms, but that was to be expected. What I wasn't expecting was His Royal Highness, Lux Wulfric. He was striding down the hall towards me, a grin too similar to his father's on his face. He came to a stop before me. He was impeccably dressed in black robes with white crane patterns sewn throughout. The smile was where the resemblance with his father stopped; he was more lean, midnight hair and dark brown eyes on a handsome face, and he was noticeably darker skinned than his father. Everything about him was darker, and I wondered if his heart was too. He took my hand and leaned down to kiss it. His lips brushed my knuckles, and it took all my self control not to yank my hand away.

He stood up. "You look magnificent, Valine."

I made a show of looking him up and down. "I am still a princess, so you should address me as such."

Lux chuckled. "How cute. You think that you are still important."

I so badly wanted to punch him. Instead, I began walking towards the dining room, Lux and the entourage of guards following after.

I hated him, and I hated that he wouldn't shut up.

"How was your trip here?" he asked.

I kept walking. "Fine, for a prisoner."

He gave up asking me questions and began talking about all the changes that his father had made. New staff, new decorations, new laws. With all the talk about a larger military and grand parties, I grew more and more frustrated. He had no idea, or simply did not care to know, about how poor the state of Racour had become. Vukan had killed the four other kings, and I heard he'd hand picked puppets to inherit them. He had also wiped out all the nobles who were loyal to the High Queen, even down to the children.

He'd also outlawed religion, claiming himself to be a deity. Anyone who opposed him or whom he simply did not like were thrown into the mines to work as slaves or killed in public executions. He spent money in exorbitant amounts on parties and increasing military power. Right before I was captured, I had heard rumors that he was preparing to invade the other countries on the continent, and yet Lux had the audacity to talk about the newest wine Vukan had procured from the southern region.

We finally reached the dining room doors, and it couldn't have happened sooner. Two guards clad in red and gray opened the doors for us. It should have been purple instead of red.

The dining hall was a long, rectangular room with pillars and tapestries along the walls. The table was also the same shape as the room with the ruler's seat at the top and the richest and most important nobles seated closest and the lesser lords and wealthy merchants seated at the ends. I wasn't surprised that Vukan hadn't arrived, as he seemed the type to want to make a grand entrance.

However, I was surprised to see that Gabrys and Sebastien were already seated at the head of the table. Lux walked me to my seat, even pulling out my chair. He had seated me next to himself, and he took his place next to his father's. Across from me sat Sebastien, but he didn't look at me. Gabrys, on the other hand, didn't look away from me. In fact, his eyes had never left me since I entered the room.

He smiled, and it made his face look a little younger. "You look so much like Ariella. Such beautiful eyes, and your hair is her color."

These men were too comfortable mentioning my mother.

"I'm not like my mother." I paused to look all three of them in the eyes. "I am still alive."

The smile on Gabrys' face disappeared. "I am sorry about that. I never... I didn't—"

He was cut off by the creak of the doors. Vukan strode in, and everyone stood, except for Gabrys, who looked at his plate with sad eyes. Sebastien finally spared me a glance, raising his eyebrow at my refusal to stand as protocol dictated. Accompanying Vukan was a pretty redhead with a tight green dress that showed all her curves and a dipping neckline that hid little. Vukan's arm was slung around her waist as they walked all the way up to the remaining seat at the head of the table. I thought that Vukan would dismiss the woman, instead he sat down and pulled her onto his lap. She laughed as he kissed her neck for an uncomfortable amount of time.

Vukan finally pulled away and lifted his hands for everyone to quiet. "Ladies and Gentlemen, I am pleased to introduce a special guest," He paused to laugh. "I suppose she isn't so much of a guest as someone who has simply returned home."

He looked at me and gestured for me to stand. I didn't move until Sebastien's glare turned deadly, and I stood, returning his sharp gaze.

Vukan continued. "Welcome home, Valine Polaris, Princess of Racour."

After everyone applauded, I sat and hissed something unsuitable for a princess.

Sebastien turned to me and leaned across, feigning to reach for some pickled cabbage. "I did you a favor, Valine. You have pushed my uncle enough for one day by not bowing or addressing him correctly. Tread carefully, or you will quickly find where his patience ends."

I didn't say anything and just turned towards my plate. A lavish feast had been prepared, pork, potatoes, bread, soup, vegetables, and the like, but I was hesitant to eat.

Lux leaned to whisper, "Don't worry, Valine. Even if it's poisoned, I will make sure to resuscitate you. I'm very good at mouth to mouth."

He winked, and I kicked his leg under the table. "Ow."

I smiled, and reached for some stir-fried pork. I hadn't eaten something so delicious in such a long time.

Yet even that was ruined for me.

Vukan, who was a few cups into some rice wine, slurred, "Your mother was so beautiful, Valine." He paused as a disgusting belch erupted from his mouth. "It's a shame that she refused me. She would have made a wonderful arm piece after I became king. Hopefully you will only take after her looks and not her folly." He fondled his female companion as he spoke.

My hand creeped towards a knife that had been left carelessly too close to me. Before I could grab and use it to part Vukan's head from his body, Lux grabbed it. He sawed at the pork belly in front of him, taking a hefty portion and placing it on his plate.

"I am so generous, aren't I? To allow the princess to come home," he drawled. Careening forward and shoving the redhead off of his lap, Vukan pointed a jewel clad finger at me. "I will grant you the ability to go anywhere in the palace, so long as you behave like a good little girl." He licked his lips. "And if you do me a favor, I may even let you take trips into Pardus." He leaned back laughing, yanking the woman back onto his lap.

I glanced towards the knife, but it was still in Lux's hand.

I wouldn't have been able to reach Vukan's throat anyways. Sebastien would have interfered, or Lux would have blocked my path.

The rest of the dinner went agonizingly slow, but eventually Gabrys dismissed himself. He hadn't mentioned my mother again. Actually, he hadn't said anything else during the dinner. Shortly after he left, Vukan grabbed his company for the night and stumbled out the door. I was thankful he left. He and his mistress had progressively gotten more affectionate as the night went on, and it was making me sick. Why couldn't he just choke on his food?

With Vukan gone, it was as good a time as any to leave. I stood and swiftly exited the dining hall, guards rushing to keep up. Unfortunately, Lux followed me. He had drunk quite a lot during dinner, so I was surprised that he was able to keep his balance.

He slung his arm around me. "So Valine, it's been a while. I haven't seen you for ages. Perhaps we should..." He drew closer, whispering in my ear, "Catch up. Ya know, see what's changed."

His arm slid from my shoulder to my waist, but I thrust my elbow into his ribs, grabbed his arm that was around me, and flipped him over my shoulder. He landed on his back with a loud smack. I threw my body on top of his, pinning his arms with my knees and placing my elbow at his throat, applying pressure.

"If you ever touch me without my permission again, I will show you just how much I've changed." I stood up and smoothed my dress.

Lux glared at me. "You—"

A figure emerged from behind a statue.

The man paid no heed to the fallen prince, only sparing him a quick glance.

Sebastien had a semblance of a smile on his face. "Aren't you just making friends with everyone today?"

I rolled my eyes.

He frowned, the hint of amusement vanishing. "You better watch yourself. I'm not sure what my Uncle wants with you, but it won't be anything good if you insult him and his son every five minutes. Lux is a naive idiot who likes women and wine far too much, but Vukan isn't so vapid. He is something else entirely."

"Hey, I am right here." Lux stood and straightened his clothes. Sebastien grabbed my arm and pulled me away, leaving an annoyed Lux behind.

After a few more steps, I ripped my arm out of his grip.

"Careful Valine, you do not want to incur the wrath of the king," Sebastien warned.

My nostrils flared, and through gritted teeth I replied, "No Sebastien, it is *he* who should not incur *my* wrath, should not tempt *my* fury."

Sebastien scoffed, "You're not the one in power. You better get used to it, or you will find yourself wishing you had heeded my advice."

"They can't do anything else to me. They have killed my family and friends and taken my home," I hissed.

Sebastien's face returned to its stoic position. "You're wrong."

I shook my head and began walking faster towards my room. Sebastien followed.

I snapped, "What do I have left to lose? What could be worse than being a homeless orphan?"

Sebastien spoke softly, "A *dead*, homeless orphan. He can take all you hold dear and destroy it."

I laughed. "Oh Sebastien. How sweet. You assume that I haven't already died."

We had reached my rooms, and Sebastien looked at me incredulously. "You at least must have something that you care about."

He didn't seem to get it.

I pointed my finger at him. "Listen here, *Legate*," I sneered. "Everything I held dear, my mother, my father, my brother, my home, my friends, my *life*, was taken." I paused and shoved his chest. "By your father and uncle. Your family stole everything from me! I have worked tirelessly so that I could get my kingdom back and save my people from *your* family. So I'll insult Vukan and Lux and every person in this damned castle! And Vukan won't be able to destroy anything, because there is nothing left to destroy."

His only reaction was a tightening of his jaw, but even that quickly dissipated. If only I was able to control my emotions that well.

He began to speak, paused, then continued. "I actually came to tell you that the king requests your presence in the throne room tomorrow afternoon. We are receiving delegates from Eboc."

"What for?"

"To discuss their surrender."

"What?" The rumor was true.

"That's all I can say. See you tomorrow."

The door clicked shut behind me, and I slid down the door, my head in my hands. I had pretended that I had nothing left in front of Sebastien, but I knew that wasn't true. There was Yanish, my faithful follower, who was like a big brother to me. And his young daughter, Fron. There was Lilik and Mahlon, an old couple who treated everyone in camp like they were their children, and Lilik had doted on me, been there for me when I had my first bleeding. Then there was the young baking couple who owned a small shop in Pardus. Korine and Sidian had been expecting when I had arrived on their doorstep. They hid me in the cellar of their bakery, risking their lives and the life of their unborn child for me. Now their little girl, Sorin, was almost eight.

There were so many people Vukan could hurt, and he could never know of their existence. All those people were part of a dream, a dream for me to sit on the throne. A dream so fragile, so delicate, so easily broken. I had to be careful. He could never know that there was still more he could take from me. And what of Eboc? I couldn't let them be conquered. Who knew what Vukan had in mind? I doubted he would stop with the country of Eboc. But what could I possibly do in my current position? I finally let myself cry.

After I had cried out my fears and frustrations, I wiped my face.

I would not give up so easily. I would get close to those I could use. To Lux, to Sebastien, to servants, to soldiers. I'd get close with anyone and everyone, and before they'd realize it, I'd be on my throne.

CHAPTER FOUR

I woke up the next morning to the sound of someone vomiting. I tossed the covers over and walked to the bathroom, rubbing my swollen eyes. Zenith was retching into a bucket, skin looking pallid. I crouched down and rubbed her back. After she seemed done, I brought her a glass of water from my nightstand. She looked up at me with grateful eyes, and as sweat slipped down her forehead, she sipped at the water.

"Thank you, Milady," she whispered.

I picked her off the floor and laid her in my bed.

She began to protest, albeit feebly due to her apparent illness, "Oh no! I couldn't you're—"

I tucked her in. "Nonsense. You aren't feeling well. I'm about to leave, so you might as well make use of this bed. And don't worry about helping me get dressed, I spent the past several years readying myself."

Zenith didn't seem to have it in her to argue, and she quickly drifted off to sleep.

I was gonna be late if I didn't hurry. I ran to the wardrobe and grabbed the first dress I could find, a pale rose gown with a golden vest. I slipped it on and applied some kohl to my eyes, but didn't have time for the rest. An impatient knock at my door almost caused me to drop the ceramic holding the cosmetic. I ripped the door open and began walking, still trying to tie my vest at the same time. Sebastien looked at me, with what I guessed was amusement.

I glared. "It's harder than it looks."

"I don't doubt it. Here let me."

He batted my hands away and deftly tied the strings behind me. He finished just as we reached the grand hall. I thanked him, doing my best to look up at him with wide eyes full of gratitude.

Whenever I had tried with Yanish, he had always told me I looked like a drowned kitten but without any of the cuteness. I hoped Sebastien would find it endearing.

The Legate cleared his throat and looked away from me as we entered the hall full of courtiers and nobles who had gathered for the Ebocian delegation's arrival.

It would be the first time Eboc had sent a group of emissaries since Vukan had taken over, as well as the first time seeing me since the coup.

Many eyes and whispers followed me as I made my way to the base of the dais with the Legate. I stared ahead, not deigning to meet the curious eyes of the crowd. I glanced at the thrones. Gabrys hadn't bothered to show up, likely absent due to planning some military strategy with his soldiers. Vukan seemed rather disinterested in his dark gray robes that looked nearly black with a lavender sash and black boots.

Purple was the color of the Polaris queens.

It wasn't his to use.

I was distracted by a man rushing to the other side of the dais. Lux hadn't even bothered to tie his tunic all the way, and it annoyed me how good he looked, his long hair a mess and simple black garments askew. The Wulfric line was physically blessed. My admiration was interrupted by the announcer's call. A lanky man stood by the doors, calling out the names of the people now entering the room.

I did my best to pay attention despite the winks Lux kept sending my way. I rolled my eyes and finally focused as the ambassadors came forward.

The Ebocian's dignitary was a woman, beautiful with her dark ebony skin and deep hazel-brown eyes. She was of average height and all soft edges with a round face and full arms, but she looked like she could handle herself in a fight. Her black hair was woven into intricate braids which were intertwined with red and yellow ribbons. She walked forward with a lethal grace.

I watched the other nobles, gauging their reactions to her and her comrades. Some men openly ogled the woman, and I wanted to punch them. The woman was wearing a wrapped skirt and a loose, red, sleeveless shirt. The whispers from the men around me were lewd in nature. She paid no heed, exuding a fierce elegance with her walking stick that likely looked ordinary to most, but I knew it was a common weapon favored by the Ebocians. They'd honed their methods over centuries, and could snap bones with a single well placed hit. The dignitary and her entourage stopped before Vukan.

The woman's party bowed low, but she only bowed her head. I was immediately inclined to like her.

Vukan's eyes flashed in irritation, but he still smiled. "Welcome, my friends! Thank you, Princess Zasper, for gracing us with your presence. I am pleased that your Father has finally agreed to talk."

My attention was fixed.

Princess?

The Ebocian King sent his daughter to be the dignitary?

The Princess spoke with a thick accent, her speech slowed by the difficulty of the Racourian language, "I am here because my Father wishes for it. I don't want to be here long. We will talk quickly and soon."

Whispers started moving around the room. After a minute I began to pick up snippets.

"She hasn't addressed him properly."

"She is dressed like a savage."

"She can't even talk? How dare the Ebocians send such a simpleton as a delegate."

Some others that I heard were even worse. I wanted to shout at the impudent court, but it wouldn't help anything.

Vukan clapped his hands. "Well, there is plenty of time for discussion. You and your party must be tired. Please, allow my guards to show you to your rooms."

Vukan made a quick exit, I assumed all too eager to return to the redhead from the night before. The Princess began to leave, but she was quickly overrun with nobles, vying for a chance to talk to her.

I shoved my way through the crowd and stopped beside her, wrapping my arm around hers. "Excuse me, but I have been charged with seeing to her Highness' accommodations."

No one moved out of the way, and why would they? I was a captive—no longer the heir. They all kept trying to talk to the clearly annoyed Princess. Well if they wouldn't listen to my words, then I would express myself another way, one that they couldn't ignore. I shoved one courtier hard enough that she fell into two others, taking them down as she fell. Everyone finally shut their mouths.

"Thank you." I gave them my best smile. "Now if you would all get out of my way, it would be much appreciated."

The courtiers made the wise decision to move, many hurling insults under their breath as we walked past them. I was making a wonderful first impression.

After we finally made it to the hall, Zasper asked me, "You like it here? You do not look... what's the word... uncomfortable with Vukan and his family."

I met her stare, and tried to discern if she would be willing to help me. I had to tread carefully; just because I was willing to fight didn't mean she would be too.

"Please, Princess," I said, "do not mistake my calm demeanor with complacency. I am not content to watch someone else sit on my throne."

The corners of Zasper's mouth turned up. "Perhaps you and I could become good friends."

I smiled back. "I think we shall."

Zasper nodded. "I will see you later, *Chui.*"

I lifted my eyebrow at her farewell, but she walked away with the rest of her entourage before I could ask what it meant. I hoped that I would become friends with the Ebocian woman. She had a light in her eyes that I had yet to see in this place. I forced the hope that was sprouting in my heart down and disappeared into my rooms.

The next morning, I awoke to the smell of steaming eggs and sausage. Zenith was nowhere to be found, so I took the tray of food and sat on the couch. I spent the rest of my morning exploring my room, studying anything that could be an escape route or used as a weapon, but all too soon I became bored. I had just arrived, but since I was a "welcomed guest" as Vukan had put it, maybe I could wander until I found something to do. I threw on a pair of black pants that Zenith had scrounged up at my request along with a long cotton shirt and layered a thicker one on top.

Although I was born in the palace, some renovations and time made it hard to recognize where things were. My wandering took me to a doorway leading outside, and a cacophony of noises lured me to a courtyard.

Men sweated despite the morning chill, drilling in one corner and cleaning gear in another. I spotted a rack of weapons and walked over, unsure if anyone would stop me. Spears, bows, and swords stared back at me. I picked up a bow, since they did not have crossbows, and walked over to the target range. I drew an arrow, fingers running over the feathers like two long lost lovers meeting again. I used to be very skilled with one growing up. However, right before the coup occurred, crossbows had been introduced into Racour, and I became accustomed to the more common, newer weapon over the last several years.

I notched the arrow, pulled my arm back, and released it. The arrow found its mark in the chest of the dummy in front of me. I shot three more in rapid succession, hitting the dummy in the stomach and head, only one arrow missing by a small margin.

"Remind me never to get on your bad side."

I rolled my shoulders. I needed to stretch more. "I don't have a bad side. They're all equally amazing."

The wheezing laughter caused me to turn. A man, a guard by the looks of the wolf crest emblazoned on his tunic, with ochre eyes and dark hair stood behind me.

"I'd agree with that." He stuck out his hand. "I'm Sokah Jang."

I cocked a brow, but reached out and gripped his hand. "Nice to meet you."

He frowned. "Don't I get to know your name?"

I turned back towards the dummies. "Only my friends and my enemies get to know my name," I stated dryly.

"And which am I?" Sokah asked.

I launched another arrow, hitting a dummy a bit further away. "Which one?" I leaned towards him. "That, Sokah, depends entirely upon you." I walked away and placed the bow back on the rack.

Sokah followed me across the training pit. "Well, I definitely don't want to be on the other side of that arrow, so how about a friend?"

I shrugged. "We'll see."

Sokah smiled. It was a pleasant sight, his mouth slightly favoring his right. It was quite adorable.

"Hey! You!" A voice shouted from across the arena.

I turned towards the shouting. I knew who it was before I saw him, recognized his voice. "Great, here comes Ugly Eyes."

Sokah sputtered, "What?"

I jutted my chin towards the man stalking towards us. Sokah gawked, "You called Hagan Alberon, 'Ugly Eyes'?"

"I think it's a pretty tame name for someone so vile."

Sokah shook his head laughing. "You've got more balls than me."

I smirked. "Some call me stupid, some call me brave. I'm not dead yet, so maybe I'm a bit of both."

Hagan finally reached us. His face was red as he snarled, "You bitch! I got put on latrine duty for a month because of you."

I rolled my eyes while keeping my hands loose and my knees slightly bent in case he tried anything. "No, you got latrine duty because you couldn't keep it in your pants."

He narrowed his eyes. "I'll teach you to show some more respect to a man."

I looked to Sokah. "Do you see a man in front of me, Sokah? I don't." I pushed my finger against Hagan's chest. "All I see is an arrogant pig." I reached behind me and grabbed for the rod that had been on the armory wall. "Although that would be insulting to all the pigs of the world." I wrapped my fingers around the staff, my courage strengthened as I let the hard wood meld to my hand, and shoved Ugly Eyes back with my free hand. "And just so I can prove my point, grab a weapon and meet me in the sparring pit."

Hagan's eyes widened and appeared to bulge with rage. I wasn't sure his face was capable of reaching a darker shade of red. "I'll make you regret ever opening that mouth of yours," he threatened.

As I walked past him, Hagan whispered into my ear, "I'll make you beg for forgiveness on your knees before me, and while you're down there, you can do something else."

I shoved him and stomped into the arena. Rubbing my thumb along the wood, I felt confidence flow through me—it was smooth, strong, steadfast. It would not break easily, nor would I.

I walked into the circle of dirt that two men had previously been sparring in. I ripped a strip of cloth from my top and tied my hair back. Sokah cheered and gave me a thumbs up as I cracked my neck and rotated my shoulders. I focused on my breathing. In and out. I forced myself into a calm state. I could not use adrenaline, not yet. I put my left foot behind me and twisted the staff in my hand.

Hagan grabbed a short sword from the wall. So that's how it was gonna be? He stepped into the dirt ring. He spat at me, saliva just missing my feet. I looked down, and then looked back up, wearing a grin. Hagan shouted some insults too demeaning and childish to dwell on.

And so it began.

I decided to take it easy at first, let him tire himself out. Hagan was as stupid as he was arrogant. He'd picked a short sword, which meant I could easily whack him while keeping my distance with my long staff. He was physically stronger than me, so it would be better to keep some space between us. I would attack just enough to irritate him, enough to make him so mad he got clumsy.

Quintus was a retired regiment leader in the army, and thus he was in charge of the combat training for our ragtag group. He always emphasized the mind games. A battle started from the moment there was a challenge, and one should take advantage of every opportunity to manipulate the opponent. Infuriating one's enemy to the point that they became blind with rage was the easiest, particularly with men. Injure their pride. Insult their ability. Their tactics would grow imprecise and allow the chance to strike.

He charged and swung, attempting to hit my right side. I parried and whacked the back of his knee. He caught himself from collapsing but didn't manage to block the top of my staff as it slammed into his shoulder with enough force to leave a bruise. I took a couple steps back and waited for my opponent to gain his composure.

I guess I was wrong—Hagan's face could get redder.

We continued that way for a while, Sokah cheering me on the whole time. Sweat dripped down my back, but Hagan was already drenched with it, anger causing him to overexert himself. Jaw clenched and eyes filled with fury, he closed the distance between us, faking a swipe at my feet before thrusting at my stomach. I managed to jump and block the brunt of his hit, but hissed in pain as his sword cut my thigh.

I unleashed myself upon him, using my speed where my strength was lacking. As the next swipe came, I rolled, his blade missing by inches and slammed my staff into his face as I stood. He cursed me and thrusted his blade again. With ease hard won by years of practice, I parried with my staff and twisted, bringing the other end down on his wrist in full force.

Hagan dropped his weapon with a clank.

He clutched his right arm, yelling, "You broke my wrist. I am going to kill you! Someone—"

Some soldiers came to drag him away, likely to the infirmary. One of them chided, "Just shut up and accept your loss, Hagan."

I smirked and waved as he was pulled out of the courtyard, satisfaction sweeping over me at the sight of it.

Sokah watched with a giddy expression, along with a few other men who had joined his cheer team. Before I could thank them for their support, a frowning figure entered my peripheral vision.

Sebastien looked pissed. He glared at his men standing nearby, and they quickly found somewhere else to be. Sokah gave me another thumbs up as he walked away, and I smiled genuinely at him. I'd have to remember to tell him my name.

I ignored the Legate as I walked to set the rod back in its place.

Sebastien cleared his throat and spoke like a father scolding a child. "What was that?"

I looked at him innocently. "What was what?"

Sebastien's voice raised ever so slightly. "You shouldn't have done that. Hagan was being punished. You didn't need to hurt and humiliate him."

"Hurt? I barely touched him! And punishment? You call a month of poop duty punishment?" I shoved Sebastien's chest. "You want to scold me for humiliating a man who is literal scum? How about the women he has assaulted? I doubt I was the only one since you yourself even admitted he has "issues". What about them, Sebastien? He shouldn't just get latrine duty. He should get kicked out of the army and thrown in prison!" My heart was beating harder now than it had during the fight, a raging fire of indignation spreading over my body. "And if that's the kind of man you employ, the kind of man you allow to be in a position of power, then you are no better by allowing such intolerable actions to occur," I seethed.

The Legate slammed his fist against the wall, causing the whole structure to shake and the swords to rattle.

"You. Are. Not. Queen."

He stepped forward, forcing me backwards. "You are going to earn the wrath of the King and myself if you continue to be so stupid and arrogant."

I stopped retreating. "How dare you? As if the Wulfric family deserves the power they currently possess!" I stepped forward so that we were face to face. "I may not have a throne to sit on, but make no mistake, I will always be *queen*." I looked up into his eyes. "I will not be tamed, I will not be timid. Make no mistake, Sebastien, I will get my kingdom back."

Sebastien narrowed his eyes. "You may not have realized this Princess, but the people don't care that you aren't the one sitting on the throne. My Uncle is a fair enough ruler, and more importantly, he keeps order."

"Order? You mean his executions?" I scoffed.

Sebastien crossed his arms. "A necessary evil. Besides, no one truly innocent is killed."

"How about the poor suffering under the burden of Vukan's high taxes? How about the widows caused by his pointless war?"

Sebastien scratched his head. "Of course I empathize with them, but there is nothing I can do about it. And what makes you think your mother was so great? Racour became weak under her."

He was just asking to be punched in the face. "I have no delusions about my mother. She was indecisive, perhaps even negligent, but she was never cruel."

Sebastien opened his mouth to speak again, but I'd had enough. "If you say one more word, I will kill you now. Consequences be damned."

I shoved passed him and headed back to my room.

CHAPTER FIVE

The next morning, I decided it would be best not to return to the soldiers' courtyard. There was another place I was longing to visit. I knew that I should be attempting to gain more valuable information before escaping, but I couldn't help myself. I wasn't sure if the gardens were even there anymore, but as a child, I had loved to hide out among the flowers, trees and bushes and just read or play with Tagon, my mother's leopard. I got a little turned around on my way, and I made a mental note of the ways in which the castle layout had changed.

I happened upon some guards who were in the midst of a conversation.

"The war with Indo is costing too much coin and too many lives."

"You can't say such things in the castle. Do you want to end up like Zimmion? Poor fellow left behind a widow and three children just for speaking ill about Vukan's pension for women."

"Well even if we don't say it, we all think it."

"And on top of the war, the pirate problem is getting worse."

"Can't say I haven't been tempted to join em myself. The pirates seem better off than us."

"If it were up to me—"

Their words ended abruptly as I rounded the corner and came into view.

The oldest looking of them, with a graying beard and a ragged scar on his cheek addressed me first. "Princess Valine, how can we help you?"

"You know me?" I asked, puzzled.

His lips curled into a smile, causing the wrinkles on his face to smush together. "Of course. I was a soldier under your mother, The Creator grant her entry, and saw you a few times whenever I had a rotation in Pardus."

I was shocked by his blessing to my mother.

He continued. "Where are you headed, Your Highness?"

"The gardens. Although it seems I have lost my way." I laughed.

One of the other men, who had seen me beat Hagan the previous day, congratulated me and offered to escort me to the gardens.

I thanked him and took his arm.

His name was Falchor, and although he was on the older side, he'd recently become a father after he and his wife had tried for years. We talked the whole way, and it was rather endearing to hear him brag about his beautiful wife Ari, who could make delicious blackberry tarts and their little boy, Draque, who according to Falchor was going to become a genius.

When we got to the gardens I thanked him, and congratulated him on his son and wished him and his family well. He offered to stay and watch over me while I was in the garden, but I politely declined. Before he disappeared back into the castle, I shouted for him to bring me some of Ari's tarts one day. His bellowing laugh echoed as he promised he would bring me some. I smiled and yelled back that I'd hold him to that promise.

The gardens had changed since I had been there last. My mother had loved roses. There used to be rose bushes scattered chaotically in a variety of colors. Perhaps if she'd tended to her official affairs and less to her flowers, she would have made a better queen. Still, they had been famously beautiful, and foreign diplomats had always been jealous of them. But Vukan had ripped them all out. For hundreds of feet in each direction were shrubs and statues depicting various people and creatures. In the center of them all was a giant, opal blossom tree. At least that remained. I walked over to the familiar tree, brushing my hand against the bark and resting my forehead on it.

"Hello, old friend," I whispered.

The bark was dark gray, and the leaves were a creamy white like the moon. Legend had it that it was where Constella had been buried, and that her companion guarded her grave, refusing to leave, until she too faded away. Their bond had apparently fed the unique tree, the only one in existence that I knew of.

I smiled and took a step away. I twirled, my skirt swirling around me, and raised my face to the sky. Even though I didn't have my crown back yet, I was still home, and it felt great. I finally stopped from dizziness and collapsed onto the grass. I laid back and laughed at my situation. I was a prisoner in my home, a queen without a throne, but I wasn't hungry for once, and I wasn't concerned about where I was going to sleep. In that moment, I could just relax; for at least a breath, I was just a girl in a pretty dress.

I laid in the grass, gazing at the autumn trees blowing in the breeze.

Someone giggled. I closed my eyes, trying to ignore them, hoping whoever it was would go away. Instead, I felt feet brush against my skirts, and the grass rustled as they sat.

"What was so funny?"

I sat up to see Princess Zasper's smiling face.

I shrugged. "I'm not quite sure why I was laughing."

Zasper's eyes sparkled. "I think that those are the best kinds of laughs." Her Racourian had suddenly improved, albeit her accent remained.

I sat up and brushed the grass from my back, Zasper helping pick off some pieces.

"Why are you here?"

Zasper tossed her braid behind her shoulder. "I needed some fresh air."

I clicked my tongue. "I know you know what I was asking."

Zasper smiled. "I don't speak your language perfectly, so most people think I am not smart."

I shrugged. "Most of the nobles here only speak one language. You definitely aren't the stupid one."

"You're a very kind Princess. I will tell you my reasons."

I wasn't sure I could believe whatever words came out of her mouth, suspicion having set up camp in my mind, but I would at least listen.

Zasper crossed her legs. "I am here because I had heard there was a good leader in Racour once more."

I was flabbergasted. "Certainly you do not mean the Wulfrics."

She shook her head. "No, I do not." She stared at me.

"You mean me?"

She smiled. "Yes. My father has high hopes for you and sent me to confirm them."

I was amazed that word had traveled to Eboc so quickly. Then again, it was more than likely that word had been sent to Vukan ahead of my arrival. If that information had been relayed to the Ebocian court at that time, there would have been just enough time for Zasper to appear when she did.

"What is there to confirm? I have no throne, no power."

Zasper looked deep into my eyes. "I think you have more than you know. Anyways, at least you won't be like your mother. She was horrible at diplomacy." She looked at me almost pityingly now. "Your mother was not very good at ruling."

I flinched. "I think I have heard that more than I care to."

Zasper rested her hand on my shoulder. "You can still love her. Just because she made a bad queen doesn't mean she made a bad mother."

"She wasn't good at parenting either," I murmured.

Zasper patted my hand. "Even then, we often love people who do nothing to deserve it."

I fiddled with a piece of grass. "Many said she only had me out of duty. Our conversations were few and always full of awkward silences. If it hadn't been for Tagon, I think I would have been very lonely. After my father died, he was the only one to really keep me company."

Zasper gave a comforting look. "I am sure she felt overwhelmed with motherhood and running a kingdom."

I nodded in agreement. "That's why she always escaped to her roses or paintings. I think that she just never wanted any of it. A kingdom or children. I suppose that being born royalty doesn't necessarily come with the ability to rule."

Zasper picked a nearby rose. "Authority doesn't equal capability."

"Couldn't have said it better myself."

Zasper handed me the rose. "What happened to your father and brother? I had heard many rumors, but..."

I twirled the flower in my hand. "My father died a year or so after my brother was born. A carriage accident. And my brother from poison not long later. After the coup, I found out that both were orchestrated by Vukan. I am sure there had also been many attempts on my life that I was unaware of at the time."

Vukan had planned for a long time, strategically weakening my mother. In all honesty, she was already inept to begin with.

Zasper said nothing. I looked up, but unable to meet her gaze, I instead studied her hair. It was so beautiful, the way the hair intertwined with each other and the adorning accessories like an intricate dance.

Noticing my staring, she said, "I'll do your hair for you."

A smile cracked my somber expression. "I'd like that very much."

Zasper grinned back, and I stood and offered a hand to help her up. "I'm Valine by the way. Although I am sure you already knew that."

Zasper thought for a second, then replied, "I shall keep calling you *Chui*. In Eboc, we don't use the letter *v* often."

She grabbed my arm and I yanked her up. "I don't know that word. What does it mean?"

"One day you will know."

A week. A week of avoiding Sebastien after our encounter, although technically he was the one avoiding me, which also meant that I was stuck with Lux during dinners. That man could talk about himself for hours, bragging about his new horse, hound, or hawk. He once even gave a discourse on the history of rice wine. Every once in a while I feigned interest, but by the end of the week, I was blatantly rude to him. Albeit he was better than Gabrys' relentless stares. He only tried to talk to me once, to ask how I was liking being home. I snapped at him about how it would be much nicer if I had my throne and family back. He gave up after that. Vukan only showed up for dinner twice, apparently too busy with his nobles, King Dumas in particular staying in Pardus more than his own castle, and a harem of women.

Aside from the awkward dinners, I was finding ways to enjoy myself while planning my escape. I had asked many guards and servants about pertinent information that I could use against the Wulfrics, but they were all reluctant to share no matter how innocently I phrased the question. Zasper stopped by my room daily to braid mine and Zenith's hair in different styles while we talked. I learned quite a bit about both of them.

I already knew about Zenith's parents, but she told me more about growing up in a noble's household. She said that they treated her and her mother well, even after her father died. The lady of their house was an older woman whose husband owned a small, yet profitable sheep farm outside of Pardus under King Sosoni. Zenith spoke fondly of her time there, and explained that the noblewoman had purposely brought her to the palace in order to secure a more prestigious position. Poor thing was stuck with a prisoner princess.

I held my tongue while she gushed over the King. "On the day I first arrived as a chambermaid, His Majesty saw me cleaning some linens. He came over to talk to me and told me how I was so lovely."

I rolled my eyes.

Zenith lovingly sighed. "Ever since, he always tells me sweet things." She fumbled with a braid that Zasper had finished. "I know what all the others say. That I'm naive and foolish—that His Majesty couldn't possibly love me—but he does."

Zasper attempted to placate her. "I'm not saying that you're foolish, he may like you," She turned the girl so that they could face each other. "But he will never be able to marry you. He will never cherish you and you alone. You must be aware that he has many women."

Zenith shifted, placing her hands a top Zasper's. "But I could be his mistress!"

Zasper's eyes flicked to me.

I leaned forward and sighed. "Zenith, Vukan is a slimy womanizer. He wants you for only one thing. He is old enough to be your father."

Zenith's eyes widened. "You can't talk about His Majesty that way!"

I tossed my legs over the arm of my chair and popped a cube of cheese into my mouth. "I'll talk about him any way I please. The crown he wears was mine long before it was his."

Zenith turned her face towards the floor, but I could see her ears were red. Zasper looked at me, then her, and back again. I was of the mind that we couldn't force Zenith to do anything, and she would learn her lesson eventually. But Zasper seemed to think differently. Her eyes urged me to say more.

I stood and knelt next to Zenith. "I'm sorry. I'm sure he is very good to you—"

Her head snapped up. "He is!"

I put my hand on her shoulder. "But please also try to understand why I don't like him."

Zenith cocked her head. "I really don't actually. I mean, King Vukan may be... a little lavish, but the Wulfrics saved Racour from the High Queen."

My hand dropped. "What?"

Zenith scooted back. "Yeah... The king saved us from... from your mother."

I clenched my teeth. "Why would Racour need saving from my mother?"

Zenith's eyes darted between me and Zasper as she mumbled, "Your mother was a bad ruler, King Vukan is the savior of Racour. The old queen was wasteful and selfish. And the king, in all his benevolence, wanted to free the kingdom from her rule, and when he confronted her, she killed herself rather than answer for her crimes. And she had you sent away to kill you because she was afraid people would want to replace her. And that she had assassinated the other kings due to her greed for money. He... he showed great mercy by welcoming you back. The Polaris' were the reason for all of our suffering." Zenith bit her lip.

I could feel my skin heating up and my heart beating furiously.

"Who told you these things?" I hissed.

Zenith's voice trembled. "It was posted all over the city. The king sent couriers out into all the kingdom, so that we would know what really happened in The Great Coup. He wanted to dispel the lies that some of the people were saying. Lies about how *he* had killed the four kings and High Queen, and tried to kill you. Obviously that was all fabricated. Look at how generous he has been with you."

I slammed my fist on the table, the shuttering causing juice to spill and a pile of fruit to tumble. Zenith flinched. "The King is a monster!" I threw an apple at the window, glass shattering everywhere.

Zasper jerked out of her seat. "Valine! Calm down." I opened my mouth to shout back, but Zasper shoved me away from Zenith and towards the bed.

Had I not been so irate, I would have complimented her on the improved pronunciation of my name.

She brushed the maid's hair away from her face. "Ignore her. She is mad because not all that is true."

"More like none of it," I grumbled, which prompted Zasper to throw an apple at my back.

"Ouch!" I rubbed the back of my shoulder. Obviously the older Racourians would know what had truly occurred since a giant army sweeping across the nation wasn't exactly inconspicuous, but Vukan was trying to ruin the Polaris reputation while improving his own to those too young to remember.

Zasper wrapped an arm around Zenith. "It's true that the previous queen wasn't the best at ruling, but she was never cruel. She just wasn't properly groomed for the position. She never wanted her people to suffer, she just didn't know how to make decisions to help. She was very young, about your age. But she was also very timid, so the nobles did all of the ruling, many of whom were very selfish. They passed policies that only benefited themselves." She paused and looked at me.

I pushed off the wall and sat in front of Zenith, grabbing her hand and gently squeezing it. "I cannot speak for my mother, but I do know what I saw."

I pulled Zenith up and walked her over to the wardrobe, opening the doors and shoving some dresses aside. I patted the wooden bottom and motioned for her to sit, and she shuffled inside and pulled her knees to her chest.

I pointed towards the bed which was half obscured by the wardrobe's door. "I saw Vukan slit my mother's throat as I hid in a wardrobe just like this one. I saw him execute servants that helped me escape. And now I have seen him bring my kingdom to ruin."

Zenith's eyes were filled with tears, her voice soft and quiet. "I didn't know."

I sat on the floor in front of her. "No, you didn't. No one does. Because Vukan kills anyone who dares tell the truth. I am sure most of the citizens aren't foolish enough to believe such a poor attempt at rewriting history."

Zasper narrowed her eyes at the comment.

I ignored her. "I saw him hunt down those who protected me. But of course you don't know. You work in the castle, and before that in a kind noble's house. You have never gone hungry, have never seen the slums of the city.

You don't ask questions because you are content and as long as your life is fine, that's all that matters."

I felt the rage building inside of me, as the images of the horrors I had seen flashed in my mind.

"She's had enough," Zasper scolded.

"No, I've had enough."

I bolted up and stormed towards the door, but Zasper quickly blocked my path. "What are you going to do?"

She already knew what I was going to do.

"Move."

Zasper's brows furrowed, creating wrinkles in her twilight skin. "Don't be dumb."

I walked around her and out the door. "I thrive on my own stupidity."

Part of me wanted to go back to my room, apologize to Zenith for being so harsh, and return to eating food and braiding hair. But I ignored that part of me.

I wished I hadn't.

As I stalked out the door, the surprised guards jerked into attention, following me all the way to the king's quarters.

The pounding of my fist against the door could likely be heard throughout the entire castle. Good. I hoped every person in the bloodied palace could hear the sound, the sound of rage and retribution.

His face was red when the door swung open.

I invited myself in.

It was a room deep in the palace with no windows, less danger from would be assassins, but also one less escape route.

It was significantly larger and newer, having been constructed after Vukan became king. It was covered in portraits of nude women, and jars and bottles of alcohol littered the desk and bed tables. It was dark, and the stench of opium and wine clung to the air, the only light coming from the lanterns on the hearth and on the nightstands.

I noticed a woman, well she was barely that, a girl probably a few years younger than myself, lying on the King's bed.

Vukan slurred from where he stood near the entrance to his bathing room. "Those guards are good for nothing."

I glanced over my shoulder. "Oh, don't blame them Vukan. I told them that the Crown Prince was giving his prize horse to whoever beat him in an arm wrestle. Too bad your soldiers are as unintelligent as their king."

I looked back to the girl who was only covered by a thin silky dress, not looking very happy to be there. I tossed her a silk robe that had been draped over the foot of the bed, and she hastily slipped into it.

"What's your name?"

She didn't meet my eyes.

"A-Ariella."

My head whipped towards Vukan.

He came over to the bed and sat next to the girl and caressed her face. "Well, that's what I call her." Vukan stared at me as he kissed the girl's cheek.

Revulsion spread in my veins and a furious heat flared in the pit of my stomach. My eyes scanned the room, finally resting on a set of golden chalices—small jewels adorning the base of each cup. I swiped both of them, tucking one under my arm, and walked up to Vukan and the girl.

I pulled her away from him, to Vukan's dismay.

"What are you doing?" he asked drunkenly.

I led her towards the door. "Don't worry, these were a gift for my 1st birthday, so I can do what I want with my property." I handed the girl the twin chalices. "Sell these, and then leave the capital."

She finally looked up at me, her eyes shimmering with tears and gratitude. "Silba, my name is Silba. Thank you."

She flung her arms around me before slipping out the door with the jeweled cups. Her bare feet slapping against the stone floor echoed down the halls until it eventually disappeared.

I turned slowly, wondering why Vukan hadn't done anything to stop me. He had moved to a table and poured some alcohol into a small glass. His garments were untied, leaving his chest bare, and I was thankful that he at least had his pants on.

He swirled his drink. "Poor Ariella, such a quiet little thing."

I dug my nails into my palm. "Her name is Silba."

Vukan sipped his glass. "Oh, that whore? No, I was referring to your mother."

"You don't get to say her name," I growled.

He clicked his tongue. "That's where you're wrong my dear. I get to do whatever I want." Vukan reclined back and propped up his feet.

I crept up behind him. "Not whatever."

He held his breath as a sharp pressure appeared against his neck. A sliver of glass from my broken window had been easily hidden in the sleeve of my top.

"Heard you've been telling stories."

Vukan had the audacity to laugh. "I'm known for being quite good with my mouth, in more ways than one."

"You have lied to the people, selling yourself as some kind of hero," I snarled in his ear.

He turned his head, so that his lips brushed my cheek, the glass cutting his skin. He didn't seem to care. His breath was rank with alcohol. "Those with power paint the picture, those who survive get to dictate the story." Rotating his head forward, he licked his finger and slid it around the lid of his glass, creating a high pitched squeal.

I slowly leaned away. "I will ensure that history will not remember you kindly."

The guards' thundering footsteps and shouts rung in the corridor.

The distraction was enough opportunity for Vukan to rip the shard from my grip. He stood and flung the rest of his drink down his throat as guards appeared in the doorway, swords drawn.

Vukan laughed. "You didn't do anything special tonight. I still have all the power, and I'll just find some other girl to warm my bed."

He motioned to the guards, and they grabbed my arms. I said nothing as they dragged me to my room, internally seething. I scolded myself for barging in without a proper plan.

It was so stupid of me to confront Vukan like I had. He was right. I hadn't helped that girl, not really. She could just as easily be captured and killed, and I had nothing to barter with and no one to help me in this place. I would have to lay low for a while and figure out what to do.

I made it two weeks without making anyone mad, at least that I knew of. Vukan hadn't reprimanded me for the stunt I had pulled, which was a huge relief. Even if I had killed him that night, it wouldn't change anything. I would've immediately been executed for treason, and Gabrys or Lux would have taken over. I was both thankful and bored of the quiet. I wished something would happen, the next play in my dangerous game. I should have been more grateful for the lull.

CHAPTER SIX

My *door was ajar.* I never left it open and neither did Zenith. I crept slowly and quietly inside, noticing the lack of guards in the corridor. Something was wrong.

Why did it smell like metal?

An uncontrolled scream escaped my throat, harsh and animal like.

I fell to the floor and scooped the girl onto my lap. Zenith's body was already drained of color, a sickening pale white like baker's flour. Blood covered my arms and made my clothes stick to my body.

I brushed the hair away from her face as she looked up at me with wide eyes. She tried to speak, but I hushed her. "Shh... Don't try to talk."

I grabbed her hand. "Don't worry. I'm here. You don't have to be scared. You're going to be okay."

I wanted to cry, but couldn't, not wanting Zenith to see. She nodded, causing more blood to spill from her wounds. I fumbled one hand across her body, searching for the source. I had not been able to study the healing arts, but Quintus had taught us the basics about injuries and the best locations to strike on a human body.

I found a gash on her side between her third and fourth rib. Her lung was likely punctured, her wheezing and labored breathing a confirmation of my suspicions. My hand went down to her abdomen that was soaked in scarlet. Another wound was just above her navel.

The neck, the heart, the thigh.

Any of those would have been a quicker and more painless death. These were calculated for the most damage drawn out over an agonizingly long time.

At least she seemed to be in shock. I prayed that she wouldn't feel anything.

"I'm sorry..." she managed to whisper.

"You have nothing to be sorry for."

"I shouldn't have said those things about your mom. I should have never come—" Her words were cut short by her cough. Blood sputtered from her mouth. "Please... tell my mom... I love her."

I nodded, sniffling. "Of course."

She didn't say anything else. Her breathing became more shallow and slow.

I didn't realize it, but I started humming. It was a song I used to sing with my rebels whenever someone had a birthday—or died, as such events in life were linked. I hummed, and some of the fear left her face. I rocked her back and forth, doing my best to comfort her in her final moments.

With the amount of blood loss no healer could save her.

Whispers escaped her mouth. "You were... so kind. You would have been a good queen."

She struggled to breathe, and as the realization of the severity of her wounds, the reality of death knocking on the door. was comprehended, fear clouded her face.

"Please... I don't want to die..." Her eyes pleaded.

A drop of water landed on her chest. Someone was crying. *I* was crying. I tried to stop it. All I could do was hum and hold Zenith as her breathing weakened.

She tried to speak, but the words could not come out.

I softly kissed her forehead. When I pulled back, she didn't move.

I couldn't stop the tears now. I sobbed as I held her, muted screams trapped in my throat.

A snicker.

I looked up to see Vukan smile, who as he emerged from the bathing room, dropped the bloodied knife he had used to stab Zenith and leaned against the door. He had been watching me while I was too wrapped up in death to notice his presence. Behind him was someone else. Lux stood there with a look of boredom, although his skin looked ashen, and his eyes averted the gruesome scene.

Vukan turned to where I was looking. "I wanted him to do it, but he was too weak."

I said nothing.

He continued. "Come now, Valine. You can't be that surprised. Did you really think you could get away with all the blatant disrespect? I've treated you so well, but you did not appreciate it. I need you to know your place." Vukan stared at the blood on his hands with a sick fascination. His voice turned dark and deep. "I brought you here to stop you from causing trouble with that little rebel group of yours." He licked the blood from one of his fingers. "And to finally own a Polaris Queen, to have the dynastic line under my rule." He inhaled, eyes sparking with satisfaction. "And it truly feels wonderful to have accomplished it. To have the servant become the master and the master the servant."

Blood stained his lips, and my face reddened to match the color. A knot of tension formed in my chest like a volcano before exploding.

I laid her gently onto the ground.

I slowly stood up, blood dripping from my hands. Zenith's blood.

Her eyes stared up at me, void of life.

I stepped over her body and clambered over to where Vukan stood. Lux's look of boredom disappeared, switched to one of wariness and discomfort. He quickly bent and retrieved his father's knife from where it lay discarded at his feet. He brought it in front of him, eyes darting between me and his father. He was a fool if he thought that would save him. I no longer cared about being executed for treason.

"Valine." His voice shook. "Don't do anything else to anger the King. You've seen how he deals with that."

I stopped short.

Vukan reached out, perhaps to grab me, but Lux got me first, catching my wrist and yanking me close to his body. I jerked, trying to fight him, but he was stronger than I expected. I shuddered at his touch, the hairs on my neck standing upright. He put the weapon against my throat, and I squirmed, refusing to let the knife break my skin as he pulled me tight against him, his arm now around my waist.

From the corner of my vision, I saw Vukan move towards us. Lux's gaze darted to my mouth and then to his father who was approaching. He crushed his lips to mine.

My body tensed, and my muscles shocked into submission.

As bile rose in my throat and my mind screamed at my body to move, to do something, Vukan's laugh bellowed through the air.

"Please don't become a problem, Valine. You are too pretty to be killed," Vukan cackled.

Lux finally pulled back, the knife still firmly in his grip. I slid my hand up to Lux's chest and gripped his collar. I yanked him towards me and kissed him. Vukan laughed in delight and Lux dug his fingers into my back. After a few moments, I pushed him away. He looked shocked, only now noticing what I had taken while he was distracted.

The knife I held to his throat was still stained with blood.

I saw him swallow, look to his father for help and, realizing that he would offer none, Lux scrambled to get out of the situation. "Valine, if you kill me, you won't make it out of this room alive."

I put more pressure on his throat. "I wouldn't care if I did."

I applied more pressure, but something inside me whispered, *stop*. I had to bottle my anger. If I died, I wouldn't be able to help anyone. Silba, my friends, Zasper. They would likely all be killed too.

I whispered into his ear, "Know this, Lux Wulfric, I will kill you. I promise that you will not die a peaceful death. I swear on my throne that I will slit your throat with as little care as your father had when he killed an innocent girl. And then I'll kill your father. Wulfric blood will drench this place."

Lux looked offended. "How could you hate me so much?"

"You're a monster," I hissed.

Hurt flashed in his eyes but quickly dissipated, replaced by fire. "I am my father's son," Lux spat.

I backed away while he rubbed his neck and glared daggers at me. I turned to leave before I killed one of them and sealed my execution, but my departure wasn't quick enough, and Vukan wrapped his hand around my arm, the jarring motion causing the knife to slip from my grip. With his other hand, still stained crimson, he grabbed my chin.

He turned my face to his. "My dear, never disobey me again. Never *defy* me again. As much as I enjoy tormenting you, I am not against killing you. A horse that refuses to bend to the will of its rider is worthless." He glanced at his son. "And never threaten what's mine."

I didn't say anything, and Vukan snorted and let me go.

The last thing I heard as I walked out was Vukan's scolding. "You're pathetic, Lux, letting her get the best of you. If you ever let a woman get the best of you again, I'll let you die. You are such a disappointment. If only Sebastien were my..."

I ran through the halls until I could no longer hear their voices.

I had to be anywhere else, anywhere except the place where her body was. I stumbled into a random person's quarters and made my way to the bathing room. I vomited into the chamber pot until my stomach was empty.

When I was done retching, I crawled to the bathtub and pumped. Steaming water filled the tub, and I pulled myself into it, not bothering to remove my clothes. The water was quickly colored red. If I could have vomited anymore I would have.

"What are you doing here?"

I jerked my head towards the voice. Sebastien stood in the doorway, lips pursed and brows drawn. I didn't say anything, turning my head to gaze at the blank wall.

After a moment of silence, I heard him approach.

"Is that your blood?"

I didn't have the energy to reply. Sebastien kneeled beside the bath. He gently turned my chin towards him. I flinched, my face bruised from Vukan's rough grip.

"What happened, Valine?"

My eyes watered. I wouldn't let him see me cry. I had already cried in front of Lux and his father. But my eyes, they betrayed me and tears started to drip down my face.

I managed to whisper a reply, "Vukan. Lux. Zen..."

I couldn't say her name as the tears threatened to turn into sobs.

Sebastien frowned. "I'll be right back." He quickly stood and left, the door clicking shut behind him.

After a few minutes, I heard muffled voices arguing outside the door to the bathing room. I didn't want to hear it, so I dunked my head underwater until all the air had left my lungs. I emerged from the water and gasped for breath, the burning sensation in my chest signaling I was alive. Someone cleared their throat.

A portly woman, middle aged with graying hair and olive skin, stepped forward. "My name is Rosalva. I will help you bathe and dress."

Her voice was gentle, like a mother's.

I nodded, and Rosalva came forward and released the plug to empty the scarlet water.

She helped strip me of my wet clothes and draw a new bath. As it filled, she scrubbed the crusted blood from my hands. I wasn't sure how much time had passed when she pulled me from the tub. She helped me dry and change into some man's shirt that smelled like honey soap. I wondered but didn't care enough to ask who it belonged to. Rosalva carefully grabbed my arm and led me to the bed.

I stopped short. "I can't. This isn't my bed," I whispered with a hoarse voice.

Rosalva urged me into the already folded back sheets. "His Highness specifically instructed that you were to stay here for the night."

I didn't have the strength to resist as she lay me into the canopied bed.

As she was about to put the blankets on top of me, I shook my head. "No blankets. Too hot."

The room was probably quite cold, but she smiled and complied nonetheless.

"I will go tell His Highness that you are…" She paused and gazed at me with sympathetic eyes. "As well as can be expected."

I managed to muster a little strength and reached out to grasp her hand. "Thank you."

Rosalva gave a sad smile, squeezed my hand and left.

I looked around the room. It was the same layout as my own, except it was significantly larger. There was the wide bed on which I was laying, although this one had black sheets and an indigo coverlet with a white canopy, and there were sofas, chairs, tables, and a fireplace. On the hearth sat two dragon statues. One made from a green jade and the other some sort of cobalt stone.

Even from the bed, I could make out the individual scales and well sculpted talons that looked like they could tear through wood. They were eerily lifelike.

There were a few paintings on the walls, each beautiful and exquisitely made, but one caught my eye above the rest. It was the smallest painting, hanging next to the bed. It depicted a starry night with a flat landscape, and in the middle there stood a solitary tree. There appeared to be a man looking at the stars while a leopard lay at the foot of the tree.

It made me think of my own companion, and I wished that they were here with me. I hadn't met my companion before my mother died, but I remembered the bond between Tagon and myself, who seemed to love me more than my mother did. I was surprised that Sebastien would have such a decorated room. He seemed like a minimalistic man.

But I didn't have time to ponder it. As sleep beckoned me, offering a haven from the horrible reality, I made a mental note to thank Sebastien for his help.

Blood. *There was blood* everywhere, and it was choking me. I tried to call for help but the metallic liquid filled my mouth. Crimson was the only thing I could see. I was going to die.

I woke up panting, sweat dripping down my forehead. Footsteps padded towards me, but I couldn't see who it was in the pitch black room.

A grumbling voice spoke from the darkness, "Drink this."

I couldn't see very well, but a cup full of a warm liquid found its way into my hands. I didn't know who had given it to me, and it very well could have been poison. Either way I would drink it, and either way it would end my nightmare. Originally, I had wanted to sleep because it was the only place where my suffering did not follow me. But now even my dreams were no longer a sanctuary, ceasing to offer a reprieve. I gulped down the liquid. In the drug induced darkness there was peace. Rest. I was so tired of the pain.

"That's it. Good girl."

The voice sounded familiar. The liquid must have been a potent concoction because I was already drifting off.

"It's going to be okay," the voice spoke again.

I knew that voice, but I was already half asleep.

The last thing I heard before I fell asleep was, "I'm sorry, Little Bird."

I awoke in my own bed the next morning.

But I didn't get up that day. Or the next. Or the next. Days went by, all merging together. My nights were filled with ghosts of the past and monsters of my memories. A couple weeks went by, and I could only manage to sleep, eat, and bathe. The latter two were not of my own volition, as Rosalva forced me to consume something nutritional at least twice a day and threatened to throw water on me as I slept if I refused to get into the bath.

I received a message from Vukan, conveying his *condolences*. I ripped it up and threw them into the fire. Lux sent flowers, which I threw to the floor. Zasper came to my room often, but I had no desire to talk. She did her best to comfort me, but it was futile.

"I'm so tired of people telling me that I am brave, or good, or strong. I am none of those things. I am a failure. I've wanted to be extraordinary since I was a child, but I am not. I am nothing!" I yelled.

Zasper reached out, patting my back. "Those who are strong have often gone through terrible tragedies. The wise have made many mistakes. And those who laugh the most, often have been in the darkest places. Being happy when life pounds you with its fists is not the only sign of strength. Sometimes, those who simply get up each morning to live another day, are the most brave," Zasper encouraged.

Had I heard such words at another time, under different circumstances, perhaps I could have appreciated the sentiment. Of course, such words would never be said during happy situations. I didn't want to hear them. Life was hard. It was unfair. I didn't want it.

I demanded that she leave me alone.

And she did just that.

I fell back asleep, praying that I would be able to escape to a dreamless abyss.

I was never that lucky though.

Another nightmare. I clutched my chest and beat the sweat soaked pillows. I yanked my hair, and tears cascaded down my face. The pain I felt was so terrible. I clawed at my clothes. They were choking me. I couldn't breathe.

The pain was unbearable, but then it slowly faded away.

And I felt nothing.

Eventually, after days of numbness and nightmares, I got up. Zasper had urged me to do something, anything, having refused to give up on me. Rosalva and Zasper were relentless. So I dressed and headed for the sparring ring. I didn't grab any weapons, simply headed for the nearest dummy and started throwing punches.

"What did the poor guy do to deserve that?"

I kept throwing my arms. Left hook, right side, undercut.

Quintus and Yanish both made sure we all trained with both hands, in the unfortunate event that our dominant hand was incapacitated.

"I've said it once and I'll say it again, I never want to get on your bad side."

Throat, block, stomach, knee. Wood creaked and the post keened and snapped. The dummy fell to the floor, straw spilling from its insides.

Sokah kicked it with his foot. "I never liked this one anyways. Always looked at me funny."

I looked up at him. "What do you want, Sokah?'

Sokah looked concerned, sympathy soaking his features. He hugged me before I could move, and surprisingly, I was warmed by it, comforted. I melted into his embrace, my cheek resting on the course tunic of his uniform. As Sokah held me, I noticed a figure in the shadows. Lux looked on at us with a blank expression, but realizing that I had seen him, he quickly walked away. I wished I could pound him into the ground too.

Sokah pulled away, giving me one of his lopsided smiles. The corner of my mouth twitched up. He grabbed my hand and dragged me over to the wall of weapons. He opened his mouth to say something but was interrupted. I hadn't noticed The Legate emerge from behind the rack. He coughed, standing awkwardly, and Sokah squeezed my hand before dropping it and walking away. I wished he hadn't left.

Sebastien stepped closer, his expression looking uncharacteristically worried. He reached out a hand towards my face, but he quickly dropped it back to his side. "I am sorry Valine. It's unfortunate—" He sighed. "I'm sorry."

I was surprised by his attempt at comforting me, and despite my hesitance to believe his sincerity, I ever so slowly took the hand he had intended to offer me. It was calloused and rough, his fingernails cut down to the nail bed. I didn't say anything, but he seemed to understand my silent thanks.

"Well this is certainly a surprise, Cousin."

Sebastien took a step back, our hands disconnecting.

I turned and glared at Lux. "What are you doing here?"

Lux stepped forward and stared with fiery eyes at Sebastien. "I came to offer my condolences to Princess Valine, but apparently I interrupted some sort of intimate moment."

Sebastien stumbled over his words, the first I'd ever heard him do so. "I... uh... It wasn't anything. I was... just being polite."

My breath hitched for a moment. He had seemed so sincere. I had actually let myself forget for a moment that he was a Wulfric. A few kind words. That's all it had taken for him to soften my heart.

I clenched my fists at my side, my teeth grinding together. "Right, nothing special."

Lux leaned towards Sebastien and pretended to whisper, "But we kissed."

I felt my body heat up, and without thinking I grabbed an arrow from the quiver that was nearby and slashed at Lux's face. His eyes widened as he tried to evade my unexpected weapon.

I clipped his brow, and blood gushed out. A pity. I was aiming for the eye.

"Valine!"

Sebastien grabbed my wrist and wrenched the arrow from my grip.

"Don't you ever come near me again!" I seethed.

Lux touched the blood seeping from his wound, and when he pulled his hand away, he looked at the crimson coating his fingers and laughed. He actually laughed.

"I guess that's your way of saying I am a bad kisser."

The flaming rage boiled inside me and turned my vision red like the blood now pouring from the Crown Prince's forehead. I wanted to kill him, and if it weren't for Sebastien holding me back I probably would have.

"I suggest you leave, Cousin," Sebastien warned sternly.

Lux had one eye closed now to stop the blood from entering it. "Alas, it seems I must attend to some important matter. Tis a shame, as I was looking forward to spending more time with our lovely Princess."

Lux looked at me, his lips curling. "I would kiss your hand to say good-bye, but I don't want any more scars for today." Lux turned, hand plastered to his brow.

I couldn't stand another minute in this place.

Sebastien grabbed my arm. "Valine—"

I glared at him. "Leave me alone."

I ripped my arm from his grip and stormed away. I turned right instead of left, heading for the palace doors that would lead to the gates, to outside. If I stayed one more minute in the castle, I was likely to do something to get me killed. If I hadn't done so already.

I had to work on patience.

My lack of self control had been disastrous in the past. A couple years ago, during a raid on a small military outpost, I unintentionally caused the death of one of my comrades.

We had studied the shift rotations, how many soldiers were stationed, and how often they came and went. However forming plans was easier than sticking to them.

We snuck in during the early hours right before sunrise. The darkness was waning, which meant we had less cover, but it was also the time when the man on guard duty would be the most tired as well as when the commander of the outpost would be out on dawn patrol.

We entered from a hole we dug under the wood wall and made our way to where the supplies were stored. We grabbed valuable medicines and weapons, as much as the six of us could carry. As we snuck by the commanding officer's room, I noticed something that piqued my curiosity. I slipped inside and walked towards a large leather map that was strewn across the back wall. A red circle marked a location on the outskirts of the forest in Stallian territory. It was one of the camping spots we used in summer.

Panicked, I fumbled at the nails that were holding the map up, but they wouldn't budge. I tugged on the leather, pulling with all my strength. Finally, one side gave out, tearing away from the wall. There were still three more.

Callar, a hunter who was a few years older than me and had known Yanish from trading furs and meats, burst into the office. "Val, what are you doing? We have to go now! The commander will return any minute."

I didn't bother to look at him as I continued to yank at the map. Whoever made it was annoyingly skilled at their craft. "It has one of our camp locations on it. We can't leave it here."

Callar's voice was filled with urgency and tension. "If it's on the map it means they already know, just leave it. We have to go. *Now.*"

I hadn't thought of that. I left the map, one corner slumped over itself. We ran back out into the wooden makeshift hall and sprinted towards the exit.

As we came out of the building, I saw another rebel's feet disappear under the log wall. Callar and I checked to make sure that there were no soldiers around, and we darted to the hole. I crouched to crawl beneath when shouts rang out. My blood froze, and I turned my head.

Across the outpost, the gate opened to reveal the commander and eight other soldiers. We were easily spotted, and they charged at us, weapons drawn.

I looked up at Callar with wide eyes, fear gripping my body. If only my fast beating heart had wings; it could have flown us up and out of danger. If only magic still existed, then I could have blasted through the wall, and we could have made a quick escape.

His face was filled with sorrow, a solid resignation in his voice. "You better become queen after this, Val."

He kissed my head, and then his rough hands shoved me towards the ground. My face smashed into the dirt as my arms scrambled to pull me under the wall, my body working faster than my mind.

A pair of soil coated hands grabbed me and dragged me the rest of the way. The rebels asked no questions. As the yelling on the other side grew louder and Callar's absence obvious, they all knew what had occurred.

I wanted to protest, to insist that we wait for Callar, but the others shoved me forward silently. We sprinted towards the tree line, flinging past bushes and shoving the foliage from our faces. We stopped when we could no longer hear the commotion from the outpost.

We panted, keeled over with hands on our knees or resting against the tree trunks.

"It's all my fault. If I had stuck to the plan... If I hadn't tried to rip that damn map..."

Gavid, a tall and slender man with blond hair, a decade older than myself, stood upright, wiping the sweat from his brow. "You're right. It is your fault, Val. I hope you don't repeat your mistake." He stated it matter-of-factly. He would not lie in order to protect my feelings. With that he turned to leave, the others giving me a wide berth as they followed after our mission leader.

They all blamed me, and rightly so.

If I kept acting out, I would be executed before I could get my crown back. Then Callar's sacrifice would have been for nothing. I had to do better, for myself, for girls like Zenith and Silba, and for all who still dreamed of a better future.

I needed to get out and cool my head.

CHAPTER SEVEN

I was slightly insulted that only two guards had been sent to follow me. Once we reached the city, they were too easy to lose. I wove through people, shops, and streets; three minutes and I had lost them.

I climbed a roof just to make sure, gazing out over the crowd of nobles, merchants, and laborers. The nobles were easy to spot with their extravagant garments and large entourages of servants and guards. The workers were identifiable by their weathered skin, worn clothes, and weary faces. The more wealthy merchants were somewhere in between, believing themselves to be above their fellow commoners while ignorant that the nobles would never view them as equals. There on the far side of the avenue were my guards, hopelessly searching for me amongst the crowd. I smiled and climbed down.

As I let my feet touch the ground, I noticed a paper plastered to the wall. An inked sketch of a young woman with chubby cheeks and hair in a bun stared back at me with doe-like eyes. Beneath the image was written: *Hedelia Tark, Age 18, Missing.*

I had seen such posters around the whole country, steadily increasing in number over the past few years.

I was startled by a hand grabbing my shoulder. Assuming some other guards had somehow found me, or worse—a couple of vagrants who were looking to take advantage—I spun around, dagger in hand. Sebastien hadn't even noticed me take it and slip it up my sleeve. But it didn't look like I would need it.

The man wore a thick brown tunic with a gray sash wrapped around his waist. The fabric looked coarse and well worn. He had umber skin and the feet that poked from under his tunic and standing atop rope sandals were covered in calluses. He had wise looking eyes, as if he had seen many things, horrors and miracles alike, throughout his life.

The man laughed, dry and raspy. "You won't be needing that, girl. I doubt an old man like me could do much harm."

I shrugged. "I have learned never to underestimate anyone."

The man laughed again, a rather strange sound, like paper rubbed together or dry leaves being stepped on.

I smiled kindly, taking in his haggard and filthy appearance. "Sir, would you like something to eat? Something to drink perhaps?" According to the ways of The Creator that my father had instilled in me from childhood, one was encouraged to perform acts of service without expecting anything in return, and the old man looked like he had nothing to offer anyways.

He grinned. "That would be very nice."

I tucked an arm around his and led him into a nearby tavern. I sat him down at a table and went to the bar to order some congee and water. I brushed past obnoxious men and friendly barmaids and set the food and drink in front of the man. I sat across from him as he began to consume his meal. He grabbed the spoon and began to devour it, white goop dripping from the corner of his mouth and precariously close to seeping into his beard. I held out a piece of cloth to him, and he took it graciously and wiped his mouth. I smiled as he finally slowed and looked up at me.

"So Valine, how's life?"

My smile disappeared, and I carefully unsheathed the dagger that I had stolen.

The man chuckled. "Child, put that away. I'm an old man. What danger do I pose to you?"

I stared warily, eyes glancing around in case of an ambush. "How do you know my name?"

He took his finger to his teeth, digging for some unknown substance. After a second, he removed it and met my gaze.

"He told me."

I shifted the dagger from one palm to another and leaned closer. "Who told you?"

He leaned close enough that I could smell his breath. It smelled like some sort of herb.

"The Creator told me," he said with complete seriousness.

I sat back and laughed. I was sitting in front of a lunatic. I shook my head and rubbed my brow. The man grabbed my wrist. I jerked away, but he was strong for his age and held on.

"Look at me, child," he said, "I am not a fool. He sent me to you, to help you."

"I am sure He exists, but I've never heard of Him actually talking to someone before," I scoffed.

He explained, "The Creator has instructed me to teach you."

"Teach me what?"

The old man grinned, stood up, and limped out the door with his staff.

I had to follow him. Curiosity was another pesky trait of mine, like a fish easily caught on a line that dangled something tantalizing. I pushed past the people streaming into the tavern and came out onto the street. I looked around for a moment and saw a man with a staff and dreadlocks disappear around a corner. I walked swiftly, afraid to run and draw too much attention to myself. The crafty old man was hard to follow, but after a few minutes I was able to catch up to him. I slowed my breathing and my pace as I came up beside him.

I whispered as we walked, people brushing past us. "Teach me what?"

He didn't reply.

I sighed and continued to follow him. I had set out at a little before noon, but by the time we stopped walking the sun was well past the middle of the sky. Before I knew it, we were on the outskirts of town near the base of Sanguis Mountain. I had no idea what I was doing, and this was likely a waste of my precious time. I still had to contact some friends located in Pardus and get back to my band of rebels. Vukan would be furious knowing I'd left the confines of the castle and shook off my guards, and I certainly wouldn't have the chance to escape again.

There was an ancient, warped oak on the side of the path we traveled, and the man sat beneath it. He crossed his legs and closed his eyes.

"I have followed you all morning, sir, so will you please tell me what it is The Creator told you to teach me?" I forced myself to remain respectful in hopes of getting an answer.

He didn't say anything in reply. I mumbled to myself and sat down before him. I should have left, shouldn't have wasted my breath with him, but something deep inside drove me to stay.

I rested my head on my hand. "Will you at least tell me your name?"

He opened one eye. "Egann."

I was finally getting somewhere. "Why did The Creator instruct you to help me?"

He's never bothered to help me before.

Egann didn't open either eye this time. "Because He loves all his creations, and it is His will for you to be restored to your throne."

I was glad he couldn't see me when I rolled my eyes.

He frowned. "Don't scoff."

My cheeks heated as my face turned red. "I wasn't..."

"Don't lie either child."

I bowed my head. "My apologies."

He nodded in acceptance.

We had sat there for an annoying amount of time, Egann barely deigning to respond to my questions.

I lazily drew my finger through the dirt. "So what are you supposed to teach me?"

He was silent. I grumbled and continued doodling in the dirt. My mother may not have made a good queen, but she was an exemplary artist. She had taught me to paint and draw from a young age, but I never was able to reach her skill level. Although, maybe she should have spent a little less time lost in galleries and more time paying attention to her kingdom, especially her subservient kings. Then perhaps she would still be alive.

I was startled when a cold pierced my spine and spread through my entire body. I began to shiver, my teeth clattering. It was only autumn, so it shouldn't be this frigid. I looked up at Egann, who hadn't stirred. I opened my mouth and a cloud of cold air left it. Ice sprouted around me, and I yelped and hastily stood. I looked around me. The ground where I had been sitting was covered in ice, and it was spreading like fire every second. The ice crawled up the tree and down to the path. Soon it would reach the old man.

"Egann!"

I lurched toward the man and shook him. "Egann, we must go!"

The only movement he made was the rising and falling of his chest and shaking caused by me.

I grabbed his staff that he had set next to him and placed it in one hand. "Egann, hurry! Something is happening."

The ice had engrossed half the tree trunk and continued to spread further, only inches from his body. I looked around, my heart starting to beat wildly.

My face panic stricken, I turned to Egann who was now smiling. "There's nothing humorous about this situation!"

Egann finally opened his eyes and slowly stood, leaning heavily on his staff. "Peace child."

My jaw dropped. "Peace? Egann, I don't know if you've noticed or not, but some sort of crazy ice thing is happening."

Egann chuckled. which I noticed he did annoyingly often. "It's magic."

This guy was insane. "Oh, so I have magic, do I?"

Egann nodded. "Precisely."

I groaned, slapping my hand to my forehead. What had I gotten myself into? Magic was not completely unheard of, but it had been a good century since someone in Racour had been born with it. Most assumed whatever caused it to have simply vanished, like a stream ran dry. If anyone else in Saego had it, they kept it quiet.

A distant ancestor had the gift, or curse, of seeing glimpses of potential futures, but no one believed her. She had the shortest reign of all the Polaris queens, having been driven mad and disappearing into the mountains, never to be seen again. I didn't want to end up like her.

When I pulled my hand from my face, I noted that my panic was gone, as was the ice. I peered at the strange old man. "Egann... what is going on?"

Egann motioned around him. "Listen, child. I untethered your magic, the ice bloomed within you, you panicked, the ice exploded with you, and when you calmed, so did the ice."

He said it so nonchalantly, like I was the fool for not knowing. I shook my head. "I don't understand. You're just crazy."

I tried to think through what had just occurred. Was there merit to his words? Well obviously there was. Ice didn't just suddenly appear out of nowhere. I decided to entertain the idea for a moment as I sifted through my thoughts.

"Okay, Egann. So this magic came from me. How? Why hasn't this happened before? How did I get it? How does it work? Why—"

Egann lifted his hand. "Silence."

I obeyed, clamping my mouth shut.

He sat once more beneath the tree and motioned for me to do the same. I was getting frustrated and impatient with Egann, but with this new revelation, I couldn't just walk away. He had answers that I desperately needed now.

Egann laid his staff across his knees and placed his hands palms up. His eyes darted from his hands to mine and back. I guessed that he wanted me to lay my hands atop of his, and although I was reluctant to, I did it anyway.

Egann looked at me curiously. "What are you doing?"

I removed my hands quickly. "I, uh, I thought..."

Egann chuckled. "No, I just wanted you to copy me."

"You could have just said so..." I mumbled.

Egann shushed me. "No more talking. Just listen."

I bowed my head in compliance. He seemed to swing from laughter to seriousness often.

He began again.

"The Creator told me in a vision that I was to find a young woman and help her. He told me where to find you and what I was to do once I did. He showed me this tree and seasons passing underneath it. I was to untether the magic hidden within you, and then instruct you in your gift and in the ways of The Creator. And so here we are. I have released the bond that suppressed your magic, and I shall begin to train you in the disciplines of it on the morrow at this tree."

My head hurt and my thoughts were reeling. "May...m..." I stuttered. I cleared my throat. "May I ask questions now?"

Egann dipped his head.

"How do I have magic? How is this true?"

Egann rubbed his hair covered chin. "Well, He didn't tell me why you have magic."

"Figures."

He stared at me, seeming to know that I had more questions.

They came pouring out like water from an overflowing cup. "Why is He helping me now? Where was He when my family died? When Vukan slaughtered thousands of innocents?" My voice was beginning to rise. "Where was He when I was—" Unbidden tears were coming out. "When I was hiding in that damn closet while Vukan abused my mother and slit her throat?"

Egann pulled out a handkerchief and handed it to me. "What humans do is their choice. He does not control us like mindless creatures. We all have the choice, the potential, for good and for evil. If he zapped someone as soon as they had the intention to commit an evil act, would that truly be free will?"

I wiped at my face. His reason made sense, but it didn't help the frustration and pain.

He patted my knee. "There are many mysteries, many things we cannot possibly understand, but we must have faith. We must trust Him. He is always watching, and He always makes a way. And now He has chosen you."

I was overwhelmed with emotions and questions, my mind buzzing and my chest tight. "How though?"

He ignored my question and looked to the mountains. "There is something you need there."

I turned to follow his gaze. He was looking to Sanguis Mountain.

What could possibly be there?

I turned back to inquire what he meant, but he was already up and walking away.

"Wait!" I shouted.

I didn't think he would stop, but to my surprise he did. "How will you teach me? How can I contact you?"

"I will meet you again here."

My head was spinning. I closed my eyes, inhaled deeply, and faced the mountain that would hopefully have what I needed. But I didn't know what I needed, so how would I recognize it? I looked around once more to ask him another question, but he was gone. I cursed to myself and began my trek back into town.

Stupid man. Stupid magic. Stupid mountain.

I sat on my bed, door obstructed by a chair since it only locked from the outside, and stared at my fingers. I turned my hand over and studied my veins and arteries, tracing them up my arm. How could I have magic? More importantly, how desperate was I for answers? I had lost my chance to escape, the guards having caught me on my way to contact an old friend. My thoughts had been so consumed with Egann and his strange words and revelations, that I had failed to properly observe my surroundings.

There was likely to be a tightened watch on me from now on. If another opportunity to leave the castle arose, would it be better to just escape or should I continue to stay in the castle, obtaining information and gaining the support of those who worked within it? If I chose the latter, how would I be able to meet with Egann again? Vukan wasn't likely to approve of outings to train with some magic teacher.

I sighed. unsure of what to do. I hadn't tried to use my magic since Egann had untethered it, whatever that meant, and I was afraid to try. But as I sat there, I decided that I didn't want to wait for the old man to cryptically tell me how to use it. So I slowed my breathing, focused on the bench at the foot of my bed, closed my eyes, and willed ice to appear. For a few moments, nothing happened, and I almost gave up. Then I felt the cold in me, and I heard a crack and opened my eyes. A murky ice covered my entire sitting area and even crusted the door. I hadn't meant to create that much.

I should have probably waited for Egann.

A pounding sounded on my door. "The King requires your presence immediately!"

Panic gripped my heart. Crap. I was in such deep crap.

"Princess, open the door."

My heart pounded as my mind scrambled. "Give me a moment!"

I jumped off my bed, my feet slipping on the ice. I grabbed the pillar of my bed, regaining my balance and carefully walked over to the door, unable to move the frozen handle or the chair that blocked it. I gritted my teeth.

"Please go away," I whispered to the magic ice.

"Princess, open the door now!"

Technically, it wasn't locked, just frozen shut.

I closed my eyes, urging the ice to melt, and attempted to twist the knob. I felt something give and opened my eyes. An annoyed guard stood in front of me, the chair pushed to the side.

"I—"

"It's about time. The King is waiting."

My eyes widened. Did he not notice the frozen room behind me? Was he stupid or blind? I glanced over my shoulder to see the ice had vanished.

As we walked towards the king's quarters, my relief that the ice had disappeared was replaced with annoyance and indignation. The guard had acted rather rudely. Albeit, his attitude reflected my situation, that I was a princess in name only, at the mercy of the king. It was pointless to scold his behavior.

The guard brought me to Vukan's rooms, my arm aching where his grip was too tight. He knocked on the door and a voice told him to enter. The guard opened the door, shoving me through with no consideration. Vukan lounged upon a cushioned chair in front of the fireplace. He smiled and held out a hand towards me.

I could smell the alcohol from where I stood.

"Valine," he drawled, "please come in, make yourself comfortable."

I was forced to walk in front of him to get to the other chair, but his hand grabbed my wrist and yanked me down. He held me on his lap, my attempts to push away proving futile. The smell of rice wine was obnoxious.

He grinned. "I have wonderful news for you. I have routed your little rebel group. We found them hiding in the forests outside of Pardus. Apparently your gang of ruffians were hoping to attempt some kind of noble rescue for their royal rebel leader."

I stopped moving and so did my heart.

His smile grew wider, more maniacal. "Oh, now I have your attention? Well..." He leaned closer, breath warm against my face. "I killed them all."

I didn't move. I didn't react.

But the ice in my veins awoke, ready to carry out the bidding of its host.

The pain and rage that gripped my heart threatened to overwhelm me, but I couldn't let it. There were others he could kill as a punishment if I failed to wield my magic. I had to control myself, for them. I didn't have enough knowledge about my powers to guarantee I could successfully kill Vukan where he sat, even if I wanted to. For all I knew, I was just as likely to freeze myself along with him.

Not now, please Creator, not yet.

I felt it quiet. It was still there, but not about to burst.

Vukan cocked a brow. "Not even the slightest twitch? Not a single tear? Did you care nothing for them? Perhaps I shall tell you more tantalizing tidbits then."

His mouth was now next to my ear, his breath hot. "What was your friend's name? Yunip? Yakish? Oh right... Yanish. Well Yanish was the last one captured, a sneaky fool, and when we found him, oh did we have fun! I personally went out to the cell where he was being held and... acquainted myself with him. You know, I have to respect him at least a little. He didn't beg during the lashings, the drownings, or even the brandings. No, he only broke when we brought his daughter in, a sweet little redhead, you know I love those, and had her ravaged over and over by my men in front of him. Then he screamed, pleaded, begged for her. And being the merciful man I am, I stopped her suffering with a quick slice to her throat. I'm sure you can picture it well. Unfortunately, Yanish never spoke again, though that may have been from me cutting out his tongue."

He paused, his fingers wrapping around my hair, curling it like one would with their lover. "Hmm... I guess I got too carried away with fun. Without the ability to speak, he was useless, so I just stuck his head on a pike near the entrance to Pardus. You know, so that no one else would try to rebel. Had to make an example out of him."

The ice reached a crescendo, threatening to erupt in a storm of fury that rumbled in my bones. I bit my cheek so hard it started to bleed. I wouldn't give him the satisfaction he desired. I wouldn't cry, nor would I let the anger control me. He could not know about my magic, not until I was ready to kill him with it.

Vukan laughed. "My, my. Darling, you have such an ice cold heart." He shrugged. "Since you obviously feel nothing at the news of your comrades' deaths, perhaps this will elicit some sort of emotion from you. In celebration of the suppression of the rebels, I am throwing a party in a few days. Oh, I do love parties. And you shall have the honor of accompanying me!'

I thought that Vukan's punishment for me had ended with Zenith, but I had mistaken his quiet for some sort of forgiveness. The whole time he had been working on much worse. Chills ran down my spine, my stomach twisting as I shifted in his lap.

He grinned, tightening his hold on me. "Finally! I'm glad you can feel something, Valine. I was beginning to get worried."

I couldn't worm my way out of his grip, but I turned my head away from him. His blue fingernails clutched my chin, forcing me to look at him. "You should count yourself lucky Valine, women have killed each other over the privilege of being my companion for a night. I suppose I technically killed them."

"I am not worthy of such an honor," I said through gritted teeth.

He tsked, "So little passion. You know, I'm an avid supporter of it. You shouldn't do anything if you won't do it with vigor. Everything I do, whether it be killing or love making, is carried out with enthusiasm."

He crushed his lips to mine, and my entire body tensed, my joints locking together. I wanted to kill him. But I couldn't get myself to move, and even my magic seemed to cower in a deep corner inside of me. I had thought that if I had ever been in such a scenario as the one I was in, I would kill the perpetrator, even if they had a weapon, I would fight until they killed me. I thought death was better than a man assaulting me.

Even when Hagan had attempted, I had fought back then. But for some unknown reason I froze. I was unable to move, to scream, to do anything. I'm not sure if the urge to vomit was due to him or my own cowardice. He pressed me against himself and ran his fingers through my hair.

My body finally responded, and I tried to push away. But his fingers dug painfully into my sides. Relief came when the door slammed opened and clashed with the wall.

I took the opportunity to bite his lip. Vukan cried out, fingers going to where his mouth was now oozing blood. I jerked away and jumped up, backing up until I felt the solid wall behind me.

Sebastien and Lux stood in the doorway.

Lux looked shocked, eyes wide and fists clenched so tight his knuckles turned white, while Sebastien looked at me and then his uncle with no emotion. He looked no different than one observing the clouds, unbothered and unimportant.

Lux stepped forward, but Sebastien braced his arm in front of him. "Uncle, Father requires your assistance with some matters."

He rarely used the familial term with his unfortunate blood relative.

Vukan leaned back in his chair, wiping away the blood from his lip. "It can't be that important—"

"It is," Sebastien cut him off. He cleared his throat. "I'm sorry. I mean that it is extremely important issues that he needs to discuss with you. Military and um..." His eyes darted to me for a second. "Rebel issues."

Vukan rolled his eyes and stood nonchalantly. "Very well."

He turned to me where I was pressed against the wall, fighting for control of my breath. He strode over and slapped me so hard that it felt like my orbital bone had broken. "I shall see you at the party." He paused just as he reached the doorway. "And Valine..."

I glared at him, holding a hand to my already swollen face.

"Make sure to cover up that bruise. It's very unbecoming."

The silence was deafening as he disappeared out of the room.

I looked at Sebastien, hoping for... I didn't know what. But he wouldn't meet my gaze. He stalked out the door, his back erect like the soldier he was. Lux stood for a moment, hands in his pockets, head cast down.

He ran one hand through his long hair. "Valine, never come to my father's rooms alone."

I barely registered what he said. He took a step towards me and reached out a hand, but he quickly withdrew it once I flinched.

He began to talk to me, but I didn't really hear him. I slipped down the wall and stared blankly at Vukan's bed. I didn't know how much time had passed, but eventually my focus cleared.

I was alone.

My eyes were drawn to a gray rug with black spots that lay atop of Vukan's bed. I slowly stood, hand braced against the wall, and padded towards it. My vision blurred, and I swayed on my feet. My stomach became nauseous again, and I turned and ran out the door.

I sprinted down the halls until I came to my rooms. I slammed the door and walked straight towards the balcony, kicking and kicking at the lock until it broke. I thrust the doors open and made towards the railing, throwing my legs over and climbing down the side of the castle, which was made easier by the eroded stone, giving plenty of footholds and crevices for my fingers to grip.

I wasn't sure how long I ran, but when I finally regained my bearings, I was at the tree where I had met Egann. I collapsed at the base of the tree and folded my body into itself. I wasn't cold. Maybe it was the magic thrumming through my veins, or perhaps I had become sick from what had happened.

I didn't care either way.

CHAPTER EIGHT

I awoke the next morning with a fur cloak over me. I sat up quickly, whipping my head back and forth.

"It's about time you woke up."

I recognized the grumbling, old voice. Soon after he spoke, Egann hobbled around from the other side of the tree, leaning heavily on his staff.

"Come on child, we have a lot of training to do."

I didn't get up.

Egann reached down to help me up. "Come on—"

"No!" I screamed, recoiling away from his outstretched hand.

He frowned, his knees cracking as he kneeled. I looked away from his face, unable to meet his perceptive gaze.

"Do you want to talk about it?"

I drew the cloak tight around me in hopes of hiding. I had never frozen like that, had always been a woman of action, but at that moment I couldn't get myself to move.

"How do you feel?"

Tired. Filthy. Ashamed.

I had let Vukan do that to me. I had fighting skills and magic, yet I did nothing. I could have killed him then and there. But I didn't.

Egann nodded as if in understanding.

"You don't even know what I thought," I croaked.

Egann wrapped the cloak around me tighter, careful not to make contact with my skin. "You feel that it is your fault... that you should have resisted, tried harder to keep him away. You're afraid it might happen again. And on top of that, you feel the weight of your friends' deaths."

My throat was dry, my lips cracked, and my voice hoarse. "Did *He* tell you that too?"

Egann shook his head. "No. I saw the heads spiked in front of the city. But the rest... I know what it's like."

I furrowed my brow. "What?"

Egann sat across from me, setting his staff between us. It was a small comfort—a barrier to keep us apart—a simple yet appreciated gesture.

"I was only a young boy when it happened. Never told anyone, should have, but all too soon I had convinced myself that it was normal. He kept telling me that I had brought it upon myself. That no one would believe me. Took place for a long time. One day, my father died, but I still felt his phantom hands, felt the grime that covered my soul. Hated him and myself for years."

I let the cloak loosen just a bit. "What did you do afterwards?"

Egann sighed. "Well, I became a prostitute."

He laughed at my shocked face. "I felt like that was all I was good for, and no one had bothered to tell me otherwise. Until one day, this kind old lady with a stick dropped her basket in town. I helped her pick up her apples, and she was so grateful she invited me to her house. We made an apple pie together, and it was the first time I had been hugged in five years and felt truly cared for—no other intention or desire behind it other than warmth and safety. I visited that old woman often, and she would tell me of The Creator, who loved me, and wished to heal my heart. I scoffed at her at first, but I kept coming back, if nothing more than for delicious pies and kind words. She kept telling me how much I was loved. On one of my visits, I finally faced my pain. She taught me to forgive."

Tears welled in my eyes as he continued his story.

"She explained that forgiveness is the first step in healing. If you refuse it, then bitterness will infect you, festering and tainting even the good moments of life. If you allow hatred to take up residence, then you will have sentenced yourself to suffering. If I refused to forgive, then he would continue to steal my joy and win. She insisted that forgiveness is freeing their hold on you. I wanted that. Freedom. So I forgave. My father and myself. Eventually, I left the "service" and moved in with her."

He paused, gazing lovingly at his stick. "She told me everyday I was loved, and when she died, she left everything to me. I decided I would sell everything and travel, sharing with people the love of The Creator."

He smiled as he ran his hand over his staff, fingers tracing every chip and crack.

The cloak fell off my shoulders, crumpling around me, and tears streamed down my face. Egann smiled, his wrinkled face smushing together. I crawled over to him and he enveloped me in his arms. I didn't flinch as our skin made contact. His dreads fell into my face, and they were a welcome wall to cover me as I cried.

After an hour or so of comforting me, Egann said, "The trauma will always be a part of you. The sharpness of it will dull, but it will likely always be there. Somedays you may forget about it completely, and other moments you will be overwhelmed with the terrible memories like an unexpected flash flood. But you will survive. You will laugh again. For now, you just need to keep going."

He paused, waiting for me to wipe away the tears and snot. "No matter how dark the night, the morning is sure to come, child."

And with that we stood and began to train. He encouraged that it would help with more than just controlling my magic, that it would help me work out my emotions. It would make me stronger too, so I would not be helpless like so many times before.

"Magic is easily beckoned and dismissed. The difficult part is controlling it. It responds to your emotions and thoughts, so if you are scared or angry or happy, it may appear. For example, if you were particularly angry, perhaps some hail would rain down, or the person you were angry at could become covered in ice."

"Sounds cool," I whispered.

"It's not. It's dangerous." He had good hearing for his age.

He also made a good point. Could ice be anything but destructive? What good would ice do for me in a place where it was never lacking? The very mountain tops in front of us were covered in snow almost year round. Of course ice magic would be useful for fighting, but what about in times of peace? What did peace even look like? I would train and hone my magic into a weapon capable of defeating my enemies, then I could figure out how to apply it to ruling, to tranquility. Maybe I could make little ice sculptures to sell to other countries as additional income. I shook my head, flinging the thoughts away and retuning to Egann's instructions.

He continued. "But you have to be careful, not only to control your emotions, but also on how to use it. Just like the physical body tires after tedious labor, your magic will also wane. You have a limited amount you can use at one time, and it will take a toll on your body as well."

I furrowed my brows. "Well if I train, does that mean I can increase my capacity?"

He shook his head. "No. The amount of magic will not increase. What you are born with is what you will always have. Think of it like an existing jar that has limited volume and needs time to refill."

"Then what's the point of training?" I mumbled.

"Because you don't want to accidentally freeze some-one, and what you are able to do with the magic you have depends on training," he scolded.

He gave an example. "If you never train, then perhaps you can freeze some things, make some hail, maybe even make some ice float in the air. But if you train, you can make things out of it."

"Like weapons?" I asked excitedly.

Egann nodded.

"Awesome!" I exclaimed.

Egann tsked. "But as of right now, you'd be lucky to freeze a puddle of your own volition."

"I freezed my whole sitting area in my room."

"Did you intend to do that?" Egann questioned.

"No," I mumbled.

"My point exactly," he responded.

At the revelation of such information, I began to take the training more seriously.

Fron's red pigtails bounced around as she ran through the garden. I smiled as I chased her, the warm sun bathing us in light. Behind me, I could hear Yanish's deep laugh. I looked back to see the big barrel chested man's long beard shaking along with his laughs. I turned back to Fron, who was hiding behind a tomato bush.

"Hmmm... Where did she go?" I pondered aloud.

I heard her muffled giggles as I pretended to look around confused. I disappeared behind some corn stalks, careful to not bend them, lest they give my position away.

Squealing as I grabbed her shoulders, Fron turned with an expression of faux fear, a smile revealing her crooked front teeth. I fell on my butt laughing as her pale freckled face turned red. We both giggled as we threw dirt at each other, the soil sticking to her face. But suddenly the dirt looked more red and wet. Her laughing ceased as a red line formed across her neck. Crimson blood poured from the wound and stained her green frock. I whipped my head around to call for Yanish, but only a body lay slumped against the back door, a decapitated head in its lap—the tongue missing from it.

I stood up quickly, but all around me lay bodies. The crops turned into corpses. They were dead. All my friends dead.

I ran into the woods as fast as I could, but the trees suddenly reached out and grabbed me. Their branches gripped my body and turned me around, forcing me to stare at the blood drenched farm in the middle of the woods. The only people I had as a family, the one place that seemed untouched by the violence of the rest of the world, was now washed in blood—the cabin ablaze in flames.

It was my fault. It was always my fault people died. I brought ruin wherever I went.

I screamed, but no one was there to help.

I woke up abruptly, sweat dripping down my face and back.

If ruin was all I could bring, then I would bring it to this castle and the monsters within its walls. I would bring ruin to them all.

I noticed that my guards had changed, and I recognized one of them was in the rotation more than others. I had heard someone call his name once. Citadel. Only Sebastien could orchestrate such a thing, seeing as he was in charge of the palace guards. I didn't know Sebastien's reasons for helping me, or if it was even help at all. He could very well be spying on me, but I didn't care at the moment because his guards never followed me past the city limits or tried to stop me from leaving the castle.

I went to the tree every day for three weeks. Since I had no rebel comrades to get back to, as those who hadn't been killed by Vukan were spread out and all had families or friends who I could not risk being found out by my presence, I simply went back to the castle after I was done.

And every night for three weeks, I had the same recurring nightmares. Every night I would find myself covered in blood, my friends' corpses hanging from the castle gates or the forest farm covered in crimson. It was my fault, but I would do my best to train so that no one else would die because of me. I would become strong enough to protect everyone who put their faith in me.

Once again I was practicing, and my head ached from our sessions and lack of sleep. We had spent hours out there, most of them filled with silence as I tried to create pillars and walls of ice or whirling tornadoes of ice shards. It was difficult, and Egann rarely spoke.

One of the few times in which he decided to open his mouth was to scold me.

"You are trying too hard."

I dropped my hands to my sides. "Before you said I wasn't trying hard enough. Now I'm trying too hard."

Egann nodded.

I huffed and crossed my arms over my chest.

Egann sat cross legged, as he often did. "You are being too forceful. You do not own the magic; it is a gift. You are the steward of the cold and ice. You ask and so it shall be. Do not beat the wildness out of it."

I rolled my eyes. "Well how come I am having such a hard time with it? It appears easy enough, but it won't do what I want."

Egann closed his eyes, letting the breath slowly enter and leave his body. He was always meditating, although he said it was simply his way of talking to The Creator.

Why did he take so long to answer my questions?

After a few more moments of impatient silence, he opened his eyes. "Because you want to control it, but you cannot. It is something to be worked *with*."

My muscles tensed, his words hitting closer to home than I would have liked. Home. Huh. What was home anymore?

Egann's brow furrowed. "You do not think you have a home?"

A soft wind started to blow. "Stop doing that!"

Egann brushed the locks from his face. "Doing what?"

I stalked towards him, shoving my finger in his face. "You know what. You think you always know what I am feeling and thinking, but you don't!"

Egann used his staff to push my hand away. "I know many things, how you feel all the time isn't one of them. Occasionally, I can guess correctly."

The wind was starting to blow harder, leaves ripping from the branches of the oak tree. "You think that because we share some tragedy that it means we are the same. But we are not!"

Egann smiled sympathetically, sadness filling his eyes. "Are we not the same? We are both people. Do you think your sorrowful past makes you special?"

I took a step back. "I—"

He continued. "You think you are the only one to know pain? Grief? Well you are not. Everyone has experienced some sort of affliction, some sort of sorrow. Do not isolate yourself because you think you do not deserve love, or worse, afraid to lose it. You have been through such terrible darkness, just like so many others. But, dear child, do not let yourself *melt*, rather, let yourself *morph*. Be stronger. Be kinder. Be better. You are doing a disservice to yourself and your kingdom if you allow bitterness to reside in you, if you let all that has been done to you fester. Be free, child. Let yourself love, laugh, and have joy. Do not deprive yourself of people to love because you are angry or hurt or find yourself unworthy. Because you are not. You are a queen, whether or not you wear a crown. And most importantly, do not let fear rule you when *you* were made to rule."

It was snowing. I was crying.

I looked up to the sky, where white crystals were falling, the wind having calmed to a whisper. I looked back to Egann. I wanted to believe all he had said, that I was valued, that I was allowed to be happy, and that I was worthy of love. Perhaps in time I would come to truly believe those things. For now, it was enough for the old man just to say it.

Snowflakes floated above us. Egann smiled, the sadness leaving his eyes. "You asked, and it came."

I only had a couple more hours before I had to get back to the palace or my absence would be noticed.

Egann said farewell with a pat on my head. I would see him in a few days, as he had something to attend to. In the meantime, he told me to continue to train my skills privately in my room. I vowed that I would, but first I had another mission to accomplish.

I gazed up to the summit of the mountain. I had to do something for my kingdom, something for the people who had pledged their lives to me. I had to do something for Yanish and Fron and all the others, who had become my family and died for it. And so I began my trek up the mountain, to find whatever lay in its vastness.

After my conversation with Egann, I felt something warm inside.

Hope.

It was a small light in my heart, sparked by all that the old man had said to me. I smiled and started to climb.

Hope was dandy and all, but it sure didn't keep you warm when walking up a mountain that was always covered in snow. Why was it freezing already? The cold seared my fingers, much like the sight of the gray pelt on Vukan's bed. The skin was that of an ice leopard, the creatures that lived in the mountains above Pardus.

The huge predators had guarded the Queens for centuries, and my mother had one, a companion as they were referred to. He had been small for a leopard, at least that's what the court had said, but as a child I thought him to be enormous. He was fast and unsettlingly quiet, and he used to sneak up on me and tickle my face with his whiskers or his fluffy tail. His name was Tagon, and he was such a gentle creature who didn't deserve to die, even if it was to protect my mother.

I remembered it so clearly.

The doors to my mother's room shuttered as Vukan and his men rammed them. My mother ushered me into a secret compartment hidden in her wardrobe. She whispered for me to stay quiet and not come out until the room was completely empty. Then I was to escape out the secret door, just like we had practiced so many times before. I opened my mouth to say something, but the stern look she gave me quickly quieted the protest forming on my lips. I nodded, and she closed the door.

But there was a small peephole I could look through that was unnoticeable from the other side. I knew my mother wouldn't want me to watch, but I never was very good at following directions.

I stared wide eyed. Vukan and three men broke the door open, splinters of wood flying everywhere. My mother stood with a dagger in hand, but her body was trembling. Vukan adjusted his dark red armored vest. What were the splotches on it? Did he like to paint too?

He smiled and sauntered towards her. "Now Ariella, don't do anything stupid." A snarl was the only warning given before Tagon leaped from a shadowy corner and sunk his five inch fangs into Vukan's shoulder. Vukan yelled, falling to his knees as claws and teeth sunk into his skin. His men jumped towards the leopard, swords drawn.

Tagon released Vukan and turned to face the three men coming at him. He managed to rip the achilles of one and the throat of another before the third was able to cut a deep gash into Tagon's flank. He cried out and turned to face his opponent. While he was distracted, Vukan had snuck around behind him, managing to pin the leopard's tail to the ground.

I wanted to shout a warning, but no noise would come out of my throat.

Tagon snapped his head around but the other man had taken advantage of the opportunity and plunged his sword into Tagon's side. The big cat collapsed to the floor, panting. He growled as the two men crept towards my mother, who had backed herself into a corner. Vukan smiled and gestured for the other man to grab her. The man lunged for my mother, but somehow she managed to move and angle her dagger in just the right place to impale the man as he grabbed her. The man slumped to the floor, clutching his stomach.

Vukan rolled his eyes. "Fine, I'll just do it myself." Vukan was more agile than his soldier and easily disarmed my mother. He held both her wrists in one hand and slipped the other around her neck.

My mother's face looked so broken at that moment. Tears finally rolled down her cheeks, fear filling her eyes, but she never once looked in my direction. Vukan slowly kissed each cheek where a tear had fallen.

"So beautiful, even now," he crooned.

My mother glared at him with all the ferocity she had left. "You disgust me Vukan."

He tsked and put one finger over her lips, caressing them intimately. "Now now. This all could have been avoided if you had just married me and made me High King," he drawled.

A sudden curse escaped Vukan's mouth. Tagon had dragged himself towards my mother, her companion, her guardian, her friend. His loyalty was strong, even on the edge of death, and he dug his clawed paw into Vukan's calf. Vukan cursed at Tagon and kicked his head, and the ice leopard had no more strength left, glossy eyes fixated on my mother and her assailant.

Vukan turned his attention back to the queen. "It's too bad though," he sneered. "You are so delicious to look at." He glanced down at Tagon. "And you can watch your precious queen die. Then I think I'll turn you into a nice rug."

Tagon whimpered, and Vukan stripped my mother as she screamed, did things to her, and then, finally, slit her throat with her own dagger. Tagon growled once more, and then his body stilled, as if his soul had left to meet my mother's. He would accompany her to the afterlife where they would be companions for eternity.

Many in our kingdom didn't believe in any sort of heaven. But I believed. Somehow I just knew that there was a paradise waiting, and that there was no room for Vukan in it.

CHAPTER NINE

My *breathing was labored* by the time I reached the first caves. I needed to workout more. The past few weeks, I had focused more on magic training than exercise, and it was starting to show.

I passed by the first cave, which was more of a small hole than a proper cavern. I poked my head into a few others, wishing I had the gift of light and flame to illuminate my quickly darkening surroundings. I estimated that I had a little over an hour left before I had to leave and get back to the castle. But I had to focus on the present. I needed to find the leopard's caves, assuming that is why Egann had exhorted me to go on this never ending hike.

I searched aimlessly for the next twenty minutes, painfully aware that my time was running out. I had already searched several side caves that led to nowhere, and there were still six more. This was taking too long. When I arrived at the next one, I frustratingly threw my hand into the dark cavern, sending ice as far back as it would go. I figured that if anything in there was alive, it would make some sort of noise from the onslaught of ice crawling towards it.

Nothing. Not a single sound.

I grumbled and headed to the next one. I half heartedly did the same thing, but this time, a soft snarl echoed through the cave. More growls and hisses soon followed, the noise reverberating off the ice covered walls.

I ran into the cave but soon skidded to a halt. There was barely any light, and I had to be careful or I'd end up with a sprained ankle or worse, assuming whatever had growled wouldn't immediately kill me. I slowly crept through the cavern. Two tunnels split off from the one I was currently in, and I quieted myself and sent ice down one corridor. The gust of ice whistled past rocks, echoing off the floor and ceiling. I sent another wave down the left one. There were barely any echoes.

Using ice to discern which path I should take had not been wise. I was already fatigued from training and climbing up the mountain, and I still had to make my way back down it. I sighed, doing my best to encourage myself to keep going.

Treading faster than my eyes could adjust to the darkness, I cursed as I ran into a rock that jutted from the ground. I slammed my hand over my mouth, hoping that the leopards hadn't heard, for fear that they might run down some other tunnel and I'd never find them. Then again, I didn't want to sneak up on them. It was probably for the best that they knew I was coming. I stepped around the rock, making an obscene gesture at it.

A rumbling sounded. My skin prickled, and I peered forward. I could barely see the outline of a small leopard sitting in a shadowy alcove. The noise that emitted from it sounded like a mix between a wheeze and growl.

Was it laughing at me?

I crossed my arms. "Something funny?"

The noise cut off. Uh oh.

The creature stood.

Yes.

I leaped back and looked around. No one else was in the tunnel, but I could've sworn I heard someone talk. The creature again emitted its strange laugh. *You humans are so humorous.*

I cocked my head. "Is that you speaking?"

The leopard nodded, and I stepped forward.

How interesting. "But how?"

It shrugged, or what at least seemed like one. *I don't know. We just can. Although only some humans can hear us when we speak, those with royal blood.* The huge cat stalked towards me, sniffing. *You must be one if you can hear me.*

I nodded.

The cat was small, but its markings were similar to Tagon's. Black circles and splotches covered the light gray pelt, but what caught my attention was its eyes. They were completely icy blue. There was no iris, no other color. Just a storm of blue.

It's rude to stare.

I fumbled for words. "I, uh... I'm sorry."

The cat sniggered. *So who are you?*

I couldn't believe I was having a conversation with an animal. Tagon had never talked to me as a child, then again, he could have simply chosen not to talk to me. He seemed to have a quiet personality. First cryptic old men, then magic, and now telepathic cats. I was insane. Or maybe the world was.

"I am of the Polaris line. Valine Polaris."

The cat's ears flattened, and it hissed, *Come with me. Now.*

I was shocked that even though it spoke only in my head, I could hear its voice change. Though I was worried about *why* it changed. It was already padding away, and I had no choice but to follow.

The cat led me to a glowing cavern. I looked around, small black vines webbed over the stone walls with pur-ple, luminescent flowers. The strange plants offered just enough light for me to see the multitude of cats, varying in shades from black to white, staring at me with equally strange eyes as the leopard who had brought me here. I stumbled, bumping into the cat who stopped short. It tucked its chin to its chest, ears flattening. I peered in the direction it was facing.

Another ice leopard, bigger than the one next to me, sat on a smooth rock. Its eyes were bright blue, her pelt white as snow with pale gray circles.

It cocked its head at me, tail twitching. *Syri, who is this human that you have brought into our home?*

The cat I had met, Syri, lowered her body to the ground. *Glavnyy, this girl found our cave, and I talked to her—*

The cat jerked to her feet, claws unsheathing. *You spoke to the human?*

I raised a finger. "I can hear you, you know."

The leopard snarled at me and turned back to Syri.

Syri whimpered, *She is a Polaris Queen.*

Growls rumbled through the cavern, and I glanced around at the cats. Their hackles were raised and their lips curled. I shivered, although not from the cold. The white cat roared and a blanket of silence swept over the cave.

She turned her blue eyes to me. *A Polaris Queen, you say. What has drawn you here? Do you wish for death? Because that is the welcome your line deserves.*

I met her eyes. I pushed my shoulders back, doing my best to feign confidence. "Well technically, I'm not a queen. Which is what brings me here. I need your help."

Hisses and wheezy chuckles emanated from the cats. I crossed my arms.

I opened my mouth to voice my indignation but thought better of it.

Instead I asked, "What about Tagon?"

The snarl that came from the she-cat chilled my bones.

The leopards looked after the Polaris line for generations, and we have been taken for granted. Our lives have been wasted on you pathetic queens. Too many of you have been weak, stupid, and Tagon died due to such stupidity.

I lifted my chin. "I am not my mother, nor my ancestors. I am simply asking for the leopards' aid, as they once aided the first High Queen."

Those piercing blue eyes bore into me. *Who are you, that you compare yourself to Constella. She was the best of you, and none can compare to her. Most of her successors cannot measure up to her. Why should we aid another foolish ruler?*

I put my hands on my hips. "Because your kind swore an oath long ago, and because you cannot hold me accountable for wrongs I did not commit, for reigns that I had no control of."

She cocked her head. *Oh really?*

I nodded. "I will be High Queen Valine Polaris, and I am going to take back my throne. I will take my royal responsibility seriously, and I will not squander my power and resources like some of those whom you speak of."

I paused, sighing. "I know my mother was not fit to rule. She didn't do anything really, but Vukan is the embodiment of evil. He has his personal guards kidnap women, and then he just discards them when he is done. He is bleeding the nation dry of lives and money with his war. He is fighting with Indo who has never done anything wrong. He just wants their land! He already has plans to invade Eboc. Eventually he will go after Percia and Manchur."

I jutted a finger at her, praying she wouldn't bite my hand off, but wanting to drive home the point. "And don't delude yourself that he won't come hunting the leopards. He will want to eradicate you all, to repay what Tagon took out of his leg and for your connection to the Polaris queens." I straightened my posture. "And even if you refuse to help me, I will fight him one way or another."

She smiled, at least what I thought was an ice leopard's way of smiling. It was entirely possible she was just threatening me with those large teeth. I chose to believe it was the former. She stood, the rest of the leopards following suit. *Very well, Queen Valine, the leopards will aid you.* She leapt off the rock and padded into a dark passageway that led deeper into the cave. The large cat stopped to look back. *Until you prove to be as pathetic as all the others.*

I bowed my head. "That day will never come."

She huffed, a cloud of air escaping her nostrils. *We shall see...* She began padding away.

I called out, "What is your name? Syri called you, Glan... Glav... "

Her ears flicked. *It's* Glavnyy. *It means chief.*

"What is your real name then?" She paused, but I didn't think she would answer.

Kalosa.

She disappeared into the darkness.

A large male leopard, fur an ashy gray, walked up to me, huge furry paws making only the softest sound on the rock floor. He was enormous, far larger than Syri and even Kalosa. I felt something inside me tug.

"And who might you be?"

He peered at me with turquoise eyes. *I am Dryden. I am your companion.*

I furrowed my brow. "I thought I didn't have one."

A rumbling purr reverberated through his body. *The leopards have always bonded with a queen, but I was not allowed to seek you. Tagon wasn't supposed to go to your mother either, but he disobeyed Glavnyy and went anyway. Kalosa is not fond of the queens and refused to acknowledge the bond. I wanted to meet you, but I couldn't.* His tail curled. *Until now.*

I crouched, but he was so big that he towered over me, so I opted for standing, which still brought him past my waist.

"So how does this whole bonding thing work?"

He patted a spot in front of him with his paw, and I took it to mean he wanted me to sit. Once I was seated comfortably, he lay in front of me, and finally we were at the same eye level.

All ice leopards can speak into the minds of royal humans, but when a queen is bonded to her companion, she doesn't have to speak aloud for her leopard to hear her.

My eyes widened. "Really? Wait." *Really?*

The big cat purred, *Yes. None of the others will be able to hear your voice though, only me.*

I scooted closer to him. *How does the actual bond occur?*

His ears flicked. *When High Queen Constella saved the first clan leader's cubs from trappers, Nata, the Glavnyy at the time, decided to watch over Constella. She saw that the Queen was fair and just, and even left treats for the clan's cubs at the cave opening every once in a while, so Nata decided that she would resign as clan leader and go down into the valley to help the Queen–to grant her advice and to protect her.*

Constella and Nata decided to make a blood oath before Khristos, who I believe your people refer to him as, The Creator. They climbed to the top of the mountain of the leopards and slew a lamb, for oaths amongst us are sealed with blood. They vowed that the leopards would always send a companion to the Polaris Queens, so long as they were as fair and just as their ancestor, and that Queen and leopard were to protect each other so long as they both lived.

But after a few generations passed, the Queendom's integrity deteriorated, and eventually Kalosa banned us from going to our bonded. Tagon ignored her command. He was her mate, and we leopards mate for life. Kalosa has never been the same since.

That explained her hostility and hesitancy. I didn't know what to say, pity pouring over towards the ice leopard leader.

Dryden continued. *However, since the day I was born I've felt something missing. When I finally saw you, I just knew. You were mine.*

I smiled, finally understanding what that tug had been. *And you are mine.* I tentatively reached out a hand. *May I?*

He stretched his broad head out, and I ran my finger through his fur. On the top, it was coarse, but once past the first layer, his hair was as soft as feathers. I laid my forehead atop of his, inhaling. He smelled like the pine trees that dotted the mountain tops. He purred, and the vibration shook my head. I laughed and hugged him, and his nose nuzzled my shoulder.

I am curious about why he didn't speak to me. He played with me often as a child, but I never heard his voice.

Dryden licked a paw and ran it over his head. *I don't know. He was always quiet though, even for a leopard.*

I stroked his head, guilt rising in my chest even though I had nothing to do with Tagon's demise. *I'm sorry. He deserved better...*

He shook his big head. *He died honorably.*

I studied his clawed paws. *An honorable death is still death.*

Dryden growled, *Don't diminish his sacrifice. We all must die. How we live and how we come to an end are what define us. The merit of one is not in their length of life, but in their fulfillment of it. His life was full of integrity and so was his death.*

I supposed he was right. I gripped him tighter. He was the best thing that had happened to me in a long time, besides befriending Zasper and Sokah.

I'm glad I finally met you.

He purred, and I thought he was smiling. *When do we leave?* he asked.

I shook my head. *I'm sorry. It's not safe for you. The men who are on my throne, they'd kill you. I just got you, and I don't want to lose you.*

I stood reluctantly.

Dryden rubbed his head against my hip, leaving behind gray and white fur. I scratched his head. I didn't want to leave him, but it was already so late.

I will try to return as soon as possible.

Dryden nodded. I sighed and walked away. When I got to the tunnel exit, I looked back once more, bluish green eyes meeting mine. I waved goodbye and disappeared down the stone corridor.

As I walked down the mountain I felt the tugging sensation become stronger, as if begging me not to go. But I had to ignore it. I kept walking, and I wondered if Dryden felt the aching too.

The sun had disappeared by the time I returned, the last of its rays fighting to stay in the sky. I managed to reach my rooms with little interaction with anyone else, simply smiling at the guards that staunchly stood by my door. Speaking of guards, I would need to find Sebastien and ask why he was using specific guards for me.

Relieved to be alone in my room, I went to my balcony to ponder everything that had happened. No one had bothered to relock it.

An unexpected wave of revulsion crashed into me, a phantom of Vukan's hands crawling on my skin. My stomach twisted as the thoughts of shame and guilt creeped in once again. I replayed the conversation I'd had with Egann and imagined Dryden's soft fur and Zasper's sparkling eyes. My stomach calmed, the tumult ceasing, but all the good things that had happened, the good friends I had made, all of it, was tainted by Vukan, his sickening darkness encroaching on the flame of hope that I had so tenderly nurtured.

A hand gently brushed against my shoulder, and I jerked away, my side slamming into granite.

Zasper's mouth parted, her eyes wide with concern. "What is wrong my friend?"

My instinct was to yell at her to leave me alone like last time. I had managed to avoid her for three weeks, turning away whenever she looked at me at dinner or rushing past her with an awkward nod in the halls. I still regretted yelling at her. I didn't know why I avoided her. Perhaps I was afraid that she would think less of me, that she would judge me, or perhaps she would find me as disgusting as I thought I was.

"Will you tell me what happened?"

"I can't."

Zasper rolled her eyes, agitation winning over worry. "You know that is ridiculous. You can talk to me about anything."

I refused to let the tears escape, forcing them to stay put. "I'm afraid I can't share my vulnerabilities with anyone. It is not allowed for queens."

Zasper chided me. "Do not hide behind your crown Valine. A weak person hides their feelings, you are better than that."

The barrier, or more accurately cell, that had kept my emotions locked away burst open. The words spilled from my mouth, sobs racking my body.

By the time I finished telling her, I felt comfortable enough to let her hug me, hold me, as I cried.

Zasper tenderly grabbed my shoulders. "Look at me Valine."

I shook my head.

She used one hand to lift my chin, but I jerked away. I never wanted anyone to touch my chin again. I could still imagine his iron grip on my face.

Zasper continued without touching my head, simply wrapping a gentle arm around me. "This is not your fault. Vukan is evil, and he had no right to do that to you—no right to do anything that he does. You are beautiful, strong, and this does not define you. People will do terrible things to you, try to convince you that you are worthless, whisper lies to darken your soul. And oh how bright your soul shines. How it has burned for justice, honor, and hope. This is not a reflection of you. This is not your fault. Not the deaths and not the assault."

Zasper smiled, her eyes tearing up. "Do not let the wickedness of others dim your light. Do not let him break your spirit."

I leaned into her and apologized, "I'm sorry for yelling at you."

She squeezed my shoulder. "I understand."

I was glad she came to see me, being willing to be the first one to knock on the door, the one to break the awkward wall between us.

"Do you know about The Creator, Zasper?" I asked.

"Of course. Eboc has a weekly *Kanisa*. It is a gathering of people to hear about His ways and help encourage each other. Although I heard that in Percia they have a great temple dedicated to Him. Percia is supposedly where the first prophet was born."

"Interesting," I murmured.

The Creator. Egann spoke of Him often, The Creator that made everyone and everything. I looked to the sky, the stars just beginning to wake from their slumber. He made those too, apparently.

I looked to the heavens and whispered, hoping He would hear my plea.

It just made sense to me that there was some power, some entity that existed and brought everything into existence. But I would be a liar if I didn't admit that I had my doubts about His goodness, about His love for His creations. No one could offer a satisfying explanation either, for why there was disease or natural disasters. I could comprehend how violence and thieving, all the crimes that were done by men, were not His doing, similar to how Egann had explained. But how could He have the ability to heal sickness and stop fires, and still allow them to ravage lives? Ultimately there would be no answer in this life.

Perhaps when I went to Paradise, I could ask Him. Until then, faith alone would have to suffice. Something that was easier said than done, and something many refused.

CHAPTER TEN

*I**t was likely to* be one of the last warm days of fall, and it would be a shame to waste it by staying indoors. I headed straight to Zasper's room in the guest wing, only a few twists and turns from mine, and knocked on the door. As soon as she opened it, I grabbed her arm and drug her to the barracks. The soldiers coming and going eyed us, but didn't ask us any questions.

We stopped in front of the entrance. As a soldier exited, I leaned in front of him, my hair falling to the side.

"Excuse me, but do you know where Sokah Jang is?"

The soldier cocked a brow, looking between Zasper and I.

He sighed, calling out through the still open door. "Sokah! Some girls are here for you!"

"Girls? Does he not know who we are?" Zasper asked indignantly.

I shrugged. "Most people haven't seen me since I was twelve, and it's not like your portrait is well spread in Racour."

Sokah emerged, black tousled hair still damp from a bath. He ran his hands furiously back and forth, water droplets spraying everywhere.

"Hey! Is that how you treat two beautiful princesses?" I asked, wiping the wet spots from my face.

Zasper flicked a drop from her fingers, eyes glaring at Sokah.

His lips curled into a smile, dimples shining like stars on his round face. "My apologies, Your Highnesses. However, you were the ones who showed up without warning."

I laughed. "We were just that excited to see you."

Zasper mumbled under her breath, "Maybe you were. I didn't—"

I shoved her with my shoulder while maintaining eye contact with Sokah. "We came to ask if you wanted to have a picnic with us."

Sokah straightened, eyes shining with excitement. "Sounds great!" He held out an arm to the both of us. "What have I done to earn such a great honor?"

I slipped my arm around his, Zasper reluctantly following suit on the other side.

"Well you are one of the few people I actually enjoy being around," I explained.

Sokah's breath hitched, and he sniffled dramatically. "I truly am honored, Your Highness."

I chuckled. "You can call me Valine."

I stumbled, caught off guard by Sokah's sudden stop, his arms dropping to his sides.

He frowned. "Does that mean I am your enemy?"

I replied with a smile dancing on my lips. "Only if you don't hurry up. I haven't eaten yet today, and everyone is my enemy when I am hungry."

Sokah grinned, and with the swiftness of a seasoned soldier, he swept me up and started jogging towards the main palace.

"Hey!" Zasper shouted, forced to run to catch up.

I wrapped my arms tightly around Sokah, my hands interlocked behind him in fear that he might drop me. "What are you doing?"

He glanced down at me. "I have to get you some food before I end up busted on the floor like that dummy."

We laughed as he hurried towards the kitchens.

Poor Zasper was struggling to keep up in the cumbersome, layered garments of Racour. She had the sides of her skirts bunched in her fists as her arms pumped to keep pace with Sokah's longer legs. She looked like a crane during mating season, although I would never tell her that.

By the time we reached the kitchens, our breaths were labored. I'd laughed and giggled the whole way, and Sokah and Zasper were recovering from the unexpected exercise.

Sokah set me down gently and whispered, "I think Princess Zasper should also eat quickly."

I did my best to hold in a laugh as I looked at her irritated face. Her nostrils flared as she slowed her breathing, but her piercing glare and deep frown were what signaled her frustration.

I whispered back, "Let's go."

The cook was kind enough to prepare some rice balls, fruit, and slices of smoked duck for our picnic. Sokah carried the basket while Zasper and I walked arm in arm. We decided to go to the cove of trees that butted up against the castle walls near my rooms.

"We never really patrol here since the mountains are on the other side of the barrier. There is no way anyone could sneak in on this side," Sokah explained as we spread out the food on the ground.

I leaned back against a tree trunk, soaking in the sun that shone through the treetops. I inhaled deeply, the smell of soil, sap and smoked duck wafting into my nose.

Sokah popped a rice ball into his mouth, a bulge forming in his cheek as he chewed. Zasper tossed the peel of a slice of orange over her shoulder, a stubby pine the victim of her citrus onslaught.

"How did you become a soldier?" I asked.

Sokah replied with a mouth full of duck, "It is one of the few stable jobs and the only one not taxed. For every other profession, the taxes have increased almost every year. All for funding the military."

I chewed on dried persimmon. "I wonder why Vukan started the war with Indo."

Sokah reached for another piece of duck. "Who knows. Although word trickled down the ranks that after Indo he wants to go for Manchur."

Zasper froze mid-bite. "What about Eboc?"

Sokah winced, eyes filled with sympathy. "I heard he is hoping your father's pacifistic tendencies will make him surrender."

I shifted uncomfortably. "Sebast–I mean The Legate, said that you came to discuss such terms."

Zasper's response was suspicious, and her eyes sparkled with something mischievous. "We shall see."

She was surprisingly nonchalant about such a serious matter.

"He takes women, why not other nations?" I muttered, my thoughts wandering to Silba, praying she was safe.

Sokah sighed. "You have no idea."

"What do you mean?" Zasper and I asked in unison.

Sokah leaned forward and whispered, "There are rumors that King Vukan has a special unit of soldiers whose sole purpose is to gather pretty women from across Racour."

There was no need to state what happened to such women.

I shuddered, chills crawling up my spine despite the warm sun.

Sokah's jaw clenched, and his brow furrowed. "It makes me worry about my little sister. She has always captured the interest of the neighboring boys, and I fear that she may gain the interest of the king one day."

He paused, his voice deadly and sharp, "I would kill him if he ever touched her."

I gulped. It wasn't hard to believe that he meant it, and often the softest people became the scariest when they were pushed too far. Nor did I blame him, as I too, was resolute in my conviction to kill the king.

The tension broke as Sokah's shoulders relaxed and his voice became lighter. "Actually, you remind me a bit of my sister. She has always been stubborn while also having a sensitive heart. One time she found an abandoned cat and nursed it back to health. She would wake up extra early just to give it fresh milk from the cow. If any of us drank from the milk jar before she had given it to the cat... oh boy, she would give you a good tongue lashing."

My heart warmed as I imagined it. "She sounds lovely."

But the sweet imaginations were replaced with concern for myself.

"I wonder what Vukan wants with me."

I hadn't realized I'd spoken the words allowed, but the pitiful looks from both Sokah and Zasper let me know that they had heard.

I finally allowed my concerns to be voiced. "Honestly, I have been thinking about it a lot. Why hasn't he killed me? What does he want from me?"

Zasper replied, "Maybe he wants to look good in front of the people? Like a kind king."

I shook my head. "That doesn't make sense with how he executes people on a whim and steals women. I am fairly sure public sentiment is not in his favor, even after his poor attempts to change the history of the coup."

Zasper conceded, "That is, what was it... a good point."

Sokah offered, "Maybe it is some sick desire to have a Polaris queen beneath him? It is no secret that he had made multiple marriage proposals to the queen following her consort's death. Maybe you are his revenge for her snubbing him."

I slowly chewed on the persimmon. "Maybe."

I sat at the table near the balcony entrance, brushing my hair. A smile danced on my lips as I fondly recalled the day's events. Getting to spend time with Zasper and Sokah was one of the best memories in my adult life. I had made genuine friends.

The rebels were of varying ages, most the age to be my parents, a few others more like younger siblings. Callar had been the closest to my age, but he felt like an older brother. Zasper and Sokah were real friends though. Our relationship was not born from a common cause that united us. It was chosen of our will, for nothing other than the pleasure of each other's company. Albeit befriending a foreign princess and palace guard had its advantages when it came to planning a rebellion. A war needed soldiers to fuel it.

My heart ached at the thought of asking them, of potentially losing them, during the inevitable battle between Vukan and I. Hopefully, such a negative outcome would never occur. I would make sure they lived long and happy lives, and once I was queen, I would get to spend more time with them. Perhaps we could even do what the commoners did with their friends. Sokah wasn't royal, so he would know what all the fun things to do were. As a princess on the run, I had never been afforded such opportunities, only watching from a distance as the people celebrated solar and lunar holidays and participated in festivals.

I smiled again, imagining all the possibilities.

Knocking startled me out of my thoughts. I stood, sighing, and I strode over to the door and opened it. The new maid squeezed by. I hadn't learned the girl's name, and I didn't care to, lest she too be killed for being too acquainted with me.

She took one look at me, drew a bath, and shoved me into the water. She scrubbed me, dried me, and took me into my bedroom to dress.

She was not as gentle as Zenith, not as timid either. I was about to pick out a conservative, blue and yellow dress, but the maid shook her head. She held up a finger for me to wait and disappeared out into the hall. She returned a few minutes later with a dress slung over her arms. It was a tight looking crimson dress with a deep neckline and the four panels of the skirt were not attached to each other, leaving gaps that would show all of my legs.

I shook my head and crossed my arms. "There is no way I'm putting that thing on."

The girl frowned and took out a note from her apron. I unfolded it.

To my dearest princess, Valine,
Did you enjoy the picnic?
I was so pleased to hear that you made some friends. I don't mind if you play around in the palace, and I will even overlook your little escapade into town. You know where my room is if you ever want to express your gratitude. However, if I start to hear those pesky rebellion rumors... Well you know how I deal with those.
That Jang boy, good soldier. It would be a shame to lose such an asset over your carelessness. Or has that maid girl already faded from your mind?
Shall I name the next woman who warms my bed after you? You didn't seem to like when I used your mother's name.

Also, concerning tonight, I was worried you wouldn't know what to wear for such a special occasion, so I did you the favor of procuring a dress befitting a companion of the King.
Reminiscing your lips,
Vukan

My body trembled and my ice leapt as I threw the piece of paper into the fireplace. Too bad I didn't have fire magic to burn him and all his paper.

I held out my hand for the girl to give me the dress. "Fine. If that's how Vukan wants to play, then so be it."

I stood in front of the mirror. Smokey eye shadow surrounded my eyes, crimson lips matched the dress, the sides of my hair were slicked back, and obsidian points protruded from the braids atop my head. A knock sounded and the maid opened the door. If there was one more knock on my door, I was going to rip it off its hinges.

My irritation settled as I saw who had arrived.

"I just heard that you are to be his escort tonight."

I nodded.

"Don't let him win."

I cocked a brow. "What do you mean?" Did she want me to make a show of tonight, to fight back in my own subtle way?

"Do not lose your self-control and jeopardize your safety," Zasper warned.

We had very different interpretations of not letting Vukan win. I preferred my method.

I turned to the ambassador. She wore trailing white skirts with a matching top, and cream cords of fabric crisscrossed over her shoulders and around her neck. Her hair was braided back, her face void of cosmetics but still beautiful. I held out my arm, and she took it. We walked out arm in arm, cruel beauties ready to wreak havoc on Vukan's court.

I didn't know what to expect, but it certainly wasn't what I saw then.

Vukan had decorated the entire ballroom in shades of white, and crystal hung from the ceiling and from the ears of the noble women. Everyone was dressed in some degree of white, those wishing to be daring wearing shades of gray. I smiled though, because for now, I would play his game.

I strode towards the raised platform where an empty throne sat, knowing Vukan would be able to see me from there, if he hadn't already spotted me from the moment I walked in. It would be hard not to notice me, a splash of scarlet amongst the white ocean of courtiers. I pushed past whispering women and ogling men until I got to the steps. I strode up them and turned, eyes devouring those below. I knew he could see me. I began to sit on his throne, but a hand darted out and grabbed my arm.

"What do you think you are doing?"

I glanced towards Sebastien. "Vukan wanted to show me off, well what better place to do so than my throne, where everyone can see your uncle's wonderful hospitality?"

Sebastien hissed, "You are a fool Valine, just play nice or you'll end up like Zenith."

"You don't ever get to say that name. Ever," I growled.

I knew he was trying to keep me from doing something stupid, but I didn't appreciate it.

I ripped my arm from his grip and stormed off of the dais just to run into the second person I hated.

White robes trimmed in gold approached me.

"Valine," Lux purred, "you look ravishing."

I rolled my eyes, poison coating my words. "I'm sure I'm not the only one you've told that to tonight."

"But yours is the only one that's actually sincere."

I wasn't in the mood for his usual banter. I just wanted to leave, but I knew that was impossible, as a guard would surely drag me back here and chain me to a pillar if need be. Music started, and I hoped I could find some courtier to dance with.

Just then he held out his hand. "May I have the pleasure of this dance, Princess?"

I supposed he was better than Vukan, although not by much.

I laid my hand in Lux's, and he pulled me into him. His arm wrapped around my waist, fingers grazing my back, his other hand holding mine with a surprising gentleness. He was sure footed, leading me around the floor in elegant twirls, which I was very thankful for due to my lack of foot coordination. I had taken dancing lessons as a child, but that was so long ago and an unused skill, that I had almost completely forgotten how. Fighting moves didn't translate to dancing.

He never said a word as we moved to the music, but his dark brown eyes gazed into mine, sparks dancing in his irises, and for the slightest second, I could appreciate his handsomeness.

But it was only for a second.

The song finished, and he bowed, kissed my hand, said his goodbyes, and turned to a crowd of young women begging for his attention. I couldn't blame them. If he hadn't been my enemy, the son of a murderer, if all those years ago his father hadn't taken everything from me... perhaps we could have met at a ball like this one.

But that was not reality. My reality was far more bitter and tragic. I would kill him, him and his whole family. I chided myself, realizing I had missed an opportunity to gather information. I shook my head and glared at Lux's back, now covered in ladies hands, and turned towards the refreshments.

Sebastien appeared beside me, and I poked at some sort of bird that had been dyed an unnatural white to match the decor. He stood straight as a pillar as usual, but his brow was slightly furrowed.

I turned to face him. "Care to dance?"

"What?" His eyes widened, showing a rare bit of emotion.

I elaborated, "Dance. You know, the thing where you grab hands and move your feet?"

Sebastien straightened his expression, his stoic face far more familiar. "Oh, well I'm not much for dancing. Lux has always been better at it than me."

I grinned, grabbed his hand from where it hung by his side and tugged him towards the floor. "Come now Legate, don't tell me you can charge into battle but can't dance a simple waltz.'

He frowned. "It's not that. I just don't..."

"Hush now." I placed his hand on my waist and put mine atop his shoulder.

His hand held my own more tightly than Lux did. Perhaps he thought I might cause some trouble and wished to prevent me from doing so. I forced a smile as we trailed along the dance floor.

Our palms were sweaty, and Sebastien wouldn't make eye contact with me, his gaze fixated on a white banner dangling from a pillar.

I put on my most dazzling and disarming smile. "What's it like being The Legate? I imagine it is difficult having *so* many men under your command."

"Nothing that arduous. I am only in charge of the palace guards. My father is in command of the rest," he said without hesitation.

"How many men exactly? I only had a few dozen, even those few were difficult to maintain. I don't know how you do it. I'm impressed with how well trained your soldiers are." I tried to keep the look of awe on my face, swallowing my pride. I hated degrading the honor of my deceased brethren, but flattery was a useful tool.

It seemed to work, and Sebastien replied without a hint of suspicion, "Only about seventy at a time, and they are required to drill at least three times a week." His chest appeared to puff out ever so slightly.

About to ask him another question, my words froze in my mouth as we were interrupted.

"Mind if I cut in?"

Vukan was dressed in all black, looking absolutely stunning, but he still reeked of wine and what I could only assume was opium. Sebastien nodded his head, throwing a glance my way as he transitioned my hand to his uncle's.

Vukan, unlike Sebastien, never took his eyes off of me. He pressed me closer to him, and my body stiffened. The bit of fowl I had eaten threatened to fly back up from my stomach. I didn't care if we were surrounded by people and guards, if he tried to kiss me again, I would kill him then and there.

He chuckled. "Loosen up, Valine darling."

"Screw off, Vukan darling."

His grip tightened to the point of hurting my hand, and my fingers turned purple as the circulation was cut off.

"My dazzling princess, you need to change your attitude. Look around."

I did. No one else was dancing. They all stared at me, especially the men.

"You are nothing now. All you have to offer is an empty title and a warm body."

I looked back to Vukan, prepared to say a nasty retort.

I wasn't expecting him to ever harm me publicly, that my title, no matter how obsolete it had become, would prevent him from harming the heir of the Polaris line—a facade of benevolence towards the daughter of the late queen. So the punch to my stomach sent me to my knees, and I gasped for air on the floor, the wind knocked out of me, surprise and whispers filling the room.

"Don't forget that you are only alive because I choose to keep you that way. Don't forget your place."

The boots by my face disappeared.

No one dared to help me. Engraving their faces in my mind, I glared at everyone in the room. I could kill them all now. I could send ice over the whole room.

But then my Egann's voice entered my head. "Forgive them, for they know not what they do."

The words he had spoken to me earlier helped me to view them in a different light. They were probably just as scared of Vukan as I was. I shouldn't hate those who were just doing their best to survive under a tyrant's reign.

I stood slowly. My legs wobbled, and a pair of hands grabbed me. Sebastien supported me as I limped out of the room; my knee had hit the ground harder than I had initially thought.

Sebastien nodded to the guards that saluted him as we passed.

I was lost on what to do. The past few years of finally building a following had been crushed, and the agony it inflicted on my heart was not one I wished to repeat. But such was the way of rulers, as I was learning over and over again. I had to do something and somehow rebuild my rebel group. Until I could formulate a proper plan, I would continue to train, continue to study my enemy, and continue to win others to my cause.

Only a few high ranking military officers and nobles were truly on Vukan's side, their motivations driven by personal gain rather than loyalty. Majority of Racourians were frustrated at the very least with the Wulfric king. However, fear was one of man's greatest masters, and I would have to work hard to convince them to overcome it.

A month passed without much occurring besides training sessions with Egann once a week. He had cut back our time together so that I wouldn't depend on him too much. Plus he said he was busy, having been directed by the Creator to go who knows where. He was a snarky man and difficult to track down, but nonetheless, I went back to the tree at the base of the mountain every seven days. Citadel always happened to be the man on guard duty those days, and since I was never hauled to the dungeons to be interrogated about magic or killed in my sleep, I could only assume he was being discreet. I pondered if he had some loyalty to my mother that I was unaware of, but I never dared to ask him outright.

It was the beginning of winter now, and my magic thrummed in my veins, seeming to welcome the cold. Coming to see me multiple times a week, Sebastien's motivations for spending time with me were still unclear. Was he keeping an eye on me for Vukan or for himself?

Some days we walked around the gardens and other times we exercised alongside the rest of the guards. After whatever event he dictated we did, I would meet with Zasper. She said she would be returning to Eboc after the New Year, promising to come when I called for her. I would miss her dearly.

Lux, however, I did not miss. He didn't talk to me often anymore, but he almost always watched Sebastien and I when we were in the soldier's courtyard or conveniently just happened to be taking a stroll in the garden whenever we were. He never looked happy then.

I too wasn't necessarily happy, but I was feeling better. With my body getting stronger with proper meals and exercise, and my magic developing exponentially, I felt more powerful. I felt like I was a true princess. But like everyone, I was still a human, no more in control than a poor shepherd.

Vukan had forgiven the incident from the party a month ago, but I hadn't. Perhaps I had grown too arrogant, and I should have been more careful. But the ice that pumped through my veins had made me confident, overly so. Perhaps it was the recurring nightmares of Zenith, Yanish and Fron's deaths that pushed me over the edge.

CHAPTER ELEVEN

V*ukan invited some nobles* to a grand fighting tournament, the first of its kind, although I had heard of some old empire on a different continent that had held similar events. I was informed attendance was mandatory. The king had chairs arranged, with an ornate one in the center for him, circled around the sparring pit in the soldier's courtyard, which had been cleared of the fresh snow. King Dumas, rotund belly protruding from his fur cloak, sat with a few of his vassal lords. His lips were upturned with a sinister expectation of brutal entertainment, eyes alight with excitement.

It was in stark contrast with the men lined by the walls, faces grim and brows contorted in concern, some clutching stomachs with skin colored the promise of vomit, sweat seeping from them despite the cold. I doubted that they volunteered for this tournament.

A guard escorted me to my seat, and I sat reluctantly. Vukan, adorned in rare furs, eyes red from either drugs or the chill of the air, stood with arms spread wide.

"Thank you for joining me for what I am sure will be an exhilarating experience. It's so dull during winter, is it not? Cooped up inside all day. So in a grand gesture of generosity and consideration for those who support my reign, I present a new form of entertainment."

He clapped his hands, and two soldiers clad entirely in black escorted a couple of their fellow guards into the arena. I had never seen those uniforms before, and my mind wandered to the words Sokah had spoken. Were they *those* kinds of soldiers?

Cheering and laughter jarred me from my thoughts, as a fist met a face. Nausea boiled in my stomach as I clutched the arms of the chair. One pair after another fought until the other either gave up or was knocked unconscious. Indignation gripped my core after watching a bloodied man get dragged out of the pit. His competitor had continued to beat him even after he had been knocked out. I worried if the poor man would ever be able to wake. After that round, I didn't know if I could take it anymore.

As two men entered, well, they could hardly be called men, they couldn't even grow a beard, I felt the rage of injustice reach a climax. They were no older than myself, likely just had come of age, and they were pale and sweaty—obviously dreading having to hurt each other. I glanced to the side where the other soldiers waited for their turn to be pitted against their comrades. They looked equally distraught, yet frozen in their positions. The boys turned towards each other, visibly shaking. Vukan nodded for them to begin. They lifted their fists and circled each other, but their hands remained in front of them. Minutes passed and they didn't throw a single punch; the noble women were beginning to whisper and the men were booing.

The two boys glanced between themselves and the king, perhaps hoping they would be dismissed from this stupid, vile game. I looked to Vukan, who hushed the courtier talking next to him.

His voice boomed through the yard as he declared, "You know, I think it's time to liven things up. We need to raise the stakes. This will be a fight to the death."

The boys' faces blanched.

"And if you refuse to fight, you'll both be executed."

Some of the noblemen cheered, while the women showed indifference, any signs of sympathy either nonexistent or well hidden, and the soldiers standing on the other side of the ring shifted uncomfortably. A shorter man with brown hair stepped forward, but another lunged, grabbing his arm and obstructing him from intervening.

Lux leaned over to whisper to his father, but Vukan must have not liked what he had to say because Lux was suddenly being escorted away. He glared at his father as two guards took him inside.

Sebastien moved to say something, but Vukan held up his hand. "Legate, if you say anything I will consider it in contempt against the King. You know well how treason is treated."

Sebastien said nothing.

I looked around for anyone who could help, but no one spoke up. Even the soldiers, although clearly upset, made no more effort to stop the looming atrocity.

Vukan slammed his fist on the arm of his chair. "Begin!"

One of the boys began to cry as he threw his fist at the other's face. Blood poured from the poor boy's nose, which was most likely broken.

Reasons to help. Reasons to stay quiet. A multitude of outcomes all flashed through my mind. Even if I made it to my throne, if I gained it while allowing something so disgusting and tragic to occur, then I was not worthy of my crown, of the trust of the leopards and the faith of Zasper and Egann. I would not stand for this.

The boy steeled himself to throw another punch.

"Stop!"

Everyone froze. Everyone looked at me.

Sebastien, who had been seated a couple chairs next to me, hissed, "Valine, what are you doing?"

Vukan narrowed his eyes. "What is the meaning of this outburst, my dear?"

I stood from my chair, gesturing to the fighting ring. "Is this what you do for fun around here, Vukan? Is this what the King of Racour chooses for entertainment?"

His face was scarily calm. "Do you have a problem with that? Does it not suit your tastes, *Princess* Valine?"

I crossed my arms. "Yes, I do."

I turned to look towards the boys, relief written across their faces, and the soldiers lining the wall, who stared at me with a mixture of gratitude and shock.

I pivoted towards the courtiers. "These men work hard to protect you all, and this is how you treat them? Forcing them to fight, fight their brothers like some crazed beasts!"

No one dared to say anything, to move.

It was well worth whatever wrath Vukan was about to rain down upon me.

"Guards, take her to the post," Vukan commanded.

My eyes widened, my heart beating faster than a mouse caught in a trap. Two men came beside me, each taking one of my arms, dragging me past my seat and knocking my chair over.

Sebastien stepped forward. "Uncle please..."

Vukan snapped his head towards his nephew, eyes blazing with fury. "I am your king before your uncle. You would do well to remember that."

He turned his attention back to me. "And someone, prepare the whip."

Shaking. Why was I shaking? I wished my body would stop, but I was unable to will the tremors into submission. Vukan smiled, and dread speared through my body.

The king had ordered everyone in the palace to come out—servants standing on one side, courtiers on the other. I was brought towards a single blood-stained post that stood in the middle of the yard. I wondered how many poor souls had bled upon that wood, how long they had to endure. Did they cry or brave it silently? My legs gave out, and the guards grunted with the effort it took to drag me.

This wasn't happening. It was just all some nightmare. I had to wake up, but I wasn't asleep. And the reality hit me, just like the whip the soldier was holding would.

The two guards pulled me the remaining feet and forced me to my knees. I could do nothing as they chained my hands to the pillar. I turned my head to the castle doors.

Vukan just grinned as he stared at me, eyes filled with a sadistic satisfaction. Sebastien's eyes were trained on me, body rigid and face contorted with concern. I looked around the crowd. Nobody here could save me.

The snap of the whip made me flinch. A soldier stalked towards me, flinging the cord with each step.

He stopped in front of me, lifting my chin. "I told you you would regret ever showing me disrespect." Hagan's face turned smug.

"You aren't a pig. You're the slime that pigs live in," I threw back.

Hagan didn't say anything as he looked at Vukan who nodded. I leaned my head against the smooth, cold wood and twisted the short chains in my hands. I gritted my teeth in anticipation of the pain. I so badly wanted to freeze Hagan and Vukan, but I could potentially hurt the others, could accidentally kill the innocent servants and soldiers that I knew didn't relish this. I had to keep the ice locked inside, for their sake. I would not sacrifice innocent people to spare myself the pain.

I heard the crack before I felt the hit, and an excruciating fire tore into my skin. A strange mixture of burning and the sensation of skin scraping against rock spread over my back. I would not scream, would not give them the satisfaction.

Vukan's voice echoed throughout the courtyard. "Thirty lashes! That is Valine Polaris' punishment for disobeying her king. Learn by her example. This is the retribution all shall pay who dare defy me!"

Five. Five lashes had bore into my skin while the king spoke. Twenty-four more to go.

I would not yield.

I managed to keep the screams buried deep inside until the thirteenth lash. A screech ripped from my throat. Blood pooled around my knees-my blood. I couldn't think about anything else except that whip and the utter agony each snap brought.

Was someone shouting my name? *SNAP!* Another scream tore from my mouth. Who was yelling? *SNAP!* Tears were pouring down my face. Had someone come to save me? *SNAP!* No, no one could stop Vukan. *SNAP!* The world was going dark...

I cracked open an eye. People were arguing. Why were there soldiers around? Was that Sokah? The boys from the ring? My head was pounding, my knees ached, and my back-was there any skin left?

So many voices were shouting, or perhaps it was all an imagination and the shouts were my own. I groaned, looking around through blurred vision. Sokah had pinned Hagan to the ground, the whip discarded on the ground next to them. People were removing my chains. The two boys from the arena smiled, their hands gently setting my arms to the cobblestone.

Someone was yelling at someone else. "This is ridiculous! She is a *princess*. If you kill her the whole country will rebel."

Whoever was talking sounded angry. "I will not let her impertinence continue. And I will not have disrespect from my own blood!"

Another voice joined. "Uncle, please. She has received enough punishment."

Vukan replied, "She has defied her King."

Someone, I thought it was Lux, cut him off. "She is a nobody. You shouldn't show that such a low life bothers you. Let this go."

"Very well, take her to her chambers or the dungeon or wherever you wish," he growled.

Someone kneeled beside me.

Sebastien brushed the hair from my eyes. His eyes were such a beautiful gold brown in the light. They were like a sweet pool of honey, like the rays that showered the earth as the sun rose, or like the shimmering of coins in the moonlight. I reached out a crimson covered hand, my fingers brushing against the arch of his cheek.

He frowned. I had never noticed it before, but he had dimples. He was so handsome. The whole damned family was good-looking. I wish I could slice their faces off. I tried to talk, but words would not come out.

"Shhh... don't try to speak."

He scooped me into his arms, and I cried out in pain, the touch sending a fiery blaze through my body as he made contact with my wounds. He whispered words I couldn't make out as he carried me into the castle. By the time we reached the wing where my rooms were located, I was barely coherent. Sebastien stopped. I felt another pair of arms, strong and steady, wrap around me. I willed my brain to focus.

I whimpered and reached for Sebastien as he stepped away. "No... don't leave..."

"I'm sorry. I have to go."

I watched as he disappeared around the corner.

I turned my face into the shirt of the man who carried me now. He smelled of honey soap. I wished Dryden was here to tear Vukan to shreds.

I awoke the next morning on my stomach. My entire body was sore, my head throbbing. I hissed, biting my tongue as something cold touched my back.

"It's ice, sweetie. To help with the swelling." Rosalva's raspy voice was a soothing sound.

She pressed more ice to my back, and I gripped my sheets in my fists, burying my face into my pillow.

"I'm so sorry honey. I'm almost done. Then I'll put a salve on it—to keep the infection away. Then I'll let you be."

I screamed into the pillow as a cold cream touched my back. I wished I could black out again, or die. Anything was better than this.

Rosalva's voice was soft as she applied the medicine.

"Almost done."

My back arched, my body felt like a thousand needles were stabbing me.

Make it stop! Make it stop!

I screamed and screamed until my voice was hoarse. I was shaking, my voice dry and cracking by the time she was done.

I laid on my stomach for the rest of the day. Rosalva returned twice more, icing and applying salve to my back. Each time I would cry and scream. Thankfully, the third time she came, she brought a sedative with her. Why couldn't she have brought it sooner? It took the edge off, but the agony was still immense. Death was too much to ask for apparently. Then again, maybe this was my punishment, maybe this was what I deserved. I had killed people before too. Like those soldiers the day I was captured.

They were pawns in Vukan's sick hand. They had families, parents, siblings, or spouses who had cared about them. I deserved to suffer more.

I'd finally drifted to sleep when the door slammed open.

"What are you doing, Vukan?" demanded a voice I could not locate.

A hand grabbed my hair and yanked my head up.

I yelped, scrambling to my knees.

Vukan ordered, "Get out of bed."

I obeyed, too weak to resist.

I was thankful for the bindings on my wounds and the light nightgown Rosalva had put on before she left, although it offered little warmth. I stumbled after Vukan, his hand still gripping my hair until my scalp also burned.

He threw open my balcony doors. It was twilight, torches lining the yard outside. A storm rumbled in the distance. People were standing on the balconies to the left and right, others lined down below. Zasper came next to me, a guard shoving her from behind. Vukan was now holding my neck in his left hand, forcing me to look down. A deck had been placed below, and a pole... with a noose.

I glanced at the King, and his grip tightened, fingers digging into my skin. I was shaking again, but not from the cold. A few guards were scattered around, grim looks blanketing their faces. My heart dropped from my chest as a lone figure was brought out in chains.

Sokah did not look scared as he was led onto the wooden stage with his manacles clanging together. He was still in his guard's uniform. His face, oh, his face. His lips were bleeding and his nose looked broken, his skin purple from bruising. He looked straight ahead as the rope was placed around his neck. I shouted his name, and he jerked his head towards me, flashing his crooked grin through bloodied teeth and cracked lips.

I was exhausted, yet I conjured all the magic I could. I had to save him. I couldn't let him die, not another friend could because of me. A hand grabbed mine. Zasper shook her head, eyes knowing and pleading with me not to do anything.

She mouthed a few words. *You will be killed.*

I released the trickle of power that I had been able to dig up. The ice dissipated. I would not be able to dredge up any more magic. I was too tired. But I couldn't not do anything. Sokah could not die for my decisions.

I grabbed at the hand holding my neck. "My king, please, don't do this. Do not punish him. It is me you should punish."

"Valine, be quiet! It's too late to save him! You will only join him if you carry on," Zasper hissed.

Vukan didn't even bother to look at me. "It seems that giving you a physical reprimand is more trouble than it's worth, so I will show you the consequences of your actions. Apparently, that servant wench wasn't enough. So every time you disobey me, I will kill someone for your mistakes."

The king's gaze darted to Zasper and Sebastien.

My breath hitched. "Please… please… Why don't you just kill me instead?"

He finally looked down at me, eyes filled with a sick delight as seeing me beg. "Because it is much more fun tormenting the daughter of Ariella. If only your mother had accepted my offer to become her King and her my consort. Then none of this would have happened. But she refused, just like how you refuse to be obedient."

"Please, I'll do anything—"

His face softened ever so slightly. Would he listen to my pleas, sparing Sokah? He caressed my face.

"Too late."

He stood upright, his voice bellowing. "The soldier, Sokah Jang, is charged with treason against his King. And for that he shall hang. Any last words, soldier?"

Sokah's voice was strong and unwavering. "Yes, sir." He met my eyes. "Long live Queen Valine Polaris! Long may she reign!"

Vukan shouted obscenities, and the floor disappeared from beneath Sokah's feet. The rope went taught. Thankfully, the drop had broken his neck. He didn't deserve to slowly suffocate. He didn't deserve any of this.

My knees buckled as his body swung, and Zasper's arms caught me, my back protesting as she made contact with my bandages. I pushed her away, my knees barking as they hit the concrete. I reached through the bars, as if I could catch him, cradle his body, save him.

Vukan kicked my ribs, and I bit my tongue, a copper tang filling my mouth.

He leaned down to whisper in my ear, "I hope, Valine, that you will learn to tame your wild side, for your defiance only leads to death. And I know why you are here, what you hope to accomplish. Give it up and accept that you are nothing and have no one."

He dug his boot into my back. Through the searing pain I saw Sebastien restrain a seething Zasper.

Vukan continued. "You are *mine*. Accept your fate, Polaris bitch. Or you'll end up like your mother."

He stood, a smile replacing his sneer. "I hope to see you all at the next party."

And with a fling of his fur-trimmed cape, Vukan left.

My mind was foggy, but I remembered Zasper helping me to my bed, yelling at Sebastien the entire time. Sebastien walked out, refusing to listen to her. I laid on the bed, screaming internally, the sound bouncing against my skull. I didn't move, but I clawed at the inside of my head.

Zasper laid beside me and held my hand as I cried.

She kept her vigil the entire night.

CHAPTER TWELVE

*I**nfection ravaged my body*, and fever sent relentless shivers down all my limbs. I would experience the heat of the Ebocian summers and the freezing cold of the harsh Pardus winters. People came and went. It was all a blur. My back hurt, but my heart hurt worse. I couldn't handle another friend's death—more blood on my already stained hands. The infection caused me to hallucinate. My friends, Yanish, Fron, Zenith, Sokah were all crying out for help. But I couldn't save them. Was my throne really worth all this? Would death take everyone I cared for while leaving me?

The cold seeped into my chambers, brushing against my cheek with a tender kiss. It soothed my back, and I swore I heard humming.

A hand rested against my forehead. "Your fever broke."

I tried to look at who it was, but it took too much energy.

"I'm sorry Little Bird."

And then I drifted into sleep.

It took another month for me to be able to move somewhat normally again. My back was already scarring, but whenever I tried to exercise, I would feel tightness and pain, so I spent more time training my magic. I spent more time with Egann too. His words were comforting for my guilt racked mind.

I had met Egann once more at the tree, but instead of the usual practice, he immediately started walking towards the tree line. He was strangely fast for an old man with a limp.

"You could slow down, ya know. I am still recovering from my injuries."

Egann paused to check. "Are you bleeding?"

"No," I replied.

He resumed his trek into the forest. "Then you're fine to walk."

I felt sore but kept padding after him.

"Where are we going?" I asked.

"You'll know when we get there."

I should have expected such an answer.

After what felt like ages of silently walking behind him, we finally stopped at a large tent set up snuggly between two oaks. He disappeared inside, and I sighed, following after him.

The interior was relatively simple. There was bedding on the ground on one side and a foldable floor table with a single candle on the other. On the back side of the tent was a shelf, or a makeshift version of one, a few planks of wood haphazardly stacked to form a couple shelves that were filled with books and scrolls and the few odd jars of ink.

"You're stronger than you look, old man."

Egann's staff bonked me in the head. "Is that how you speak to your elders?"

I rubbed the spot on my head. "Sorry."

Egann sat on the ground next to his small table, and I took up the place across from him. I was about to ask what he brought me here for, but I thought better of it. He would tell me in his own time.

Egann scratched at his wiry beard.

"Do you have any questions?"

Well that was a first. A thousand curiosities flashed in my mind before I chose one.

"I don't understand why I have magic."

Egann scurried over to the shelf and shuffled through a few stacks, pulling out a wooden scroll.

He brought it back to the table and unfurled it.

"You see here, this is a list of names of people who have had magic—that are known of that is."

I leaned in to look. "There aren't that many."

Egann grunted in agreement. "There used to be more, but soon after you were born there were no others with the gift."

I peered over the list of names; only a few queens were among those on the scroll.

"So does everyone have to have their magic awakened, like you did for me?" I asked.

Egann stood to get another parchment. "No. Only you."

He always made me ask for details. "Why only me?"

He browsed the shelf. "Because something, or maybe even someone, has been stealing magic. Perhaps The Creator was simply protecting yours."

"What? Who would do that? *Why* would they do that?"

Egann shrugged. "I don't know."

"I thought you knew everything," I huffed.

Egann whacked my arm with his staff.

"Ouch!"

I rubbed the sore spot on my arm. I would leave looking like I had lost a brawl if I didn't watch my words. "Can I ask more questions?"

"You just did," he replied flatly.

I was about to roll my eyes, but stopped myself. I didn't need another whack. "Are these *all* the names of the people who have magic?"

I looked over the scroll, one name at a time. It seemed awfully short, less than a hundred names.

Egann sighed. "No. Unfortunately these names are just the ones I have heard about or know of myself."

My mouth dropped open. Zasper's name was the second to last on the list, just above mine. I was shocked that she had kept it a secret. I wanted to ask her about it when I returned, but it would likely be best to allow her to reveal it of her own accord. It would be hypocritical of me to be upset with her as I too had kept my magic hidden.

Above both our names was another, but it was blacked out with ink. I wondered if that meant that the wielder had died, but other names on the list had passed long ago, some even centuries past. As curious as I was as to why the name would be obscured, I wasn't so interested as to use another precious question to find out. Egann rarely answered my inquiries, and I had to prioritize them.

"So why do only a few people have magic, and where did it come from?"

"The first prophet was also the first recorded magic wielder, and as to why he and others like yourself have it, I am not sure. The Creator seemingly bestows it at random."

So much of life was annoyingly ambiguous. One could spend their whole life studying the world or communing with The Creator and never know everything. It irritated me greatly. I wanted to ask Him when I met Him in Paradise. Then again, such audacity and arrogance might just get me kicked out like a drunk out of a tavern. Maybe acceptance of the unknown was simpler, but I couldn't help myself.

One more question popped into my head.

"I don't know how to balance faith and disappointment."

Egann paused his organizing of the shelf. "You trust that He can and praise Him even if he doesn't," was his only answer. The old man stood abruptly. "Alright, enough talking, back to work."

When I arrived back at the castle, I stopped by Zasper's room. Like a siege weapon battering down the gates, the intense sorrow of Sokah's death invaded my mind, and I didn't want to be alone. All desire to inquire about her magic vanished, replaced with the grief. As I made myself comfortable on her bed, I noticed the markings on her arms. I had seen her inked skin a few times before, but I took particular interest in that moment.

In Percia, women stained their skin with *hinna* as a form of adornment, and it was common for Ebocians to ink their skin both for beautification as well as ceremonies for royals. A tradition on the Galapos islands was to use the markings as a form of history, the black symbols representing their family heritage.

I asked Zasper to engrave me. Agreeing to it after I told her what I wanted, Zasper prepared the tools necessary and special ink. I prayed that I wouldn't have to add anymore flowers to my leg, that I wouldn't have to watch anyone else die from anything other than old age.

I had to hold my pillow from the scratching pain of the needle carving my skin.

Zasper looked up for a moment. "It'll only sting for a while, nothing compared to your back."

I tightened my grip on the pillow. "It's okay. I deserve it."

Zasper paused. "Don't you say that. Don't you ever even think that again, *Chui.*"

I couldn't meet her gaze. "I have done so many things... bad things, cowardice things, selfish things. And no matter how many times people tell me, I don't think The Creator loves me."

Zasper's expression softened in sympathy, brows lowered and lips squished together. "No matter what you have done that you think is so terrible, it is not so terrible that it will stop His love."

I wanted so desperately for that to be true.

The pain, loss, and thoughts I had never shared before, had kept locked away, bubbled up, yearning to be spoken aloud.

"After Vukan came and destroyed my tranquil life, I escaped thanks to a few servants and soldiers who brought me to a baker couple, Korine and Sidian. They were so gentle and comforting. Despite the danger to their own lives, they housed me for weeks. Eventually, I went to the coast, hoping to find safety. For a short time I found refuge on a ship, but then I left there too. I thought maybe I could return home and get everything back. You know, at first I wanted to regain my throne because it was my birthright, that it was an inherent entitlement that the citizens of Racour would also want me to receive. Then, as I roamed Pardus those months after returning, I didn't hear cries and mourning. No one was sad about the coup that had killed my mother or even the other kings. Although one name was whispered. Perhaps some people missed one of the Kings, but none missed my mother."

I pulled the pillow closer. "Actually, I heard many people say they were happy she was gone."

I glanced at Zasper. "Do you know what they called her?"

I didn't wait for her to respond. "Ariella the Vain, who painted fruit for her starving people instead of growing them."

Zasper didn't move as I continued. "And I cried for a few days. Denying it at first, but slowly acknowledging how unfit to rule my mother was, that the image that I had painted of her was not shared by the masses. I don't think she was necessarily vain, rather, she was just unprepared to be Queen. She just wanted to be a girl, an artist actually. She didn't know how to make decisions about matters of import. And looking back, she had it hard too. Her husband and son died, and she did the best she could. I know that doesn't excuse her actions, or lack thereof. Yet I find myself still missing her. Even though we didn't spend that much time together, she was still my mother."

I added, "Of course, everyone in Racour would find out how terrible life under the Wulfrics would be after Vukan showed his true self a year later. But at the time... they probably thought that things would improve." I sighed. "My hopes were dashed so quickly, so easily. So I left again. Although this time I ran until I found a river fast flowing, deep, with plenty of rocks. The first time I had gone to water to find safety, but that time..."

The pause was long enough that Zasper had to ask, "Why did you search for a river?"

"So I could die."

Zasper's breath hitched.

I was surprised by the absence of tears as I told her. "It was my thirteenth birthday."

I looked at her, without really seeing her. "I realized that my mother would not be missed by anyone but me and perhaps a few loyal citizens and servants, and that I didn't deserve to be queen, especially if I would be a ruler like her, if my fate would be like hers."

Zasper's eyes were watering. "What happened?'

I stared off into the distance, looking beyond my friend, beyond the walls of the castle, beyond the city and mountains.

"I jumped in. I didn't even feel the instinct to swim, to fight against the pounding of the river. It was winter, and it didn't take long for my body to go numb. I blacked out. I didn't feel the pain, or the fear, but I did feel a tinge of regret before I lost consciousness. I knew the memory of my existence would be lost into oblivion. The last of the Polaris line, the heir to the Leopard Throne... gone."

A whimper echoed. I turned to Zasper, but then I realized the pitiful sound came from me.

I had been so lost then. "But then I was found."

We stayed up late into the night, the princess listening quietly and tentatively, one by one inking flowers into my leg, as I explained how a man named Yanish, who lived with his daughter in the woods, pulled me from the river and death's grip. How after I awoke, he began training me. I worked for years, developing my hunting and fighting skills.

Once I became of age and we had gathered a few more followers, we spread rumors. Whispers of rebellion began to grow, and soon Yanish had tents outside his cabin, a whole camp of people willing to fight for their queen, in the hopes that she would be better than those who came before—better than the current bloody king. It was hard, parents sending their sons to fight pointless wars and their wages leached away through heavy taxes. Eventually we got so big that we had to leave that little clearing in the woods in favor of nomadic living. We had to constantly move to keep out of Vukan's reaches, who had also heard the rumors.

The skin of my thigh was red and swollen, now covered in rows of flowers.

"A memorial," I whispered, "so they will never be forgotten."

After she finished, I thanked her and left to go to my own room. I went to my balcony and opened the doors. Even though it was cold outside, I welcomed it, a balm to my aching back and burning thigh.

Twisting my hand and whirling my fingers, I flicked my wrist and an icy sculpture began to form on the balcony. After a few minutes and a few finishing touches, I laid my hands on my lap, only a few drops of sweat having formed on my forehead. Egann would have been proud.

I had erected an ice replica of my mother, at least what I remembered her to look like. I slipped off the railing and stood in front of it. She had been so beautiful, with long, wavy hair and caramel eyes that you could just drown in, being deemed one of the most beautiful queens to rule. She preferred spending time in her carefully cultivated gardens, where we would have the occasional picnic with my father and a brother I could barely remember, or she would paint in her room. After my father and brother passed, she never really left her room.

I sighed.

I would be a better ruler, more aware and discerning, and I would not allow myself to meet the same brutal end that she did. Then again, it was arrogant of me to think I had that kind of control. I was about to deconstruct my mother when a gasp sounded behind me.

Zasper's eyes were wide.

Her gaze moved from the ice to me. "How did you do that?"

I fumbled for the words to say, my heart beating like a hummingbird's wings. "What are you doing here?"

She revealed a small ceramic in her hand. "I wanted to give you this to put on the ink, to help it heal well. But..."

She gaped at the sculpture.

I slowly lifted my palms. "Stay calm..."

Zasper strode over to the sculpture and studied it, finger hovering over the frozen sculpture. "Stay calm? This is amazing!"

She paused her studious walk around the ice to look at me. "Valine, I knew you had magic, but I didn't realize it was this powerful."

I cocked my head. "You knew I had magic?"

Zasper nodded but didn't verbally answer my question, instead grabbing a piece of soil from a potted, now withered plant, on the balcony. She turned her palm up and twiddled her fingers, a small flower appearing in her hand.

I didn't know what to say.

Zasper shrugged. "It's not as impressive as what you can do, but I have the element of life. I can make plants grow and heal minor injuries and sickness."

"Why would you show me this? How can you be certain that I won't tell Vukan of your secret?"

Zasper gently laid the tiny flower on the rail. "Because I wanted you to trust me not to tell anyone here of your magic. Vukan would only want to exploit it. You would be a great weapon if he could break you and control you, and we both know what he would do if he couldn't."

She was right.

"Besides," she added, "if I was wrong about you, I could just as easily threaten to inform him of your own magic."

Mutually assured destruction. My friend was kind yet cautious, and I was impressed with her foresight.

"Well I am glad you came, because we now don't have to hide our magic from each other. But why didn't you heal my back?"

She looked at me unapologetically. "Because you need to learn how to live with the pain."

She could be harsh at times.

I willed the ice sculpture to melt and, faster than a thirsty man consuming water, all that remained was a puddle.

I stepped over it and picked up the pink flower Zasper had bloomed. "Did you know all along?"

Zasper nodded. "He told me before coming here. He is Ebocian too, after all."

I whipped my head up. "You know him?"

Zasper steered clear of the water and came next to me "Of course. Egann often prophesied in my father's court. We wondered where he went when he suddenly stopped visiting, but then he sent me a message one day. He told me I was needed in Racour."

My mouth dropped open.

That was a better explanation of how she was able to arrive so quickly following my capture.

We talked for a while, and she told me about Egann's past. Apparently he was just as annoyingly vague and intrusive in Eboc as he was here. Zasper told me that her magic was stronger when she was a child, but as the years passed it was gradually weakening, like a hole in a rice bag, slowly leaking. I recalled Egann's mentioning of the matter, that something seemed to be leeching magic from the world until there were so few magic wielders left that many people had written it off as old tales. However that wasn't my problem at the moment, something more immediate and urgent needed my attention.

I returned to an earlier part of our conversation. "But during the picnic you had said... So you came here because of Egann?"

She smiled. "Of course. You didn't think we were actually going to surrender, did you? It was all an excuse."

"But if Vukan finds out you aren't really here for surrender negotiations..." I grabbed Zasper's hands. "It's dangerous!"

She squeezed my hands. "I came, knowing that I could be forfeiting my life, even if he doesn't kill me, he likely won't let me leave. I am too valuable of a hostage, and he is far too keen on acquiring our land."

My eyes searched her face for any signs of fear or anxiety, yet there were no lines of worry, only a peaceful expression. "Why? Why would you do all that for me?"

Zasper went to cup my cheek but switched to a gentle hand on my shoulder.

"I have told you many times before, no? The Creator has great plans for you, and my role is to support you."

I placed my hand over hers. "Thank you, my friend."

I furrowed my brow. "Then you knew then too. At the execution."

She dropped her hand, the first time I had seen her look remorseful. "Yes. I am truly sorry about Sokah, but I don't regret stopping you."

I looked away, I didn't agree with her on that. I still felt guilty about not saving him.

I finally looked at Zasper.

"Why didn't you let me help him?"

Zasper grabbed my hand, her grip tight. "Because I also believe in you. I believe that you are the one who can get rid of the Wulfrics. You are the one to secure not only Racour's future, but also Eboc's. I know how much Sokah meant to you as a friend, but you are more important."

I tried to remove my hand, but she held on. "Not less valuable of a life, but yours is more important. You have things you must do, and you could not accomplish them if you're dead."

I couldn't keep the venom from my voice. "How could you say that?"

Zasper grabbed my other hand, as if she could diffuse understanding into them. "You overestimate your abilities. If you had saved Sokah, even killed Vukan, do you really think that would be the end of it? That one of his generals or one of the other kings wouldn't take his place and kill you? That a loyal soldier wouldn't have shot you with an arrow? You don't have enough power to freeze all your enemies. None of us do. And from what I know about you, I doubted you would have enough control to make sure no one innocent wouldn't be harmed. So yes, I stopped you from saving him because you would have both ended up dead one way or another. Those flowers, those people, they all made their choice. They chose you. They chose the future you can bring. Do you think Sokah didn't know what would happen when he intervened to help you? Do you think any of your deceased comrades followed you ignorantly? Our deaths are never in our own control, but our lives, what we do with them, is the only thing we can control. Hold their memories, but don't hold the guilt of their deaths."

I didn't know what to feel. I was sad and angry at her words. I was angry at myself, at Vukan, at life.

"I still can picture his swinging body, can still hear the sound of his neck breaking."

Zasper hugged me. "I know my *Chui*."

She kissed my cheek and whispered in my ear how much she loved me, how proud of me she was, and what a great ruler I would make, because I had seen the suffering and wanted to do something about it. That I had seen and been through so much and hadn't become indifferent and coldhearted. She told me that The Creator had saved my life so that others could live. I was intended for great things, and I was grateful for her words of encouragement. But I still needed more. More power, more people. I fell asleep thinking about how I could gain each of those

things, praying that I would not see the gallows in my
dreams.

CHAPTER THIRTEEN

The next couple days were spent in bed in a depressive spell, unable to gather the energy to get up, but soon enough Zasper came to get me. She said she had a good idea to cheer me up and take my mind off of things. I was surprised when she guided me to the soldiers sector and led me to the sparring pit.

Sokah.

The crushing grip on my heart grew more intense, and my nose tingled as my throat tightened.

Zasper wrapped her arm around me. "Are you okay? Do you want to go back?"

I shook my head. "No. I need to face it, embrace it."

I cleared my throat and forced myself to move forward, and we went to sit under a tree near the pit.

"Why did you bring me here of all places?" With a lump in my throat, my voice came out with a squeak.

Zasper pointed to the opposite end. "Because I heard a couple of wolves were going to playfight."

I followed the direction of her finger to where two men in winter tunics and loose pants were standing by the weapon wall. Sebastien ran his hand over the blade of a short sword, and Lux was deciding between a single-sided and double-sided blade.

Zasper smiled. "Who do you think will win?"

I jutted my chin towards the Legate. "Of course Sebastien. He is a military leader while Lux is... Lux."

Her narrowed eyes assessed them each carefully. "I don't know. He could surprise you. Sometimes you have to watch out for the unassuming ones."

Both men walked into the pit with weapons in hand. Sebastien met my stare, sparing a moment to acknowledge Zasper.

Lux smiled, eyes bright at the site of us. "Enjoy the show, beautiful ladies."

"I hate boys," I grumbled.

Zasper snickered. "Eh, they are not all bad. Some are even good."

We watched as Lux and Sebastien sparred, the Crown Prince surprisingly deft, able to keep up with the Legate. But soon the differences in their abilities became evident, as Sebastien flung Lux's sword from his hand. While most men would be humbled by a blatant show of inferior skills, Lux winked at me as he stood weaponless. He still had the audacity to flirt.

I switched my gaze to Sebastien. He caught me staring, and for some strange reason I blushed, lowering my head. The corner of his mouth twitched up. I thought it might be a smile but before it had the chance to bloom, a sword came swinging at him. Lux had retrieved his blade while Sebastien was distracted, but Sebastien whipped his sword up, blocking the strike.

The sound of metal clashing was like a melody, a constant rhythm of clanging. I stopped paying attention, and my mind wandered. I thought about Egann, who I hadn't seen in weeks, and Dryden, who I had only met that once yet was inexplicably bound to. I missed them both. But at least I could see them again in this life. For Sokah, Yanish, Fron, my family and all the others who had passed, I would have to wait for a long time. I was almost certain I would live a long, tedious life before we could reunite. I felt almost cursed to live.

Zasper's prodding elbow brought me back to the present. Lux had disappeared, but Sebastien approached us. He stood before us, sweat dripping down his neck.

I teased, "Sebastien, I must say, I expected you to beat Lux much faster."

Sebastien finally smiled, white teeth shining like a crescent moon across his tanned face. "Well, Valine, I am sure you could do no better."

I feigned offense, hand clutching my heart. "I beg to differ."

He lifted a brow, causing a drop of sweat to fall down his temple. Moving without fully thinking, I stood, and wiped the drop from his face. Sebastien seemed shocked by the contact of our skin. I was too. I wasn't sure why I felt the need to do that.

I stepped back and held out my hand to Zasper while maintaining eye-contact with the Legate. "I hope you won't disappoint me next time."

Zasper grabbed my hand and stood. "I am here too."

Sebastien coughed. "Ah, yes. My apologies Princess Zasper. I, uh…"

Zasper laughed. waving her hand in the air. "Well now that the show is over, we will take our leave."

Sebastien bowed slightly, and I nodded good-bye.

As we walked back inside, Zasper reached over, a finger grazing my temple. "Oh, you have a little bit of sweat. Let me get that for you."

I swatted her hand away. "Very funny."

Zasper giggled, and we headed towards her room.

It was strange though. I had been relatively fine watching the sparring, and even on the way back, I was laughing and talking pleasantly with Zasper. But as soon as we entered Zasper's room, I broke down crying.

I felt like a blacksmith's hammer, constantly swinging up and down with my emotions. One moment I was determined and resolute like a sturdy, well crafted blade, and the next I was a melted pile of ore, wanting to disappear into a pile of useless goop.

"I'm just so tired. I can't do this anymore."

I didn't even have the energy to grip Zasper as she held me.

"I know you are tired. I know you want to quit. I know it would be easier if you settle for less, less than what you can do, less than what you *should* do. So don't settle. You are strong, and when you are weak, I shall be there to help carry you until you have regained your strength. But do not give up. For if you do, the world will be deprived of what could have been, who *you* could have been. A girl who held stars in her eyes, fire in her heart, and kindness in her fingertips." Zasper kissed my brow.

I sobbed into her chest, and she hugged me until I could cry no more. Then I pulled back, wiped my tears, stood, and prepared myself to face the rest of the day.

And that's how I would live, day by day, keeping an image of the future in my head, a future where Racour was at peace and the world was a gentler place. Each day I would remind myself of that image, to inspire me, and when I could not conjure the motivation from within, I would go to my friends who would help me reach that better world. And I would look to my Creator, who Egann and Zasper spoke so fondly of.

It had been a few months since Sokah died. I still missed him, missed his lopsided smile and quips in the training courtyard, but the pain was dulled, although ever present. I couldn't comprehend how my heart was still beating with the loss of so many I cared about, and I was surprised it hadn't just given out. Unfortunately, I was always the one who lived.

My back had also healed, although there would likely be scars, so it was time to go back to physical training. I couldn't only depend on my magic since there was a limited amount I had access to.

The outside training courtyard was now covered in a small layer of snow, so the soldiers now trained in a building next to the barracks. I cracked open the door, the sounds of metal clanging and gruff voices greeting me. I slipped inside, my long cloak fluttering behind me, and was met almost immediately with stares. One by one every soldier in the room paused his practice to look at me. And one by one they all placed their arms over their chest and bowed.

I stared back, dumbfounded, struggling to find the words to say. "I..." My cheeks were wet. "I don't deserve... I am so sorry."

A pair of strong arms suddenly enveloped me, and my spine stiffened. A bronze haired middle aged man, tan and wrinkled by time and sun, pulled back and patted my head.

"Thank you. You tried to help us, and you saved my nephews."

Two boys came up and stood on each side of him. One was tall and lanky with red hair and freckles to match, the other had bronze hair, hazel eyes, and a stocky figure. They were the two boys from the fighting tournament.

They both grinned.

"I'm Ferrum." The red head held out his hand.

"And I'm Talom," the shorter boy said while offering his hand.

"And I'm Mordris. And these are," he wrapped his arms around the boys as he spoke, "my sister's rambunctious boys."

I smiled and wiped an arm across my face, sleeve coming away wet. "It's a pleasure to meet you. I am glad you two are okay now."

I glanced past them to the rest of the soldiers who stood still, watching us. "But I don't think it's appropriate. Such appreciation when Sokah..."

Mordris's big hands shook my shoulders. "That's not your fault. It's—"

Talom elbowed his uncle. "Don't say it."

Mordris huffed, "We all know where the fault truly lies. Despicable bastard."

"Uncle!" The boys cried out in unison.

Mordris turned, one hand still on my shoulder. "All these men here don't blame you. It's completely the opposite. All of us are grateful."

He paused to whisper in my ear, "Grateful for such a wonderful future queen of Racour."

My eyes widened. "You—"

He put a finger to his mouth.

I didn't know what to say.

Mordris brought me over to a corner as the rest of the men resumed their training. He double-checked, ensuring no one was in earshot. Even so, his voice was cautiously quiet. "I've put up with that son of a bitch for too long. I already lost my brother to Vukan's futile war with Indo in the south. Those boys already lost their father, and then they almost lost their lives. I would have stepped in if I hadn't been out on patrol. But luckily someone else did."

"Were you not all aware of the tournament beforehand?" I inquired.

Mordris' tone darkened and his eyes narrowed.

"Vukan isn't dull. He managed to overthrow and kill the other kings and the late High Queen, as you are aware. This time too he arranged for the guards who he suspected would interfere to be stationed elsewhere or on patrol, unable to intervene. Those who were forced to participate were informed by Vukan's personal squad just before it started. They had no choice and no time."

Mordris' voice was bitter, and his gaze promised violence. "I would have cut down anyone to get to my nephews and keep them safe." The words were as sharp as the steel he threatened to embed in his enemies.

I couldn't help but voice my thoughts. "I wonder why Vukan didn't kill Talom and Ferrum too."

"My guess is he is wary of his own military turning against him. The tournament and Sokah's *execution* were enough to unsettle most men as it is. If he pushes the ranks too far..."

"Even fear won't be enough to keep them under his control," I finished.

He smiled, the corners of his eyes crinkling. "For some, it's too late. And for saving my nephews I am eternally grateful and willing to pledge my life for you."

I took a step back. "I can't accept that."

He frowned. "And why not?"

I wrung my hands together, something catching in my throat. "Because so many have already died on behalf of me, on behalf of my ill-fated plan."

Mordris shook his head, hands waving in conviction. "We already are dying on behalf of Vukan. Look at what he does. Start useless wars and throw us in a ring to beat each other to death for his own sick pleasure. At least this way I can die for something noble and worthy."

Once again I felt the all too familiar sting in my nose and eyes. He was right. Just like Zasper. People were dying anyway, and if they wanted to grant me their lives for my cause, for my throne, for hope, then I would need to accept it. If there was any chance at getting my kingdom back from Vukan, I couldn't do it alone. I had to accept people's help, accept people's loyalty, and accept people's lives. And with that I would have to accept their deaths.

"Then I will receive your pledge."

As I went to leave, a familiar face stopped me. Falchor looked older than when we had last met. Then again, a lot had transpired between now and then. He gave me a smile, but his eyes were soaked in sorrow.

He handed me a folded piece of paper. "Sokah is—was—my dear friend. And I know he was yours too."

His eyes watered. "He wanted to give you this. He wrote it while in the dungeon. He slipped it to me before... before he was taken away."

I nodded, unable to find the words. Falchor squeezed my hand once before walking away.

I slipped out the door and headed back to my room.

Later that night, Zasper and I went back to the sparring yard. She promised to teach me how to better use a staff. During my days with Yanish, I had practiced with every blade. bow, and baton, but the Ebocian style of fighting with their favored weapon was unmatched.

To others, it may look suspicious to see two princess-es—both who had reasons to not like Vukan—practicing together. Going on a picnic or taking a stroll in the gardens was one thing, but training together in fighting skills was another thing entirely, and something that would likely invoke Vukan's anger. So we made sure to come at night while also avoiding the indoor training hall. They never stationed guards at the training area at night, so it was the best time for us to go. The barracks were detached from the castle structure and far enough away that we wouldn't be heard, and it was so cold outside that we assumed no one else would brave the low temperatures, even on the off chance they noticed us.

The only light that was provided was that of the full moon and the torches lining the courtyard. Zasper and I made our way to the weapons rack. It did seem rather foolish to keep weapons unlocked and left open to the elements, but Vukan was likely too arrogant to think it was dangerous or too irresponsible to care about the expenses of replacing them. Sebastien should have known, however, but perhaps he too thought it was inconsequential, seeing as all the training weapons here were dulled for practice.

As we approached, we heard scuffling. We threw ourselves behind a pillar, forcing our breaths to quiet, but there was still no one in sight. Suddenly the noise got louder, the sound of punches and groans. We looked at each other, nodded, and quietly crept towards the source of the fighting.

In a small alcove, the torchlight illuminated two men fighting. One had his shirt almost torn off of him, but both had bruises on their faces and blood dripping from somewhere. It took me a few moments to realize who they were. Lux and Sebastien were locked in a violent argument. Lux pinned Sebastien to the wall, and the little bit of cloth covering his back was ripped by The Legate as he grappled for the upperhand.

Lux's back was covered in black markings. There was a name on his back, and two small dragons circled around it. It wasn't quite light enough for me to make out the inked name. Thinking back, I had seen Sebastien without his shirt on multiple occasions near the barracks, but not Lux.

A sneeze broke the two men apart. I looked over my shoulder to see Zasper, an apologetic look on her face. I turned back towards the two Wulfric men, but Lux was already halfway to the door, hands scrambling to pull the remnants of his shirt back together.

Sebastien rotated his shoulder and smoothed back his ruffled hair. "What are you two doing here?"

His voice was gruff and strained.

I glanced at Zasper. "We, uh… We were just going to exercise."

Sebastien wiped the blood from his cracked lip. "In this freezing weather?" he asked incredulously. And then, without giving us time to come up with an excuse, he said, "You should return to your rooms now." It was a command, not a suggestion.

Zasper and I made no argument and quickly turned and hastily made our way to our rooms.

After I closed my door and changed into my nightgown, I tucked myself into bed. Sleep didn't come though, as a picture was seared into my brain. Beneath Lux's tattoos were white scars, some long, some smaller—perhaps created by an arrow or knife. I wondered what had caused each of the marks, wondered if Vukan's cruelty touched even his own blood.

CHAPTER FOURTEEN

It was now well into winter, and as the snowfall was increasing, so was my impatience. I sat in my room with a quill and a paper hidden between the pages of a boring book, writing out the names of all the soldiers who had secretly pledged themselves to me the past couple weeks. I knew it was risky, but it was helpful for me to write things out rather than trying to keep track in my head. I kept the page well hidden when I left, just in case someone secretly searched my things while I was out.

Every time I went to the training room, Mordris or his nephews would bring me someone new. As I fumbled with the quill, a piece of paper fell out from another set of pages. The folded letter had remained closed, as I was unable to gather the courage to read it.

Would it be condemnation waiting in the ink?

As I looked over the list of names, I knew that I had to read it. Mordris and Falchor both had told me multiple times not to feel ashamed, to blame myself. It was hard not to. My fingers reached for the tips of the letter, and I unfolded it.

Dear Valine,

Although our friendship was brief, I was grateful for it. I don't know how much time I have left, so I will keep this short. I am certain that you will feel guilty for my death, but don't. When he came to fetch me, he informed me that you had courageously stood up for Ferrum and Talom, I suspect you just like the attention, but then I saw you getting whipped for it. I couldn't help myself, as I didn't want only you to be known as the chivalrous one, so I had to step in for my queen. Just don't let it go to waste. And one day, when you succeed, please take care of my family. My parents and little sister will have to work harder now that they won't have me to help. When you rebuild your kingdom, keep them in mind. I have to go now.

Don't cry too much. But also not too little; since that would be insulting to me.

May we meet again,
Sokah Jang
Your friend and loyal soldier

A wet dot soaked the paper, followed by two more. I read the letter again. He was so brave, so generous, so beautiful inside and out. He had forgiven me, no, he had insinuated that there was nothing to forgive. Snot dripped from my nose as I laughed and cried all at the same time. I felt the pressure on my shoulders lighten just a bit. Yanish, Fron, Sokah, Tagon and even my mother. Every single one of them had stood for something greater than themselves. My mother may have only gathered such courage to save me, but it was more than most. I would not let them be forgotten, nor would their deaths be in vain. A great evil such as Vukan had arisen, and so maybe The Creator had been preparing me, willing to use me to combat such darkness. I looked back to the list of names. He had inspired so many to rise alongside me.

Knocking on the door forced me to scramble. I shoved the letter and paper back inside the book and slammed it shut.

I rushed to cram the book in between the cushions of the couch. I stood and opened the door, hoping my response time had not been suspiciously long.

Sebastien stood in the doorway, holding something behind his back.

I raised a brow. "To what do I owe the pleasure that the great Legate would visit me?"

Sebastien shifted. "I, uh…"

He was uncharacteristically inarticulate. I couldn't help but smile a bit.

"I was worried about your, uh, back." He continued. "So I brought you something."

He finally revealed what was behind him—a ceramic. I took it from his calloused hand and opened it, an off-white cream with green flecks swirled inside. I lifted it to my nose, inhaling the scent of some sort of mixture of herbs and oils.

"It will help heal the scars."

I put the lid back on. "And who said I wanted to make my scars go away?"

Sebastien ran a hand through his hair, which had grown a bit longer, but not nearly as long as Lux's, which almost reached his waist.

"You know, women are sensitive about their appearance."

The warm sentiment dissipated. "I didn't know you were so *knowledgeable* about women."

A confused expression clouded his face. I turned and walked towards my desk, setting it next to my other cosmetics.

"But I suppose I should be grateful. Thanks."

I turned back around, Sebastien still standing in the doorframe, hands awkwardly dangling at his sides.

"You know, you could have just had Rosalva deliver it."

Sebastien opened his mouth to reply, but I cut him off, "Well you should at least sit down."

"Ah, yes."

Sebastien strode towards the sofa, bending his knees at the perfect angle—a sharp soldier. I sat on the armchair opposite him.

"I was worried about you."

My heart skipped a beat, and I shifted in my seat. "And why would you be worried about a little ole prisoner? Shouldn't you be disappointed that I am not dead yet?"

Sebastien frowned, which he did more often than smiling. "I don't want that. I don't want you hurt, Valine."

I rolled my eyes, ignoring the leap in my chest.

He leaned forwards, putting his elbows on his knees. "I mean it, Valine. Why do you think I allow you to train? You, who is the biggest threat to the Wulfrics. It's because I want you to be safe, to be able to protect yourself."

I stared at his eyes. "And what if I am protecting myself against your family?"

He leaned away, hands clasped in his lap. "My loyalty will always be to my Commander and to King Vukan."

"So formal for someone you call family," I sneered.

Sebastien stood suddenly, hands waving. "Lux wanted you sent to be a servant in some low noble's family. *I* kept that from happening."

Lux wanted me to become a servant? Not that it was inherently a job one should be ashamed about, but for a royal to become a servant, especially for a lower house, would be an obvious humiliation. Any pity his scars had caused to form inside me vanished.

But why would Sebastien help me? He was a constant contradiction.

I looked up at him, refusing to stand. "I think you wanted to keep me here because you can keep an eye on me and make sure I'm not causing any trouble, no?"

Approaching, Sebastien put both his arms on the back of my chair, one on each side. "Yes, but not for the reason you think."

Before I could respond he pulled away, but I had seen his eyes. They had roamed dangerously in the direction of my lips. Had he wanted to kiss me? How ridiculous. I whipped my head away.

"Thank you then. Maybe."

I felt the light touch of a hand on my face. And all too quickly it disappeared.

"There was a piece of dust."

Sebastien made a hasty exit, leaving me to dissect his words and intentions.

The next day was a strangely warm one for the middle of winter. The sun reflected off the snow, and a few stubborn birds that refused to migrate for the cold months sang outside, and it was too nice of a day to stay inside. I was tired of being cooped up in the castle, since I was no longer meeting with Egann. I had enough control of my power for now, and it had become much too dangerous to continue to slip in and out of the castle.

I was certain that Vukan had ordered the guards to keep a tighter watch on me, and Citadel was appearing less often. On one such occasion when I had tried to leave, the soldiers on duty had stopped me. A while later when I had successfully slipped out, I was unable to shake the trailing guards, so I was forced to return back to the palace.

I decided that the easiest and safest way to have some fun was to convince Sebastien to be the one on guard duty. He had some sort of affection for me, but whether it was simply a strange moral obligation or something else, I wasn't sure.

I made my way towards his rooms, but I bumped into him in the hall before I reached them. He was wearing his military uniform with the addition of a fur lined cape, his eyes stern and jaw clenched, looking lost in serious thought. His hair was slicked back and the scent of cinnamon wafted off of him. My heart skipped a beat, but I attributed it to the over-consumption of sugar from the pastries I ate earlier.

I bent my torso to the side, my hair waving in the air as I looked up at him. I did my best to goad Sebastien into sparring with me. "You know they always say to work out your pent up emotions before they explode. Some training would be perfect."

Sebastien assessed me, eyes boring deep, burning holes, as if searching for my true intentions.

I wanted to cross my arms, to put up a wall between me and his analyzing gaze, but I knew that it was better to remain in a relaxed and open stance.

"Fine," he finally replied with no enthusiasm in his voice.

I padded after him as we strode through the halls towards the in-door training center, having to leave the warmth of the main palace to reach the detached set of buildings.

As we entered, the soldiers who were drilling paused to salute their Legate. Although I noticed that after Sokah's death, there was less admiration in their eyes, some outright refusing to make eye-contact, faces glued elsewhere.

Sebastien nodded, and the men resumed their practice.

Passing by the weapons, we went straight towards the sparring rug, which was thin and well worn, barely offering any cushion. Casting his cloak aside and rolling up his sleeves, Sebastien shifted into a fighting stance. I followed suit, tossing my own cape on top of his.

Observing stances, grips, and tells, we circled each other, arms raised. Some told their next move in their eyes, others couldn't hide what their abdomen and feet were revealing. It was harder to know in advance when neither of us held weapons, as it was easier to look at fingers or wrists to know when a blade or bow would be used. Training my eyes on his, soaking in the rest of his form in my peripheral, I was determined to not allow my own to give me away.

But there was only so much one could do to mask their intentions. I shifted my weight onto my back left foot, and exploded towards him. I brought my right foot towards his knee, attempting to kick it in. He launched up, jumping higher than I ever could, and avoided my attack. As he came back down, he stretched out a leg, attempting to kick me in the head. Headshots must be a staple in Wulfric training.

I lunged to the side, narrowly avoiding his boot. I recovered in a crouch, lightly bracing myself with my hand in front of me. I flashed out my leg once more, pivoting on my wrist. I made contact, Sebastien having had no time to recover from his previous move. The Legate thudded to the ground on his back. I pounced on top of him, knees pinning his forearms to the ground.

I smirked. "Is this the best The Legate has to offer?"

A spark glinted in his eyes, and my smile dissolved.

A pair of legs wrapped around my head, and all the air expelled from my lungs as I was slammed onto the ground. Now Sebastien was on top of me, his weight forcing my back into the dirt floor. There was a small rock that had somehow found its way inside, likely brought in by a boot, protruding painfully into my lower back. I squirmed but was unable to free myself. I tried to emulate the move he had used on me, but my legs flung feebly, tapping his back uselessly.

His head towering over my own, smirk plastered on his face, he asked, "Do you yield?"

My face flushed, and my heart was beating so hard that I wouldn't have been surprised if the whole room heard it.

"I surrender."

He stood, offering me a hand. I took it, and he yanked me up, almost causing me to crash into his chest. We released our grip on each other, and I wiped the sweat from my hands onto my clothes, hoping he hadn't noticed. Then again, why did I care if he did? Sweating was natural and nothing to be embarrassed about.

I looked out towards the window, longing for my eyes to be anywhere but his handsome face.

Outside, the sun was reflecting off the snow. I turned back to face Sebastien, who was tying his cloak back together.

"Let's go outside!" I suggested.

Sebastien smoothed his ruffled hair back down. "I have some matters to attend to, Valine."

I grabbed his arm, my cape slung over his other, and pulled him towards the door.

"Come on. This is likely the only warm day we will have until spring."

His brows furrowed in contemplation.

"Please..." I said with pouty lips.

He acquiesced, "Fine. But only for a few minutes."

I skipped outside and spun in a circle, inhaling the fresh air.

"What's the difference between this and the gardens?"

I stopped to look at him. "Because I see them all the time. They're one of the few places I am allowed to go freely."

Sebastien still looked puzzled. "I still don't see why you begged me to bring you out here."

I took a few steps towards him. "I was bored and didn't want to go back into the palace yet."

He cocked a brow. "Is it really that hard to bear? I used to keep watch for hours at a time in some of the most mundane places."

I stepped forward again, so close that our noses were almost touching. "Boredom is a dangerous thing, Legate. Especially in the hands of those who have power."

Sebastien didn't reply. His eyes glanced from my own to my lips as he leaned forward. The corner of my mouth twitched. His lips brushed mine. Then his breath hitched, and he reeled backwards. He pulled on the lapels of his cloak, opened his mouth to speak, stopped, cleared his throat, and spoke again, "You're right Valine, boredom is a dangerous thing." He looked away, voice low. "But you are far more so."

The bright light of the sun was extinguished by Sebastien, who had thrown my cloak on my head. My hands batted at it wildly, my hair becoming frizzy from the friction. I unveiled myself just in time to see Sebastien slip into the castle.

I shook my head.

I couldn't believe that Sebastien had tried to kiss me. And that I had wanted him to.

I reluctantly followed him back inside, our venture outdoors cut far too short.

The next time I was at the training hall, the room was strangely empty. Talom was the only one I recognized out of the few soldiers drilling.

I pulled his sleeve. "Where is everyone? Why is it so quiet here today?"

Talom turned to answer. "It's the Legate's birthday, so there is going to be a small banquet."

I was surprised that I hadn't realized it was Sebastien's birthday. To be honest, I didn't know much about him, except the ways I could kill him. But he had been strangely considerate, perhaps even caring, so I figured I should prepare something for him.

"Who will be there?"

Talom picked at his acne ridden skin. "Only nobles and some high ranking soldiers. But afterwards the men will drink all together in the barracks."

Sebastien may have been born of murderers, but he had the respect of his men, and either enough time had passed to lessen the sting or they simply did not blame The Legate for Sokah, and that had to mean something. Still, I doubted their loyalties were as strong as they once were. Even if they admired the Legate, the king who he was serving caused his men to defect to me.

"What about Vukan and Gabrys?"

Talom wiped away the blood that oozed from a now open pimple. "Of course His Majesty will be there. But Commander Gabrys has been down at the border fighting with Indo. He hasn't been here since the end of fall."

So that explained why I hadn't seen him. I wondered if Sebastien would be disappointed that his own father wouldn't be there for his birthday.

I thanked Talom and forfeited training in favor of going into town. If I was able to get Citadel to go with me, I wouldn't have any problem. It would be my first time outside the castle in a long while, and I needed to find something suitable for a present.

I had barely made it back in time for the banquet. It was similar to the one that greeted me when I first came back home. Although this time Vukan had a willowy woman with short black hair instead of the voluptuous redhead. Lux once again tried to flirt, and I once again ignored him. I was still furious, knowing that he wanted me gone and in such a humiliating way.

The food, on the other hand, was delicious. There was a roasted deer, pickled vegetables and sweet jams that paired perfectly with the freshly baked buns.

As soon as Vukan and his companion left, everyone else quickly exited, except for Sebastien. He stared towards the door, and I wondered if he was missing his father. Even if I hated him, he was Sebastien's father, and it was hard not to love your parents, or at the very least, wish for their love. I walked over to him as others filtered out the doors.

I gently tapped his shoulder. "Would you mind coming with me for a moment?"

Sebastien turned his head, expression blank. "What for?"

"I'll just take a moment of your precious time, oh most valiant and honored Legate," I said lightheartedly.

I was a little shocked when he immediately stood. "Lead the way."

I brought Sebastien to my quarters, instructing him to wait by the crackling fire that warmed the room. I retrieved his present from my wardrobe and held it out.

"Happy Birthday."

Sebastien grabbed the cloth covered object, and I smiled as I leaned onto the wall next to him. "Open it already you doof."

Sebastien's eyes flicked towards me and then back at the present. He slowly removed the cloth, careful not to tear it. Always the perfectionist. He smiled, and not a smirk, a sneer, or one of those half smiles, but a full fledged smile with teeth showing and dimples appearing on his cheeks.

"Do you like it?" I asked tentatively.

He turned his face towards me, eyes squished and lips upturned. "It's the only gift I've ever received that was given by someone who actually paid attention to what I might like."

I shifted my feet and twisted the ring on my finger. "It's only a book about the history of siege weapons, it's not like I got you a horse or a new sword or something expensive," I prattled on.

"Valine." He darted his hand out, gently gripping mine. "It's... it's..." He looked into my eyes, the dancing fire reflecting in his own.

I bit my lip and looked away, but I felt his hand move to my cheek as he turned my head towards him.

"It's wonderful. Thank you." He leaned in and kissed my other cheek. My face reddened, and my palms turned sweaty as he cleared his throat and swiftly stepped away. "I, um, I better be going. Goodnight Valine."

With that, he turned and left.

I shook my head and leapt onto the bed. "What was that?"

I was surprised by his kiss, but I was also angry. I was angry because I had wished for more, that I had wanted to kiss him too, and I was angry because he was the son and nephew of my two greatest enemies, yet that hatred towards him was slowly abating.

CHAPTER FIFTEEN

The winters in Pardus were particularly cold and brutal, and yet I welcomed it. As a young girl, my father would read me stories by the warm fire, and my mother would sit nearby, sketching some drawings, my brother asleep in a nearby cradle. But those sweet days were long gone. Now I had no family, but I did have friends. I enjoyed sitting with Zasper by the hearth, talking about her life in Eboc, even learning a few words of her language. I also looked forward to seeing Sebastien, who often stopped by to recommend a book which were always about the military or history.

That was what had brought him to my room this time too. He sat in the armchair, reading the book I had given him for his birthday, and I enjoyed our ability to sit comfortably in silence. Thinking back on when I first arrived, the me of then would have been appalled at the me now. I was sitting with my sworn enemy, even more than that, I was beginning to like him. I was beginning to want to do things with him, and they didn't include violence.

As I sat watching him, I noticed the strong jaw, the wide shoulders, and the pristine posture with which he sat, and I remembered the feeling of warmth in my face and the buzzing in my head when he had kissed my cheek that night. Would he do it again? Why did I want him to?

When had he stopped being my enemy, the epitome of my pain and vengeance? When had I gone from loathing to enjoying his company? Had it been the small moments? The nights spent discussing a book or some random story from long forgotten history? Or was it the times he had tried to help me, to protect me? I couldn't pinpoint it exactly.

All I knew was that when I first saw him in those woods, I wanted to stab him, to inflict the same agony from all my torment and loss, but now I wanted to be near him, to feel him. The heart was a fickle thing, full of contempt one moment and infatuation the next.

My reflexes were too slow, and Sebastien caught me staring.

"Do you have something to say?"

I refused to let my embarrassment show, instead playing with my hair as I responded, "Just enjoying the view."

I couldn't be sure if it was because of the fire or my words, but his face looked a little more red. He set the book on the table in front of him.

"I am curious about something though."

I cocked my head. "And what's that?"

His eyes looked everywhere in the room except at me. "How do you feel about living here?"

I was a little taken aback by the question. "Umm... I am not sure if you'll like my answer."

That caused him to finally look at me. "I want honesty. Always."

I sighed. "Of course I have mixed feelings. It's my home, but it's not. I spent almost the same amount of time outside these walls as in it, and now others occupy it. Now my family doesn't live here, only buried here."

He shifted uncomfortably.

I continued anyway. "But I also made new friends, formed new relationships. Once more there are people I care about in this castle, which is both frightening and exciting."

I thought Sebastien smiled at that comment, but his hand obstructed the view of his mouth.

I pulled my legs onto the sofa, wrapping my arms around my knees and resting my head on them. A few moments of silence ticked by.

Just when it seemed that I would have to be the one to break it, Sebastien spoke, "Well, I hope I can be counted in the group of people you care about here."

My face flushed, and I sunk further into the couch. "I am surprised to hear you say that."

I looked at the sofa cushions, suddenly enraptured by a loose thread. My fingers played with the string when I felt a weight next to me.

"Valine."

I turned my head and a small gasp escaped my lips. He was so close. I could see the tiny flecks of dark brown mixed in the sea of amber in his eyes. My own eyes followed the shape of his brows, cheek bones, and nose, coming to a stop at his lips. I wondered if he was staring at my mouth too, but I didn't dare check. I didn't move, the anticipation anchoring me down.

Ever so slowly, Sebastien's tanned and rough hand came to my face, calloused fingers brushing my cheek and ear. I didn't know if I was leaning in or he was. All I knew was that we were getting closer, and my body grew warmer as our distance lessened.

When our lips finally touched, my body tingled. His lips were slightly cracked but still soft. It was over too quickly. When he pulled away I could confirm that his face was red, as I was sure mine was too. He didn't immediately drop his hand away, but when he finally did, I missed the feeling of it. I brought my fingers to my lips.

It hadn't been my first kiss, but I was happy to erase the previous kiss with this one. Sebastien's was pleasant and wanted, the warm and fuzzy feeling the complete opposite of the sickening one with his uncle. It was welcomed, unlike with Lux. At that time it was just a tool of distraction, a strategic choice devoid of feeling. With Sebastien, the meeting of our lips was quite enjoyable, and I was already desiring another. I thought that perhaps Sebastien would as well, but before I could say anything, the door opened without so much as a knock.

A guard looked at us, but he spoke only to the Legate, "Sir, your presence is required immediately. News of the war at the southern border."

"Coming."

Sebastien stood, pausing to look at me. "I am sorry to leave so abruptly."

He walked out, unable to wait for my reply.

I was curious about the wars Vukan was waging with our neighboring countries. He still hadn't instigated a fight with Eboc, and I wondered what Zasper was saying in their *negotiations* to maintain the ruse. The king's forces were likely too spread thin as it was. However, Sebastien nor anyone else would answer my questions concerning the matter.

All I knew was that Gabrys was somewhere at the southern border, commanding troops at the channel that separated us from Indo. I wondered why Sebastien wasn't there too. He was in charge of the palace guards, but he was obviously sent out on missions, such as the one that captured me. Did he have a more important assignment keeping him here? I even dared to wonder if what was keeping him here was a person. A special person.

A strange mixture of pleasure and guilt paraded through me. Was I a terrible person, a traitor to my own cause? Shame coursed through me. It felt unfair that I couldn't have a simple crush like the other girls my age. My plans for revenge were becoming at odds with my heart, and the internal battle kept me up most of the night.

Sebastien kept coming to see me as often as he could. However, it seemed as though he was content to pretend our kiss never happened. I was disappointed.

Still, I enjoyed his company.

We sat across from each other, enjoying dumpling soup and warm red-bean buns. Both were a staple of the Wulfric territory, and it was one of the few good things Vukan had brought to the castle.

Unexpectedly, Sebastien reached over, fingers brushing against the corner of my lips. My body froze, and I wasn't sure what to do. As he brought his hand away, I saw a chunk of bean on his thumb. So that's what it was.

I tucked my chin to my chest, my ears burning. I hated the way I felt around him and scolded myself for my ridiculous expectations. I had been thinking long and hard about what I wanted over the past nights—his death or his love.

If I was honest with myself, I wanted his heart, to be wanted, to be cherished. I wanted to go for strolls by the river and listen to music together at the theatre houses in Pardus, just like other couples did. I wasn't sure if it was a general desire or if such notions had been inspired by whatever was blooming between us. It scared me just as much as it excited, like hope and doubt in a constant wrestling match.

Later in the evening, we sat next to each other on the sofa, our shoulders touching and legs brushing. But this time he was just slightly closer, the pressure of our two bodies slightly stronger. I couldn't focus on the book I was reading, my thoughts constantly going to his mouth. He must have caught me staring because he laughed. He rarely ever laughed. It was such a pleasant thing to hear.

"I think that's the first time I made you laugh."

Sebastien rotated his body, arm resting on top of the back of the sofa. "I find myself smiling more lately."

I turned, bringing one leg up to cushion. "It's a nice laugh."

Unexpected but welcomed, his thank you was in the form of a kiss. His lips once again pressed against mine faster than an arrow released from a bowstring.

This one lasted longer, and when we stopped I had to catch my breath. My cheeks warmed, and I looked down. Sebastien brushed my hair behind my ear.

"I want to know more about you, Valine. Something unique to you. I want our relationship to be deeper."

I glanced up at his face, his eyes were on me, hadn't left me. "That would be nice. Give me some time to think about it."

His fingers continued to stroke my hair. "If it helps, I will share something with you first."

I barely nodded, afraid that a sudden movement or loud word would shatter the moment.

His eyes traced my face as he spoke, "My favorite food is red bean buns."

I couldn't help the laugh that escaped my lips. "So the Legate does have a sense of humor."

He cracked a smile, making his mouth all the more appetizing. I shook the thought from my mind, refocusing on his words.

"Alright, alright. I am afraid of cramped spaces. One time when we were young, Lux locked me in a rice chest, only coming to open it when his father had given him a good lashing. I'm not exactly sure how long I was inside there, but it still haunts me."

My mouth dropped open, the laughter fading just as quickly as it came. "That's terrible, even for a child."

He ran his thumb across my knuckles absentmindedly as he said, "Our relationship was never the same after that."

I gave a sympathetic smile and squeezed his hand in return. "I'm sorry... But thank you for sharing the memory with me, even if it is a sad one."

Pressing his lips to my knuckles, he left for another debrief, leaving my hand feeling cold without the warmth of his own.

I contemplated what Sebastien said for a few days, and I had finally acknowledged that I liked him. I didn't want to kill him anymore. He was different from the rest of the Wulfrics. He hadn't chosen to be a member of their house any more than I had chosen to be a Polaris. I wanted to show how I felt, express myself. He'd put himself on the line for me, had aided me often since I came here. He had saved me from Hagan, helped me after Zenith's murder, and when I was almost whipped to death. He felt like a guardian of sorts, always coming to my aide.

I smiled, dreaming about his reaction. I wondered if he would smile and if his eyes would squish endearingly. I felt giddy, my insides dancing around in a pleasant nervousness.

I had invited Sebastien to eat dinner in my room again, and we had just finished eating. I stood, accidentally knocking a glass over in my excitement.

"Oops, sorry."

Sebastien stood and came over, placing his hand on mine. "It's fine. I'll clean it up."

I looked up at him. "Thanks for coming."

He smiled. "Thanks for inviting me."

His eyes did indeed squish adorably. I kissed his lips, and before he could do or say something I grabbed his hand and led him to the balcony doors. It was too cold to go outside, but I just needed him to see the outside roof overhang.

"Sebastien, I want to show you something. But you can't tell anyone."

Sebastien nodded. "Okay."

I smiled, inhaled, twisted my fingers, and flicked my wrist. Icicles now hung from the overhang. I turned to Sebastien, expecting to see a look of awe and wonder, or perhaps a smile, a chance to see his moon eyes again, happy that I had shared something deep and precious with him like he had asked. I was dumbfounded by the look of disgust on his face.

"What's wrong?" I reached towards him but he shied away.

Sebastien glared at me, and it was so startling compared to the affection he had just shown me. "So you have this... this... power. And what were you planning on using it for? To kill my family?"

I wanted to deny it, but he knew I couldn't, knew it would not be the truth.

Hatred burned in his eyes. "I have to go."

I reached for him again, but he jerked away. I tried to hide the hurt in my face. "Please! You can't tell anyone about this Sebastien! He'll kill me or torture me or hurt my friends!"

"I thought you said there was nothing that Vukan could do to you that would matter," he growled.

"But that changed. I told you. I found friends, people to care about. You. I found you."

For a moment I thought I had convinced him. He looked at me the way he had when I'd given him the book, but it was quickly replaced with spite, his eyes darkening and his lips turned downward in disgust.

"I can't let you kill my family. I can't let you destroy the hard work of the Wulfrics."

I couldn't believe this. "Sebastien, I thought we were friends, I thought we were—"

Sebastien looked at me, but there was not a single ounce of affection in his eyes. "You were a mission to complete. I may have strayed from it for a moment, but I am focused more than ever now. For there to be peace there must be order, and you are a threat to that order, a threat that must be controlled. Or eliminated."

He stalked out of the room, ignoring my pleas.

I fell to my knees. This would be it. I would probably be executed by dawn. Vukan would never let me live once he knew the threat I posed. I didn't know what broke me more, never seeing Zasper and Dryden again, proving to be a failure to the leopards and my people, or Sebastien's betrayal. I braced my hands against the floor. I clenched my fist and the icicles I had made for him shattered, clinking as the shards fell. I gritted my teeth and screamed. I was angry and mournful for all that I had come so close to gaining and then lost. How could Sebastien do this?

For hours I languished in my room, switching between anxious pacing and being bent over the chamber pot, yet to my surprise, no guards came. My nightmares in which I was tortured in the dungeon, or lost my head to a sword in front of all of Pardus never came to fruition.

I was constantly on edge, but my life simply continued. I didn't see Sebastien, even at the group dinners, but Zasper came to see me daily, always worried that one day she wouldn't be able to find me in my room, worried that I'd be dead. She urged me to leave, to escape, but I didn't know what to do or who to go to if I did. Most of my followers were now the soldiers in the castle. I had very little support outside of the palace, which was quite ironic. For the time being, I thought it best to just continue on as usual, waiting for some catalyst.

Sebastien finally came to see me two weeks later, asking to talk in his room. I followed him, awkward silence weighing heavy between us. My stomach was full of knots, anxiety causing a multitude of terrible scenarios to flash through my mind.

Sebastien plunging a blade through my heart. Vukan appearing from behind a corner, leering towards me, hands outstretched, ready to strangle me. His black clad squad coming to haul me away to a brothel.

I stomped the thoughts out like a pesky cockroach. Dwelling on potential outcomes would be no use, my energy would be better spent preparing to make a hasty escape.

If something happened and I needed a route to run away, the window was my best option. Sebastien looked as pristine and clean cut as usual, although perhaps more fidgety than I'd seen him before. His fists kept curling at his sides, and he would occasionally grasp at his sword handle. "You should always be aware of every weapon in the room, and watch the hands," Quintus had always said. So with eyes trained to his hands, I was about to ask him what he wanted when he finally cleared his throat.

"Well Valine..."

He grasped the hilt of his sword again. "I have been thinking a lot about what you, er... showed me a couple weeks ago, and uhhh..."

Was he finally coming around? Had our relationship not been misconstrued? Did he care for me?

"I think it could be very useful to the empire."

Apparently not.

I noticed his use of the term. Vukan had plans to create an empire, his current war with Indo and his intentions with Eboc were confirmed now.

"What do you mean 'useful'?"

He stepped closer to me. "Your powers could be helpful. And if you prove yourself useful, my uncle will never hurt you. Your position will be secure. You'll be safe."

"And what would I have to do in order to obtain these things you say?"

He scratched his head. "Well umm... you know... just help fight and show your powers to others in order to encourage other nations to submit to our empire."

"You mean Vukan would use me as a weapon. To quell rebellion and fight his wars," I snapped.

Sebastien grabbed my hand. "We would fight together, Valine. Side by side, we would help unite the land under one ruler."

I ripped my hand away. "That ruler being your uncle."

Sebastien looked a little hurt by my action but continued on. "Of course. He is the King."

"You understand that your uncle is a blood-thirsty, self-gratifying ruler, right?"

Sebastian said nothing.

"He murdered my family, my friends, and innocent citizens. He is a leech that is sucking Racour dry. You had once told me that there are rules to uphold and protocols to follow, yet Vukan follows no moral code."

"You don't understand," Sebastien insisted.

I crossed my arms. "No, I don't."

He was pacing furiously back and forth, hair dangling into his eyes. "I don't agree with everything my uncle does, or has done, but he is on the right track." He paused, stepping closer to me. "Valine, the world will never have peace unless it is forced upon people. Some one, some group, will always oppress another. Humans are never satisfied with what they have." He shook my shoulders. "People must have peace forced upon them, or they will never have it at all."

I stared, flabbergasted. "And who is to enforce that peace? And at what cost? Shall people have no choice, no free will?"

He shook his head in annoyance. "If that is the price of peace, then it is worth it."

"That is how tyrants are born. Fear. Submission. Oppression guised as righteousness. That is what you propose—what you have convinced yourself of," I hissed.

His eyes bore into mine, begging me to understand. "Valine, please. You must see that people are horrible. We are self destructive and cruel. We kill, steal, and lie. It is our very nature to be evil."

He rested his palm against my cheek. "You of all people should know. Your mother, your home, your whole life has only culminated in sorrow because of the greed of others."

He was blind to his own hypocrisy. It was revolting.

I shoved him. "You don't get to say that when it was your family who caused it!"

Sebastien reached for me, but I batted his hand away. I had never seen him look so unhinged.

He tightened his grip on the hilt of his blade, and his jaw clenched. "Once he is gone, I will restore order and morality. Vukan won't be king forever, and once he dies, I promise to give you your throne. Together we can rule. We can ensure that there is order and peace to the continent."

"You have a very dark and narrow view of the world, and you can't see your own hypocrisy."

Sebastien once more reached towards me, but I turned away, stopping in the door frame. "I don't want any part of what you propose. I will not be a weapon, and I will not delude myself into thinking that people have to be controlled for their safety." I looked back at him once more. "I pray that one day you may see the truth. Goodbye Sebastien."

"Valine!"

I paused, turning to look at him, hoping to see remorse written on his face.

"I'll give you one last chance, Valine. Give up on your throne and never use magic again. If you swear it on your mother, I will keep your secret."

I could see in his eyes his conviction. This was his last offer, my last chance to give up on my plans and pursue my own personal future. I replied with equal conviction. "I think that you will quickly discover that I would rather die than give up. It is not a trait of mine to back down in face of adversity."

"So you would rather die than relinquish your throne?" he questioned.

I growled, "That throne belongs to me. I will not rest until I sit upon it once more, for the Racour throne belongs to a Polaris Queen. No man shall sit upon it again."

Sebastien scowled. "I appreciate your honesty. It's good to know where you stand."

I flinched. "And what will you do?"

Sebastien's face betrayed nothing, a wall having been erected between us. "I think you will find that out soon enough."

I left before he did.

Something inside me knew that this time would not be like the last. I would not be allowed to live.

I slammed the door behind me, panic dictating my actions instead of logic. I ran to my balcony, throwing the doors open. I threw myself over the rails, creating ice on the side of the castle for footholds since the snow covered the stones I would normally use. My boots made a crunching sound in the snow as I made my way as quickly as I could towards the small cluster of trees that lined the castle walls.

Finally when my lungs burned and my legs became heavy I stopped. Collapsing to the ground, I crawled towards the roots of the tree where the snow had not been able to fall. The ground was cold against my backside and legs as I laid my back against the tree.

Just my luck.

In my frenzy, I had inadvertently summoned ice, and there was now a trail from the castle to where I now sat. I should have trained harder, controlled myself better. I willed the icy path to dissipate and shuffled the snow to cover my tracks. I slowed my labored breathing.

I scolded myself, for being so naive, having been willing to divulge my most precious secret, all for a man who had simply said some sweet words and gave sweet kisses. The taste in my mouth turned bitter.

I was such a failure. I was too impulsive, and I was lacking in so many ways, including intelligence. Zasper would have never revealed her magic so flippantly. She was a better leader, a better royal than me. I had gotten Callar killed because of my own stupidity, and then my whole rebel band... my found family. Then Zenith and Sokah. I had failed the palace guards who had put their trust in me, and I had wasted Egann's time and squandered Zasper's faith in me.

I was better off dead than being the source of squashed hope.

For some strange reason, a song that my mother used to sing popped into my head. I only heard her sing it when she thought I was asleep. As a child, I used to pretend to sleep when I heard her footsteps coming, in hopes that she would sing to me. I welcomed that song now, and let it flow through my blood. I began to hum it, and soon I found myself singing it.

The sun rose upon the earth
The stars hid themselves from view
The Hunter came from the forest
He came looking for you
His soul searches the expanse
He wanders the land
The wind carries his voice
He asks for your hand
The stars rose upon the earth
The sun hid himself from view
The Hunter went back to the forest
But his love is still for you

I closed my eyes, resting my head against the tree, and let the words continue to play in my heart.

"That was lovely."

My eyes snapped open. The melody ceased. I warily stood and peered around. I couldn't see anyone, the evergreens providing enough coverage to obscure a person from view even when the rest of the trees were bare. I hoped that it was reciprocated and no one could see me or the magic I had used. I knew that no guards patrolled here, but never bothered to check if any civilians came here. I was so stupid for not checking my surroundings. I should've had Zasper ink the word on my forehead.

"How did you learn to sing?"

I twisted around but still couldn't pinpoint where the sound originated from.

"Who are you?" I hissed.

"No one of importance," the voice replied.

I walked around the tree, a few feet in each direction. "Why were you eavesdropping?"

"I wasn't eavesdropping. You were the one who intruded upon my peace and quiet."

I stopped walking, too exhausted and worn to care. "Sorry, but I didn't see anyone when I came here."

"But I heard you. You made quite an entrance, storming in here."

"It's none of your business."

"Fair enough. But please answer me this, little songbird, and I'll leave you be."

I narrowed my eyes but consented. "Alright."

I sat against my tree once more. It didn't matter if someone saw my magic now. I was a dead woman walking.

"My mother used to sing it to me when I was a child when no one was listening."

"Well obviously you were listening," the voice joked.

I rolled my eyes. "Obviously."

"Why would she only sing when she thought no one would hear?"

"You said I need only answer you one question and then you'd leave me in quiet," I grumbled.

"My apologies," it replied.

There was silence for a moment.

I sighed. "My mother had many faults, one was her insecurity. Her voice wasn't elegant and perfect, not like her appearance. So she would sing in the night, softly, so that none could hear the slightly off pitch melody that was a crack in her unflawed appearance. But I heard."

The voice mumbled, but I couldn't tell what it said. Then it spoke more clearly, "Your voice is beautiful."

I shrugged, though I didn't know if the body belonging to the voice was in a position to see it.

We sat for a while, in the serenity of the woods. I tried not to think of Sebastien, or about the fact that this could be my last free moment before Vukan came to destroy the threat that I was. The daggers of shame and self-disgust dug into me, and tears began to fill my eyes again.

"Why do you cry, little songbird?"

So he did have a visual on me. I didn't bother to try to find where he was.

"I am lost," I whispered.

"Surely you aren't lost. And even if you were, your ice could find the way for you," the voice teased.

He had seen it then. What did it matter? My death was a certainty anyways.

"A dark cloud surrounds me, and I cannot see the way out." I closed my eyes, trying to stop the tears.

"And what dark cloud traps the Little Bird?" it inquired.

"A trap of my own making. I trusted someone I shouldn't have."

"There are many wolves in sheep's wool," it warned. Then with more sympathy it said, "Oh Little Bird, please don't cry."

I wiped away the tear that had fallen, sucking the snot back into my nose. "That's very kind, but your words will do little to help me now."

I stood, and I heard distant shouts and the barks of guard dogs. "The darkness draws closer." My voice was barely audible.

"There is always hope, Little Bird. Now fly, trust that there is light waiting."

I wasn't sure if that was true, but I owed it to my friends and followers to try. Conviction gripped me, and resolution rushed through my veins. I had to live. I couldn't give up.

I sprinted back to the wall and hastily climbed back into my rooms, chastising myself for having resigned to death just moments ago. I had almost wasted the sacrifices of my friends and followers.

I grabbed the book with the list of names and Sokah's letter. I was reluctant to burn the last words of my friend, but if Vukan found it, he would punish Falchor for having given it to me in the first place, and he would kill every man on the list. I threw it all in the fireplace, the flames eagerly consuming them.

My door slammed open, and I pulled a knife from the hidden sheath in my pants that I had acquired from Mordris.

Zasper stared at me, panicked and worried eyes wide.

"I heard the guards gathering. You have to go now, *Chui!*"

I resheathed my dagger, and ran to her. "Come with me. If you stay here, Vukan is likely to imprison you. He will torture you simply because you were my friend."

She looked into my eyes. "I can't leave." She brushed the hair that had fallen into my face. "I will stay for you. Someone has to be here to maintain contact with the soldiers who pledged to you."

Tears welled in my eyes. She was right, but it still felt wrong to ask such a thing of her.

She pushed me away. "Go quickly. The guards will be here any second. Be strong *Chui.*"

My heart ached as I studied my friend's features, engraving them into my mind. "Be safe, *Dada.*"

It was one of the few words I had learned.

I turned, grabbing a pack of clothes and supplies that I had kept hidden under my bed for a situation like this. I had anticipated the need for a hasty exit, but never under these circumstances.

I was back to those trees when I heard it. A blood-curdling scream rippled through the chilled air. My chest tightened and my breath hitched, but I resisted the urge to turn back, forcing my feet to carry me towards the stone barrier. I prayed for Zasper. She was in The Creator's hands now. I tried not to think about the scream as I made my way over the wall.

Please let her be alive. Don't take her from me too.

CHAPTER SIXTEEN

Screaming. There was so much screaming. Why wouldn't they stop? I clawed at my ears and hair, willing the piercing screech to stop.

But it was me. I was the one screaming, and I couldn't stop. My throat was raw and my voice was starting to crack, but still, by some unseen power my wails prevailed. What happened? The people spat as they passed me. They didn't care about me. They hated me. Gaunt faces appeared from the shadows. I reached out, but they flinched. I recoiled, looking down at my hand. It was covered in crimson. I screamed louder, but nobody heard. Nobody cared.

I bolted upright. Straw clung to my hair, and the only sounds were the cows bellowing and pigs snorting. I didn't have much money or valuables to trade, but even if I did, staying at inns would have been too dangerous. I prayed that spring would come quickly, otherwise I would have to continue to sleep in stables and abandoned buildings until the snow melted. I snuggled into Dryden's warm pelt, who I had stopped to get before leaving the capital. He was a welcome partner, a source of comfort.

However, as I made my way towards the coast, the weather got a little warmer, flower buds forming on the trees along the road. Dryden complained often about how hot it was. Since it was still snowy and cold in Pardus, his winter coat was still present, his lighter summer pelt a couple months away.

I headed towards the same place I had gone to several years ago, under laughably similar circumstances. At the port in Wulfric land, well I supposed everything was Wulfric land now, was an important resource. I had a decent amount of palace guards on my side, but most of Vukan's military force was outside of Pardus and completely unloyal to me. There was another fighting force that just might aid me and help balance the scales.

Pirates.

They were quite common around the continent, and there were plenty off the coasts of Racour. They were tough, efficient, and good at evading capture. And since there was a major river that went all the way from Gwanji Port to Pardus with a few smaller streams branching off along the way, they would be able to travel to the capital with ease. Usually small fishing vessels or the occasional trading vessels would use the Xian River. So a fleet of pirates would be suspicious, but if spread out enough, they could potentially avoid notice.

The journey had been hard, anxious thoughts about Zasper, Falchor, Mordris and the boys had plagued me the entire way. I prayed that this would work. Prayed that all my friends and allies were safe. I comforted myself knowing that if I was successful, I would have secured better odds for us. I needed to build up a viable force that could take on Vukan and Gabrys.

As luck would have it, I happened to know one pirate personally.

I had first met Kasabian when fleeing Pardus. The sweet baker couple had given me money out of the little they had and directed me to go towards the Wulfric controlled coastal region. They hoped that Vukan would not be able to contrive the notion that I would actually go to *his* land. They hoped that I could survive by such a gamble. My chances were no worse than in the capital, where Vukan had ordered soldiers to go door to door to find the lost princess.

I managed to find my way to Gwanji, and at the port I waited to find a ship to board. I'd used most of my money to get my way there, and there weren't many ships that welcomed women aboard, let alone a child. But the safest place I could be was in the middle of the sea. I stuck to the alleyways, wary of anyone wearing Wulfric crimson. Luckily, I went largely unnoticed, except by another young boy. He had rich tawny skin and dark, wavy hair along with golden brown eyes and a hooked nose. He looked cute despite the rags he wore and the dirt covering him from head to toe.

He tossed me a piece of bread, stopping a short distance away. "What's your name, gorgeous?"

I tilted my head.

"Seagull got your tongue?"

I had never heard that saying before. Perhaps it was a phrase common to the region. He approached me, but I recoiled back.

He stopped and crouched down. "It's alright, *Bibi*."

I shifted, reaching out a dirt-crusted hand towards the bread. "What's *Bibi?*"

He laughed. "So you can talk! *Bibi* is just an affectionate term in my language."

He stepped a little closer and sat back on his heels in front of me.

"Where are you from?" I asked hesitantly.

He pulled out a piece of jerky from his pocket and sniffed it. "Percia. You know it?"

I nodded, nibbling on the bread. "Of course. I heard it's very dry and hot, with lots of deserts."

He talked as he chewed the dried meat. "That's true, but we also have a beautiful capital and lush areas that have rare fruits and olives. Gosh I miss olives. And the sunsets! You can't beat a desert sunset."

I tried to imagine it in my head. "Sounds lovely."

He grinned. "Let's go see them together one day."

I smiled tentatively. "That... would be nice."

He pulled another piece of jerky out and gave it to me. It was the first food I had that day, in two days actually, and I was very grateful for the loud, raggedy boy.

After that, we found places to sleep and eat together. The streets were not a safe place, especially for girls, despite the many members of the military patrolling, so I was thankful for his presence.

Eventually we were able to convince a captain of a small ship to take us aboard. We would forgo pay for a season in exchange for food to eat and a hammock to sleep in. I hated the ship, constantly sea sick for the first half of our trading venture. However, Kasabian took to it immediately. He loved the smell of the salty water and always kept his feet despite the crashing waves rocking the ship. He quickly earned the favor of the crew and captain, and I was also fond of him, which made it all the harder to part ways when the trading season came to an end.

We had been together for almost a year out on the ocean, but when we came back into Gwanji Port where we had first met all those months ago, we had to say goodbye. He hugged me tight, and I refused to let the tears come out.

I had been through so much, and now I had to leave behind my friend and the safety of the ship and the sea. But I knew that I couldn't stay, couldn't run from what I felt I had to do. I had to somehow get back home, and if I wanted to do that, I would need more than rope-tying skills. I needed soldiers not sailors. So I walked away from

Kasabian. He was smiling, but I knew he was sad as I disappeared into the city streets.

Next I had to find a place to live and people to help me. I was only a young girl, but one day I would be a woman, and at the right time I would reclaim my home and my throne. I would kill the man who killed my mother. So I headed back towards the capital and returned to the baking couple, who once again were willing to risk their lives and that of their daughter to house me.

As I sat and reminisced back on those early years, I realized how much The Creator had assisted me, orchestrating meetings with just the right people and keeping me safe along the way. I prayed that He would continue to guide my path and protect me and those I loved and that things would one day be peaceful enough that I could go with Kasabian to see that desert sunset.

Hopefully, the desire was mutual.

That's what brought me to the dock of Lord of the Sea of Helios, praying that our past had not been forgotten. I made sure to remove all the knives from my leather vest and straps and handed them over to the man waiting by the plank. He had olive skin, almond eyes and coarse, black hair that was tied behind his head. He wore only a pair of loose pants, his sculpted chest shining in the light.

He eyed me up and down and growled, "Are those all your weapons?"

I lifted my arms and turned around. "Want to search me?" I asked.

He glared at me and then took notice of the giant ice leopard standing at my side. The man frowned but nodded for me to walk.

Are you sure about this?

I glanced at Dryden. *I'm always sure.*

Dryden's fur bristled. *As you wish. But I still hate water.*

I clamped my mouth shut to keep from laughing. Dryden's tail hit against my calf, causing me to stumble. I stuck my tongue out at him. *Watch it or I'll shove you into the ocean.*

Dryden's whiskers twitched in a mixture of annoyance and amusement, and I smiled and patted his furry head.

Men were walking across the deck, many carrying crates of rations and others repairing the ship itself. Atop the quarter deck stood the man I was looking for. A head of long, wavy black hair and caramel skin, a body sculpted for the harsh demands of the sea, arms strong to hoist sails, strong legs to steady oneself in raging waters. Kasabian was as beautiful as legend claimed, and since I had last seen him. Although some thought his many piercings detracted from his good looks, I thought them rather attractive.

He somehow seemed to sense I was there, his eyes suddenly snapping to mine, a smile spreading across his face. I waved my fingers and smirked. His chiseled cheeks were enough to make any girl fall in love. How wickedly dangerous that face was.

I walked towards him, Dryden begrudgingly following. I tossed my braid over my shoulder and came to a stop before the pirate. Kasabian whistled and all the men stopped where they were. A man with an afro stepped forward, but Kasabian pushed him back. That must be his first mate then. There were stories of him. He was known as Amnys, hailing from a small island so tiny it didn't even show up on a map, which was not very welcoming to outsiders.

Kasabian was said to have found him in the clutches of some of Vukan's soldiers—as they cut out his tongue. Kasabian was able to save his life, but not his tongue, and the man had been loyal to his lord ever since.

I took in the man with wild hair. He was also handsome, with skin darker than night and eyes a murky pool of mystery.

"I'm surprised you surround yourself with such beautiful men, Kas."

Kasabian laughed. It was a deep, sensuous sound that revealed his legendary pointed canines. "Don't worry yourself love, I'm quite confident in my own looks that I can fill my boat with the best looking men, and not worry about finding a woman to accompany me."

He had always been confident and flirtatious. He could flirt with a wall and not notice the silence.

He gestured to his face. "I make a gorgeous view as well." He winked at me. "But not quite as stunning as you."

He was an interesting character. "Kas, don't you think you flirt too much?"

Kasabian grinned. "On the contrary, I don't flirt nearly enough being around a beauty like you. Concerning my own looks, I really wish people would compliment me more because I get tired of saying it for them. You know, it's truly exhausting reminding everyone how handsome I am."

I laughed as we both ran towards each other. I threw my arms around his neck as he tightened his arms around my waist. A rumble came from Dryden's throat, and Kasabian released me.

"And who have you brought with you?" Kasabian cocked his head. "An ice leopard? Interesting. They usually only show themselves to..." Kasabian turned back to me.

Oh crap. Crap, crap, crap. I should have left him back at the port's inn.

Kasabian's eyes twinkled with delight. "A queen."

Whispers spread over the deck. Whispers of the lost Polaris Queen and her companion. Whispers of rebellion, rulers, and ransom. Well, Kasabian hadn't become one of the most powerful pirate lords for nothing. He was clever and his crew cunning. However, I was not the young, lost girl Kasabian had met all those years ago. I was a queen, and I would not be afraid.

"No need to bow," I purred.

Kasabian laughed harsher this time. "Well this is a surprise." He whistled again, a high pitched sound, and two men with scimitars appeared at my side. I eyed them both. I could take them on, if Dryden didn't devour them first. Kasabian smiled, but it did not look so inviting this time.

"Rebel royals fetch a high price."

I snickered. "Oh please, Kas, don't you think I knew you'd find out? Use that beautiful head of yours and think. Why would I come here, knowing your love of gold." I paused to gesture to myself. "And pretty things, without a reason?"

Kasabian cocked a groomed brow. "Join me in my cabin, and I'll hear you out."

I smiled as I walked past the Pirate Lord towards the stairs and patted his cheek. "Pretty *and* smart. I knew I liked you for some reason, Kas."

His hand shot out before I got to the stairs, blocking my path. He leaned into my ear, smelling of coconuts and almonds. "You better make this worth my while, Val, you may be Racour's princess but not my men's. They'll make me turn you in for a sack of jewels."

I turned my face to whisper, "Oh Kas, always money with you." I sauntered up the stairs with Dryden by my side and Amnys watching us both with narrowed eyes.

Kasabian's quarters were rather luxurious. A map of all the continents and oceans took up an entire wall of his room. Our continent, Saego, which included Racour, Manchur, Eboc, Persia, and Indo, with their respective seas, were marked in colorful scripts, and to the right lay more lands, some I had never heard of, none of which I had

ever seen. I was supposed to take a trip to some kingdom...
Obscuritas, if I recalled correctly, when I was younger.
Apparently that's where the first queen had come from,
and my mother and father had wanted to take a trip there.
We never went on that trip.

I forced my eyes and thoughts to move away from the
map. Lavish curtains, tasseled pillows, and hand crafted
rugs covered the entire cabin. The walls were painted ma-
roon, the ceiling yellow with a red sun in the center. The
polished mahogany floors screamed money. Kasabian was
rich, the wealthiest of all pirates which meant he had the
most ships and men. That's why I needed him.

I lounged in a cushioned chair, Dryden sitting next to
me. I flung my legs over the side, sprawled across the large
seat. Kasabian smiled as he walked past us and sat behind
his oak desk which was inlaid with rubies. He gestured
to the entrance and Amnys stepped in, closing the doors
behind him.

Kasabian folded his hands and stared intently. "It is
only our past friendship that has kept me from throwing
you into a cell and returning you to Vukan for a high
price."

I cocked my head. "Do you often throw friends in prison
and ransom them off?"

Kasabian's voice lost all softness. "A lot has changed
since our days together. I don't take kindly to lying, Valine."

I rolled my eyes. "Says the pirate."

His fist slammed against the desk. "We don't do it for
fun. We do it to survive."

I reached across and patted his hand. "Alright, calm
down." Leaning back again, I offered sincerely, "I am sorry
though, that I never told you. I hope you can understand
my circumstances at the time."

Kasabian's jaw clenched, but he forced his features to relax. He leaned forward and whispered, "I never would have brought you onto that ship. I never would have—"

I waved my hand. "Oh please Kas, you would still have kissed me, whether or not you knew of my lineage."

The corner of the pirate's mouth lifted up, perhaps fondly recalling the months we spent together when we were young. Then he frowned. "That may be so, but you still lied to me, Val."

I was growing weary of this game. "I never said I wasn't the daughter of Queen Ariella."

Kasabian stood and leaned over his desk. "But you never said you were."

I stood in response. "You never asked."

We were face to face now. Oh, he was handsome. Sebastien was dusty coal compared to Kasabian, perhaps only Lux and Amnys could compare. I grabbed the sides of his head and brought my lips to his forehead.

I pulled back, my hands dropping from his temples. "Do you forgive me?"

Kas chuckled and sat back down, flopping into his chair as if his legs had given out. "I suppose you have my attention now."

I smiled. "I didn't know it ever left."

We chatted for a while longer, and I filled him in on everything that had happened between our parting until now. By the time we finished the sun had retired, and the moon had taken up its position in the night sky.

We decided we could continue our conversation the next day.

I woke up the next morning having slept decently on Kasabian's soft bed, but Dryden had spent most of the night on guard, not trusting the pirates. He slept now, unable to resist the beckon of slumber, while Kasabian and

I enjoyed a morning breakfast of eggs and toast on the deck.

"So how did you go from an honest sailor to a pirate?" I asked, leaning my back against the wooden railing, taking a bite of surprisingly soft eggs.

Kasabian buttered his bread. "Well, as you are well aware, Vukass raised the tariffs so high that there was barely any profit left for my men and I."

I couldn't help but smile at Kasabian's nickname for Vukan. "But how is stealing and racketeering okay with you? The optimistic and honorable boy I knew would never have deigned to partake in such a *business*."

Kasabian paused, setting down his food. His expression was uncharacteristically somber and serious, his voice hardening. "Because my men have families to provide for, and Vukan wasn't doing anything to help us, or anyone else besides himself."

He pointed to one of the portly men who was tying knots across the deck, arms covered in markings. "That's Tetalli. He has a daughter who is sick and needs expensive medications." He pointed to another man, short and dark skinned. "That's Kovu. He has seven children who all need to be fed and clothed." Once more he gestured, this time to a man who only had one leg, the other a stump propped up by a wooden post. "Garryn used to be a soldier until an infected wound took his leg. There was no compensation for him, no aide. He was simply kicked out of the army and left to fend for himself. That was his reward for serving his country."

I had never thought of that before, of what happened to soldiers who were no longer able to perform their duties. I still didn't think stealing was right, but I could not find myself to write them all off as immoral brigands either. Now that I was forced to think about it, I too had stolen from the Wulfrics for the sake of my rebellion. I wondered where the line of ethics should be drawn, and what made one a criminal versus a righteous rebel. Ultimately, we were all trying our best to survive in a cruel world, under a selfish king.

We ate the rest of our meal in silence, the only sounds were seagulls and ocean waves.

"*Absolutely not.*"

I sighed in frustration. "But Kas, I'd pay you *and* pardon you."

Kasabian shook his head, hands planted firmly on the desk. "Val, we are talking about my ships and the lives of my crew. What you're offering isn't enough incentive for them to fight for you."

I glared. "Not enough for them or for *you?*"

Kasabian came around and crouched in front of me, placing his hands on my knees. "Val, love, I am eager to help you reclaim your throne, but my men—"

I grabbed his hands, my voice raising with enthusiasm and confidence in my idea. "They will all be integrated into the navy or I could create a new royal position for them. They would have proper jobs and be given pensions. They'll be taken care of."

Kasabian's expression turned contemplative.

After explaining my plan to Kasabian, he begrudgingly agreed. I would challenge his crew to fight, to win their respect in a duel, and then I would tell them my plan. I had to earn their respect, prove myself, before they would even consider my offer to institute them as part of my Royal Merchants or Royal Navy—depending on their preference—and they would be granted clemency and salaries.

I would also need to create such an organization, and to do that I would have to be queen.

I tossed my cloak onto the desk. Kasabian had allowed me to prepare myself in his cabin. Luckily, the coastal region was relatively warm year-round, so I wouldn't need many layers of clothing, offering more mobility. Dryden hadn't spoken to me since I'd come up with the idea.

I looked to where he sat by the door, vigilantly watching for danger, and ignoring me. *Come on, Dryden. Have a little faith in me.*

My companion didn't even bother to look at me. *I have faith that you'll get hurt.*

I sat and began to braid my hair. *I've been hurt before, but I'm still alive.*

Dryden finally looked at me, and his turquoise eyes seemed dulled with sadness. *That was before you had me. I am supposed to protect you so that you don't get hurt.*

I tied the end of my hair with a silky emerald ribbon. Kas remembered it was one of my favorite colors.

I walked over and grabbed the fur of his neck. *This companionship goes both ways. We protect each other, and together we protect our people.*

His whiskers twitched. *But does that mean you have to do this? There has to be another way.*

I rubbed my thumb across his muzzle. *I need them. I have to raise an army big enough to defeat Vukan.*

Dryden nuzzled my arm. *You have magic, you have Zasper, and all the leopards.*

I leaned my forehead against his. *That's not enough.*

A knock at the door signaled that it was time. I looked at all the weapons on the desk and chose two daggers. That meant I would have to get close to my opponent, but this was a ship and fighting would be close quarters anyways.

I walked out of the cabin, blinking at the harsh sun. The deck was full, the crew taking up all the space on the sides of the ship. Leaning against the mast was Kasabian, a grin plastered on his face, but in his eyes I could see his worry.

I sauntered forward. Feigning confidence was just as good as actually having it. "I've trained a lot since then, Kas, don't worry about me, worry about whichever of your crew takes me on."

Kasabian laughed. "The confidence looks great on you."

He gestured grandly. "Men! Our lovely little royal has a proposition. In return for fighting for her, she will transfer our occupation from pirates to traders and soldiers. She promised pay and pension for the price of our swords." He paused to turn to me. "But we value actions over words, proof over pledges."

The men cheered as Kas spun, arms open. "Who would like to challenge our ambitious princess? Who wants to make her prove her steel," he paused, winking at me as he asked, "with some steel?"

The men erupted in even louder shouts and cheers, which I hadn't thought possible.

A man stepped forward. Amnys. He made signs with his hands, and I waited.

Someone from the crowd shouted the interpretation. "He said he would only follow someone capable. He said it's easy to make promises and harder to fulfill them."

Amnys signed some more. "And he says that he has lost faith in monarchies, but that he has faith in Kasabian, and Kasabian has faith in you. So he will give you a chance." Amnys' hands dropped to his side, one hand reaching for his short sword.

It was an interesting way to give someone a chance.

The pirates encircled us, clapping and whistling. The goal was to disarm the other or put them in a position to yield. There were no rules besides no vital points, no fatal wounds. Everything else was on the table.

We circled each other for a few moments, studying each other, looking for weakness. Did he favor a leg? Did he have any tells? Did he flare his nose before a strike? He didn't. He simply did a quick spin and brought his blade to my ribs.

I side stepped him, barely avoiding his strike. He was taller and bigger than me, so I would have to be faster. There were a few moves I had learned from Quintus to disarm someone stronger than me. I would have to evade him and wait for the right opportunity to execute the move. He came at me again, and I had to use both my arms to deflect the blow, trembling under the sheer force he exerted down on me. I pushed off his sword and dropped down to try to kick the back of his knee in, but he barely stumbled, likely used to keeping his balance on uneven seas.

I backed up, conjuring some jeers from the men behind me. I tightened my grip on the daggers. Amnys had amazing stamina, endurance wrought from the hard life living on the ocean. I had to be smarter, more strategic. I couldn't use my magic, as that would be an unfair advantage and gain me no amount of admiration from the crew.

I noticed a slight bulge on the outside of his leg. The cloth of his pants was just torn enough that I could see the bandages beneath. It was a dirty trick, but worth it. I had to win them over, had to come out the victor in this challenge. After a few more blows and parries, I had worked myself into the perfect position. I brought the hilt of one of my daggers down on his old wound—luckily not so old that it didn't hurt. He winced and dropped to one knee. My other hand brought the tip of my blade to his neck, and his sword clattered to the wood. I took it that meant he yielded.

I stepped away and offered my hand, Amnys smiling as he clasped my arm. He nodded, and the rest of the crew surrounded us. Some congratulated and complimented me, while others teased Amnys for his defeat. Suddenly arms wrapped around me.

"That's my girl!" Kasabian released me and tousled my hair. "Never doubted you for a moment." He beamed.

Amnys frowned.

"I never doubted you too." Kasabian chuckled as Amnys cracked a grin.

I laughed. "I don't think that's how it works."

Kasabian shrugged. "What can I say? I have so much confidence that there's enough to go around for everyone."

I rolled my eyes, but I couldn't stop grinning.

Apparently I had misunderstood what the challenge and winning it meant.

"It is not a guarantee of fealty."

Kasabian, Amnys, Dryden and I were back in the captain's quarters.

I frowned. "Then what is it Kas? I came all the way here and worked so hard for what?"

Kasbian tied his long hair back. "You earned yourself some respect. That your words aren't empty. You increased your chances for the future."

"What does that even mean?" I asked exasperated.

"It means that once you gain some more support, my men are more likely than not to join you. They like you now, even respect you, but they aren't willing to risk their lives until the odds are more in your favor. Believe it or not, what we do now is a lot less risky than rebellion."

I nodded, understanding their position, but that didn't change the frustration that I felt.

Kasabian sat in his luxuriously cushioned chair and laced his hands behind his head. "So what's next Majesty?"

CHAPTER SEVENTEEN

I had to return to the castle. I had escaped twice, but I had to go back, had to get Zasper out. There was a chance that I would be executed on sight, that I would be thrown into the dungeon, but I had a plan. It was risky but necessary. Kasabian would pretend to turn me in, hopefully receiving compensation for it, which would solidify the pirates resolve in joining me. I just prayed that Vukan would use the opportunity to humiliate me and not kill me. He always did love to play with his prey.

We set out from Gwanji on a single ship, traveling slowly up the river to the capital. I was enjoying getting to hear the stories of the crew. They all had lived interesting lives, although some were more tragic than others. Life was a volatile being, heaping fortune and calamity in the same breath, uncaring on how much an individual received of either. They opened my eyes to issues I hadn't thought about before. I made mental notes to address each grievance when I was queen. If I became queen.

Despite the fact that we had to fight the river's current, the boat was much quicker than walking. I sat on the bow, a cloak hiding my identity.

Dryden sniffled.

I looked down at him. *Are you crying?*

He growled, *No.*

I rubbed his head, making sure to avoid his ears.

Last night, Dryden showed his displeasure at being touched there. The wide and calm river kept the boat from rocking like it tended to on the ocean. However, the nerves caused by the reality of returning to my palace prison, or my execution, was enough for my stomach to turn. I felt dizzy when I stood, so I resigned to laying down. I clutched my abdomen with one hand, the other going towards Dryden's head, who was laying beside the bed.

My fingers ran through his fur absentmindedly, his warmth and presence comforting my anxieties.

I pinched his ear gently between two fingers, surprised by the softness.

Dryden snarled, his teeth bared and eyes fierce.

I yanked my arm back before he ripped it off. *What was that, Dryden?*

His lips relaxed, covering his fangs that he'd flashed just a second ago. *Don't touch my ears.*

I would be sure not to repeat the mistake.

The irritation from the previous evening was now replaced with sadness.

I can't promise anything. All I know is that I am glad I met my companion before... I couldn't finish the sentence.

I wasn't sure if ice leopards could cry, but the voice in my head sounded somber. Dryden growled softly, *You shouldn't go.*

I kneeled next to him. *I have to.*

His claws flexed, in and out. *You could die.*

I wrapped my arms around him. *Yes.*

He rubbed his head against mine. *Your plan is terrible.*

Do you have a better one? I asked.

He didn't answer. Because there really wasn't. If I wasn't able to consolidate my forces, if I wasn't able to confirm that I still had soldiers, then any attempt of a full fledged fight would end in our defeat. I couldn't think of any alternatives, so we sailed on towards the unknown.

Once again, I was brought in chains to my home. Kasabian and a couple other pirates surrounded me as we made the somber march towards the palace. I had sent Dryden back to his clan, and the strange pain in my heart had returned with his absence. The pirate lord dragged me forward, but he didn't have to say anything to the guards who instantly recognized me. One disappeared through the doors, but I wasn't prepared for who walked out.

Sebastien stood in front of me. It had been a month since I had seen him, and he looked the same as always, a stern expression and straight posture. He made an assessing look over the pirates, finally resting his eyes on my chains. Eventually he looked at my face, his eyes widened slightly at the sight of my black eye and cracked lip, courtesy of the duel.

"Hand her over."

He reached for the chains, but Kasabian put an arm up. "No thanks. I'd like to take her to the king myself in order to ensure we are properly compensated."

Sebastien narrowed his eyes, looked at the pirates again, and finally acquiesced. "Fine. Follow me."

He led us through the doors and down the corridor. It was eerily similar to the first time he brought me, but at least this time, I came of my own accord.

Vukan sat on the throne looking disheveled. He held a long pipe in his hand, probably filled with opiates. But even with the drugs in his system, his eyes lit up when we walked through the doors. He bolted upright, and it was then that I noticed what had to be either red wine or blood stains on his robes. I prayed that it was the former.

It had only been a little over a month since I had left, the trip from the capital to Gwanji taking about three weeks, the return trip significantly less, since walking took longer than riding or sailing. Yet in that time, Vukan had seemingly become more unstable. I had seen him occasionally smoke a pipe, but never to the level of intoxication that he was now. As he stood, he swayed, catching himself on the arm of the throne. He smiled, his teeth yellowed. I looked around, but the guards gave no indication that the man before them was not the same as before. I glanced towards Sebastien, and to my surprise caught him staring at me. There was no affection in his eyes. A part of me was still regretful at how things had turned out.

But he had made his choice, and I would be the consequence.

Kasabian's voice brought my attention forward.

"Your Majesty," he drawled with an exaggerated bow.

Vukan turned his hazy eyes to him, as if only noticing his presence then. "I didn't know pirates came this far inland."

Kasabian gestured to me. "Well I am a loyal subject returning a prized possession."

Vukan sneered. "Yes. My *thing* was misplaced."

My stomach boiled at their conversation, an icy claw yearning to stretch out and rip his mouth off, but I held my tongue.

"Of course." Kasabian made a sign with his hand. "I would appreciate our magnanimous ruler providing some compensation for such a valuable item."

Dangerous.

A dangerous request of a dangerous man.

But Vukan only laughed, spit flying out of his mouth. "Yes! To show my gratitude, give these pirates some jewels. Oh, and the wench from last night."

He smiled at Kasabian. "I broke her in for you."

My hold on my disgust and rage was reaching its limit, my ice thrumming behind cracked glass, ready to break through and devour the vile king, but I had to credit Kasabian for his composure and acting skills, his face plastered with a casual and relaxed expression. "You are too generous, Your Majesty."

Vukan waved his hand. "Yes, yes. You may leave now."

Kasabian bowed, and when he turned he gave me a slight nod. I knew he would look after the poor woman that would be given to them, who had been treated worse than one of the king's horses. Kasabian, although a pirate, was much more honorable than Vukan. The woman would be okay.

I was glad Kasabian and his men made it out, that Vukan hadn't decided to kill them immediately, but it wouldn't be the last time they would be put in danger because of me. For now though, they would be safe. My fate was not so certain.

I looked at the foot of the dais. I wasn't sure what angle to play. Vukan's current state was far less predictable than previously. Would he be more inclined to spare me if I acted despondent? Or would he prefer the opportunity to hold me captive, to humiliate me into submission, relishing my torment as he had before? I guessed the latter, hoping that at his core was the monster who enjoyed breaking things before ending them. I lifted my eyes and stared daggers at him. Anger and irritation flashed in his eyes, momentarily displacing the drug induced haze.

He stumbled down the steps and stopped in front of me. He grabbed a handful of my hair and yanked my head back. I yelped in pain.

"You still haven't given up? You still dare to look at me like that, Ariella?"

"You're insane," I spat.

He threw me to the ground, hand still gripping my hair. "I am the king now! You are nothing! You may have escaped before, but it will be the last time you ever leave these palace walls."

My neck ached and my scalp burned, but I managed to retort through gritted teeth, "Not you though. I'll make sure you're buried outside this place, where no one can find your body. Where no one can remember you."

His hand released my hair as his boot simultaneously slammed into my head, and I sprawled completely to the floor. Head pounding, I resisted the urge to yelp or cry, closing my eyes in an attempt to silence the thumping inside my skull. He grabbed my hair again, forcing my head towards his.

"You bitch."

He shoved my face into the ground and stood. The agonizing pain kept me prostrate, but hands grabbed my arms and forced me upright. My head was throbbing, my face stung, and I could taste the blood that was now running from my nose into my mouth.

Vukan swayed and started laughing, causing the pain in my head to worsen as the noise scraped against my skull like steel on steel. If it weren't for the guards propping me up, I would have crashed back to the floor.

"I know the perfect thing to tame our little leopard."

I was worried what he meant, but it only took a few seconds to find out. "Congratulations on the marriage of Lux Wulfric," his bloodshot eyes bore into me as he declared, "and Valine Polaris."

He leaned towards me and whispered so only I and the guards around me could hear, "And the Polaris name will be no more. How sad an end to a dynasty of matriarchs."

Marriage. I was engaged to Lux. I would be bound to him, forced to be with him.

Bile rose in my throat.

Vukan closed his eyes and inhaled the smoke from his pipe, nose flaring. He opened his eyes again and commanded, "Take her to the Crown Prince's room. I am sure he would enjoy playing with his bride a little early."

I wanted to curse him, but I was bleeding and my mind refused to form anything coherent. Vukan stumbled his way up the dais steps and collapsed into his throne.

After being dragged to Lux's room, I was finally unchained. The guards, who I only now noticed were clad in full black, filled the prince in on his father's decree. They laughed, saying they were jealous the prince would get to have fun with me. I spat at them as they walked out. Thankfully, Lux shut the door on them before they could retaliate. He turned and approached me, eyes fixated on the blood crusted down my face. I stepped away, back colliding against the pillar of his bed. He reached out a hand, but then dropped it.

"I won't touch you without your permission. I learned from the last time." He teased the last part half-heartedly as he sat on the couch, making a show of sitting on his hands. "See? I am entirely at your mercy now."

It was enough to make me relax, but I stayed where I was, wrapping my arms around myself. "Tell me about Zasper," I demanded.

Lux looked down, almost appearing ashamed. "She has been ordered to stay in her rooms."

I gasped, "That level of mistreatment towards a foreign emissary is tantamount to a declaration of war." Of course I had known when I left that it was a possibility, and that even worse things could have been done to her. Vukan had no concern for international relations.

Lux nodded, his long hair covering his face. "Yes." His voice was so soft and quiet I could barely hear him. "As our wedding present, Vukan plans to invade Eboc. He is tired of waiting for their surrender."

"How do you know? Vukan just decided our marriage moments ago."

Lux, unable to keep sitting on his hands, ran them through his hair. "Just before you escaped, Vukan had become more paranoid concerning you, so he was already planning this back then."

I screamed in frustration, turning and pounding my fists into the mattress.

He shook his head, fingers wringing. "There is something else you must know."

I paused my assault on the bed.

He looked up at me with what looked like fear and sadness in his eyes. "My father plans for you to marry me and then kill you."

I frowned. "What are you talking about? You're drunk Lux, you don't know what you're saying."

I so badly wanted to dismiss his words as drunken rambles, but there was no alcohol present, nor did he smell of it. It was also something I knew was unavoidable, that I, unable to forfeit my goal of reclaiming my throne, would one day wear out Vukan's patience to the point where he would finally finish me off. His strange obsession with my mother, the desire to possess her, was likely what had kept me alive this long.

Lux fell onto his knees with a thud. "I'm so sorry Valine, I never wanted this to happen. I only wanted to save your life, but I've only postponed the inevitable." He covered his face with his hands.

I was still unsure as to why he would inform me. "Lux." He didn't move. I stood and grabbed his wrists and yanked him up. Now that he was standing, I looked him in the eyes. "Tell me the whole story."

He nodded, and I directed him towards the sofa. "Sit." I sat next to him, and he took a deep breath.

"I know my father. He is ruthless against his own blood, let alone others. You've shown yourself to be unbreakable, so the next step is to dispose of you. He follows the same patterns every time."

Lux moved closer, but I backed away against the armrest. "Lux, how do I know you're telling the truth?" Perhaps this was Lux's sick revenge, and he was trying to instigate me into doing something that would ensure Vukan's wrath, shoving me off a cliff of inevitable doom.

Lux's face looked genuine. "Well... you'll know it's the truth tomorrow night."

"What do you mean?" He looked to the ground and didn't reply. I grabbed his shirt and clutched it in my fists, forcing him to face me. "Lux, how will I know by tomorrow night?"

Lux peered back at me, defeat written on his face. "Tomorrow night isn't a normal party, rather Vukan will hold our wedding ceremony. The guards told me that part," he paused, the next words coming out strained, "and he will force us to consummate our marriage in front of everyone."

I slowly released him, my mind reeling. He started to say something again, some sort of apology, but I couldn't tell with the ringing that echoed in my ears as the weight of what he said settled in. Or was it from Vukan kicking my head? Damn the Wulfrics and their obsession with hits to the head.

My chest tightened, and I stood up and sprinted to the door. The panic, the disgust, the sheer vileness of it all made me want to run away. Lux called for me to wait, and I stopped. It had nothing to do with his pleading words, but more to do with the fact that I couldn't go anywhere. By the grace of The Creator, I had escaped before. But something inside me knew that would not happen again. Something internal urged me to stop, to stay.

Slowly, I turned to face Lux. His hands were outstretched. "You know you won't be able to escape so easily again. He even conscripted more soldiers just to keep the palace under tighter security."

I padded back to the sofa, falling onto the cushion with a soft thump. Refusing to let the panic dictate my actions, I forced myself to remember the reason I had returned. No more running. I had to think, which was hard with the throbbing in my skull. What were my next steps?

"I can help you meet with her," Lux offered.

In my eagerness to confirm the well being of my friend, I walked ahead of Lux. But once we had arrived at Zasper's rooms, the guards blocked my entrance.

Before I could do something rash, Lux commanded, "Move."

They reacted immediately to the Crown Prince's words, and I shoved past them, throwing the door open.

She had lost a lot of weight since I last saw her.

"I take it they haven't been feeding you well then?"

Lux said nothing, closing the door in order to grant Zasper and I some privacy. The guards protested, but he quickly silenced them with a threat of violence. It was a stark contrast to the mournful man I had been alone with moments ago. The Crown Prince was back, even his stance dripping with arrogance.

Zasper patted the spot next to her. "They usually don't feed prisoners well, but at least I'm not in the dungeon. I heard it's the same for my brethren."

I sat beside her and wrapped my arm around hers. "I'm sorry I left you behind."

She gently shoved me with her shoulder. "You have nothing to be sorry for."

I was so grateful that Lux had helped me to meet with Zasper. We laid down, continuing to catch up.

"I wonder how Egann is doing."

"He said he is fine, but he did say he was annoyed that you had stopped coming to see him."

I bolted up. "What? You talked with him? When? Wait. Annoyed? I stopped meeting with him for his safety!"

Zasper giggled. "You know how he is. And I didn't meet him, he just sent a message through his pigeon."

"He has a pigeon? He could have been messaging me this whole time? Now *I* am the annoyed one."

Zasper patted my knee. "Oh don't be like that. He has his methods, and he is just doing what he thinks is best."

I rolled my eyes, scoffing. "He must be going senile if he thinks that is what is best."

Zasper frowned, eyes filled with displeasure at my comment. "Be respectful. He has faithfully served The Creator and the court of Eboc for a long time."

I winced. "Sorry..."

I laid back down next to her.

"I'm getting married." My eyes traced the pattern of the carved stone ceiling. "What do you think about him?"

"Who?" Zasper asked.

"Lux."

She didn't reply immediately. "I don't know. He is hard to understand."

I sighed. "Yeah..."

After a few moments of silence, we changed the subject. "Lux warned me that Vukan is going to kill me." I was almost shocked at the lack of emotion in my own voice.

Zasper answered, "Then it means that the time has come to fight."

CHAPTER EIGHTEEN

The music sounded like a death knell. The veil felt like it wished to strangle me. The silk wedding dress did little to combat the cold, and I was thankful for the fur cape draping behind me. The doors to the throne room creaked open, and hundreds of eyes peered at me as I walked. I sauntered towards the altar at a pace much too fast for the music. I just wanted this to be over as soon as possible. I hated being in front of all these people, most of whom I didn't know. Every noble and dignitary had been invited to see the uniting of two great households: Polaris and Wulfric.

I strutted towards the dais, where Vukan waited to marry me to his son. I stopped beside Lux, glancing at him through the corner of my eye. He looked so composed and calm, so different than he had looked last night. It made me question if I really knew Lux, or just the facade he presented. He looked resplendent in his royal robes afforded him as Crown Prince. They were red and gold, layered and long. I turned to face the man that would be my husband in just a few minutes. He presented his palm to me, and I took it, hoping he wouldn't feel the sweat and the shaking.

Vukan nodded and the music quieted. He smiled down at us from where he stood upon the steps.

His voice boomed through the hall, the smell of perfume radiating off him, although unable to fully mask the odor of opium and alcohol. "Ladies and Gentlemen of the court, I wish to personally thank you for coming to see the joining of these two lovers. Now I know many of you were surprised by this marriage, and the rush to wed them will be more evident once you hear their story."

He paused and looked at me with what was his attempt at a loving face. "Our dear Princess Valine, daughter of her late Majesty Ariella Polaris, came to us just less than a year ago as a poor orphan, disillusioned with the idea that she was not welcome here in her home. But we remedied that when we welcomed her with open arms. Some arms were a little more welcoming than others." He winked at Lux and the whole crowd chuckled, but they were unable to see the tightened jaw of the prince and the shift of his feet.

I squeezed his hand, and he returned the gesture.

Vukan continued. "As she became more comfortable here, I learned to love her as a daughter, and my son loved her more. These two just couldn't stay away from each other, and now here we are. The orphan and the heir."

Vukan gestured to us, and Lux removed the veil from my face. He stared at me, and I held onto those eyes, an anchor to hold me down when all I wanted was to stab Vukan, to freeze his heart. He wished to reduce me to nothing more than an orphan, here by his own generosity, but Lux looked at me kindly. Those eyes didn't behold a broken girl, or some pawn to be used. They beheld a woman, a ruler, a free entity.

I knew from yesterday that he could be trusted. Where Sebastien had thrown me away for his family, Lux had thrown his family away for me. The Legate had only been willing to go so far to help me, unwilling to oppose his uncle and father, but Lux had defied them in more ways than one. He had not asked to know my secrets, instead divulging his own.

It seemed like some sort of divine protection. Vukan had gotten himself drunk past the point of consciousness before he could give the command for our public consummation. I was grateful that instead some guards had guided us back to Lux's rooms. *Our* rooms.

"Don't even think about it."

Lux rolled his eyes and slumped onto the bed, setting the glass of wine on the table next to him.

"I wouldn't dream of it," he drawled.

I glared at him and stalked over to the bed. I crawled underneath the blankets but sat as far away from Lux as I could manage. I had no other clothes to change into, but luckily the dress was comfortable. It was likely meant for sleep wear more than a wedding anyways.

Lux eyed me. "I'm not going to do anything."

"Good."

Part of me recoiled at him, but a bigger part of me wasn't so disappointed with this arrangement.

At least he wasn't a drunk. He seemed to have a high tolerance, unlike myself. Although I had refused to consume any food or drink at the party for fear that Vukan might want to poison me sooner rather than later.

Lux got out of the bed and grabbed a blanket from the closet. He took it and laid on the couch, tucking his arms behind his head and closing his eyes. I sat up, and as I reached to grab a glass of water from the nightstand, I noticed something was behind the table. I shoved my hand down and grabbed the object. It was the painting of the leopard and man stargazing, apparently having fallen between the nightstand and the wall. I walked over to the sofa.

"Lux?"

"Hmm?"

"How'd this get in here?"

Lux opened his eyes, and I held the painting in front of him.

"Oh," he said, "I took it off the wall and must have forgotten to put it back."

My brow furrowed, my head churning to comprehend. "Why'd you take it from Sebastien's room?'

Lux looked at me like I was crazy. "Why would Sebastien have one of my paintings in his room?"

I bit my lip. I thought I had been in Sebastien's room after Zenith but... "That was *your* room?'

Lux nodded, quickly grasping the situation I was referring to, and closed his eyes again. I mindlessly walked back to the nightstand to set the painting down. That was Lux's room? He had been that voice in the dark? Then again, Rosalva had referred to the owner of those quarters as "His Highness", and no one ever referred to Sebastien as that, using his military title over his royal one. I looked over my shoulder to where he lay.

I was confused by him.

I looked around Lux's room. I still couldn't believe that it had been him to help me all those months ago. Now that I really focused, everything was the same. Except for the hearth.

I searched my memories. "Where are the two dragon statues?"

Lux hesitated. "Uh… about that. There is one more thing I need to tell you."

He whistled and suddenly the wardrobe doors flung open. A flash of emerald green and dark blue ran past me.

"What the—"

I turned to Lux, two dragons no bigger than a large house cat sitting on each one of his shoulders.

"A gift. From my mother."

"I thought they weren't real."

He shrugged his shoulders, and the pair of dragons slithered down his body and crawled back to their original place on the hearth. The green one stared at me while the cobalt one looked tired and uninterested.

"What are their names? How can they communicate? How can they *be real*?"

Lux feigned offense. "I'm hurt that you don't show the same interest in me."

I ignored his quip. Instead I studied them, the strange scaled creatures of old stories and legends.

"The green one is Sol and the dark one is Bahm. They were only eggs when my mother gave them to me. I kept them warm until they hatched."

The blue one yawned, revealing dozens of sharp teeth. It curled into a ball and closed its eyes.

"How big will they get?"

Lux sat on the couch and propped up his feet. "Hard to say. My mother mentioned that they were from her home country. Most likely they will be as big as a horse."

"Can they fly?"

"Glide."

The green one finally laid down too, but kept its eyes pinned on me. Was it wary of me?

"Can they talk?"

Lux shook his head. "No. I communicate with them by whistling. It's a poor attempt at imitating the noises they make. Although I think that they can understand our words sometimes. Unfortunately, my mother didn't leave a guide, so it's impossible to know for sure."

Lux let out a low, soft whistle, and the green one, Sol, finally stopped staring at me.

"I don't think I'll ever get used to them."

"But the queens' giant ice leopards are normal," he scoffed.

He had a point.

I cautiously walked towards him.

"The view is much better the closer you get," he purred.

I walked around to the end of the sofa where his feet rested and gently pushed them aside.

Lux sat up and braced an arm on the back of the couch. "I gave you the bed already, and now you want the couch too?"

Somehow I knew at that moment that Lux wasn't the same as the rest of his family. One could be blood related but that didn't make them the same, didn't make them complicit. I had thought the same of the Legate, but I knew this time it was real. I refused to allow the betrayals of the past to affect my future, so as I stared into his eyes, I was grateful that it was not Sebastien that sat before me, but Lux. He had been just as much a victim as I was and had to hide the kindness he possessed. Wolves sniff out the weakness and cast it out. He had much more patience than I, waiting for the right opportunity, like a leopard readying itself to pounce from the darkness.

I stared into his eyes, and he cocked a brow.

Ice slowly crawled up his fingers resting on the back of the sofa. It slid in swirls up his arm all the way to his neck where it circled, creating a necklace of frozen crystal. He didn't panic, didn't speak. He just sat still. And he smirked. He had an ice necklace that I could command to constrict his throat and still he had that expression plastered across his face.

My brow furrowed. "You are not scared or disgusted?"

His smirk only widened. "I already knew."

For a moment my heart stopped beating and my breath inhaled sharply, worried that Sebastien had told them about my magic. But that didn't make sense since I was not killed or thrown in the dungeon.

My mouth gaping open, I watched an orange flame spread from his neck all the way down his arm, steam rising where the ice melted.

I gasped, "What? How?"

"When I was eleven, a strange old man found me and told me about my gift. He also told me that I had a job to do when I grew older."

I was shocked. Egann, that sly old man. He sure did travel a lot.

"And what were you supposed to do?"

Lux slid towards me, holding up two fingers. "Two things. First, I was to do no harm, with or without magic."

My eyes widened. "But Zenith..."

The smirk finally disappeared, replaced by a sad frown. "I had no part in her death. When I learned of my father's plans, I was going to try to get her out, but I was too late."

He lay a hand on my knee, and I didn't refuse it. "I'm sorry that I couldn't save her, and for all the terrible things I had to do to convince my father that I was not a threat."

I set a hand atop of his and gazed back up at him. "And what was the second thing?"

He leaned closer, the light of the lanterns illuminating his head and reflecting off of his obsidian hair. "The man then told me that I was to find a girl and help her."

I swallowed. "Help her how?"

Lux shrugged, releasing my hand and leaning back. "He never explained. He was an annoyingly cryptic man, and I only saw him a few times." A smile tugged his lips upward. "But I think I know what he meant now."

I held my breath.

"I think I have found a way to use my light to help my Little Bird."

Little Bird.

It was either some strange coincidence or a divinely orchestrated meeting. He had been there when Sebastien and I fought. He knew about Sebastien then.

My face turned red. "So that was you in the cove of trees."

He nodded. "Oh yes. It has been one of my favorite hiding places since coming here." Lux flicked his fingers and fire roared to life in the fireplace.

I rubbed my temples. "I still can't believe—"

Lux interrupted, "That your husband is so handsome *and* talented?"

I punched his leg and he yelped, rubbing the sore spot.

"Why did you hide your powers? I mean, I know Egann told you not to use them, but why listen to him?"

Lux sat up and rotated his body so he was facing the fire. "Honestly, no one needed to tell me to hide it. Even as a young boy I was terrified of him. I knew what he would do if he found out, what he would use me for. Although I had contemplated ending him a few times throughout my life."

My eyes widened and Lux continued. "But he had too many close followers who would continue his plans, who would hurt me, hurt the rest of our family."

I stared at his back. "I don't know what to say."

Lux sighed. "I know you hate him, but I hate him too. I hate *me* too."

I tentatively touched his back. "I did. I used to, hate you that is. But now..."

Lux turned his head, looking hopeful.

I patted his back. "Now I don't."

The tension visibly left him, his shoulders sagging. "Thank you."

I pulled my legs up, crossing them.

Lux stated, "Well I'm not surprised you don't hate me. You liked Sebastien, and both my looks and personality are far superior to his."

He always made jokes when things got serious. Looking back, he made light of many things, breaking tense situations, carefully crafting his reputation.

"Sorry. I know it hasn't been that long." His voice interrupted my thoughts.

"It's okay. He showed his true loyalties. I could never love someone who thinks the way he does."

"And me?"

I was shocked by his question. "You?"

Lux peered at me. "Am I unlovable?"

I shook my head. "You're not... I don't know. I just know that I don't hate you. And maybe had I known this all along we could have been good allies, even friends."

Lux grinned. "Well that's a start. Means there is a chance."

I plucked at the split-ends of my hair, hesitant to ask what was on my mind. From last night to now, Lux had been nothing but honest, and I was reluctant to have the tentative trust between us broken. I breathed deeply. "Sebastien mentioned that you locked him in a rice chest when you were younger. Why did you do that? I know children often prank each other, but that was too much."

Lux replied indignantly, "Figures he would only think the worst of me." He crossed his arms. "When my father would return from drinking, he often was violent, breaking jars, throwing bowls and..." he paused. Lux ran his fingers over his shoulder. "And people."

"You don't mean…" I didn't want to finish the sentence. The image of Lux's bare back flashed in my mind, all the tiny white scars and pink slashes. I put the puzzle together before his words confirmed it. My body shuddered as bumps formed on my arms.

Lux sighed. "I suppose it is my fault for not telling him why I put him in the chest."

I pulled the blanket that Lux had been using over my legs, trying to think of another topic.

"What about you? Any tragic love story for you?" I asked, trying to make light of my own poor excuse for a relationship.

The smile disappeared from his face.

"The first girl I ever loved didn't love me back. I mean, of course I thought she did, or maybe I convinced myself of that because I was so lonely, so desperate." His face flushed in what I could only guess was embarrassment. But it wasn't his fault, and there was nothing to be ashamed of for loving and trusting another.

His gaze fixated on the floor, his voice cracked as he spoke, "It turned out she was my fathers informant. I only found out because my father wanted me to. I've always been at the mercy of him. He brought her in before me one night, and she confessed that she was a spy, only pretending to love me for the money my father had promised her. Then my father stabbed her, killed her, right in front of me. Even though she never truly cared for me, I did for her. I remember the blood, the shock in her eyes. I wondered what she thought in those final moments. Of the money she had been promised? Of our time together? Of some other man? From that point forward I knew I couldn't love anyone or anything because that thing would become the target of my father if I displeased him."

He glanced at me. "Then you showed up. I remember you, from our childhood. We only met a handful of occasions, but each one stuck in my mind, like a lighthouse in the tumultuous stormy ocean, those times were lanterns in an otherwise bleak and dark existence. Your pretty pink dress that you stained with tart filling that you had swiped from the kitchens. Your two braids with the yellow ribbons intertwined. Your admonishment of a noble who was berating a servant. I believe your exact words were, "If you treat any of my servants like that you will switch places with them.""

His high pitched imitation made me laugh, causing his eyes to fix on me, looking as if he was drinking in the sound like an ill man's life-saving medicine.

"You were so brave, even as a little girl. Unlike me... I am a coward. Even when I felt the desire to protect you, the only thing I could think of was to convince my father to send you away as a servant. I knew it'd be humiliating, but you would be alive, be safe. And then when you were whipped I couldn't help myself, I had to step in. And when I was dragged away, I went and got Sokah. I'm so sorry about that. It's my fault he died."

So the "he" in Sokah's letter was the Crown Prince. I grabbed Lux's hand instinctively. "Don't say that. It's your fa–Vukan's fault. Not yours, not mine."

I finally believed that. Finally let go of the guilt, letting it melt away. "You are not guilty of your fathers crimes. Each man is responsible for himself and what he has the power to control. You had no power, and even though you had none, you still fought, still tried, in your own way. Thank you."

Tears were in his eyes. "I–I've never been told that."

I couldn't help myself. I wrapped my arms around him and held him. I scolded myself for being so judgmental, so hateful and prejudiced and selfish. I had refused to see his suffering, solely focused on mine and those who I wanted to see. Revenge had blinded me on so many things. I had refused to see certain things, refused to do certain things, all for my revenge.

I could no longer live like that.

My plans would remain the same, but the motivation would be different from now on. Justice was a worthy endeavor. Revenge was not.

I pulled away and brushed his long, raven hair out of his face. "Let's talk about something else."

I thought for a moment, finally landing on something that had caused his face to soften and tone to warm. "What about your mother? I remember meeting her once when we were little. She seemed kind."

The tears that had just ceased returned as he spoke, "She killed herself."

I berated myself on my once again poor choice of subject matter. I said nothing because there were no words truly proper for such a thing. I just sat and held his hand.

"She never showed her inner sadness. How lonely she must have been, isolated in the shadows of her mind. And yet she always smiled. I try not to remember her hanging from the rafters where I found her and my aunt. Instead, I try to think about her laugh, her soft hands that always picked me up when I scraped a knee or her sweet voice as she sang us lullabies."

His voice grew taut. "My father neglected her, yet she never did us, as if she was determined to give us all the love she was refused by her husband. Yet I can't help but wonder how many times she cried alone, how much agony she must have been in to tie the rope around her neck."

I was shocked, my tongue unable to form any words.

"I wouldn't be surprised if my father had something to do with her death too." Lux's voice trailed off.

Lux and Sebastien had been through so much, but they had turned out very differently. It made me ponder, made both of them more pitiful. Ultimately, no tragedy was an excuse to inflict the same upon others. Sebastien had been hardened by his past, Lux, although on the outside appeared to do the same, was actually still soft, still compassionate.

I looked down at my hands, my thoughts returning back to his mother.

"Do you think they were selfish for it?"

I felt the sympathy and sadness in his voice. "No."

My voice came out quietly. "I can relate to the despair, and the desire to end it."

Lux enveloped me in his arms, the sudden movement causing my limbs to lock. "Never. Please. You can think me selfish or strange for asking such a thing, but for my sake, please don't. Don't leave me."

"I promise." It came out without thinking, but I always did my best to keep my word.

We were both so broken, still suffering from physical and mental anguish. Maybe that made us suitable for one another, we could understand each other, help each other. Only those who had suffered similarly could be truly empathetic and patient on the long journey towards healing. That's what healing was, a journey, one that was long and filled with obstacles and side paths, where getting lost and going backwards were all possibilities. Just maybe, we could walk together.

The tender moment was ended by a predictable quip. "Not the way everyone expects to spend their wedding night," Lux cracked.

I softly shoved him away. "I guess I better get used to your humor."

"Oh so you do find it humorous?" he asked with a grin.

I rolled my eyes, but my mouth curled into a smile. I thought back on what Lux had done for me. Kept my secrets that I didn't even know he knew, comforted me, saved me from death.

"Oh by the way," Lux threw out, "Citadel was *my* personal guard. I don't need Sebastien taking any more of the credit."

My mouth dropped open, and my head was starting to ache with the bombardment of revelations. "Then who was protecting you?"

"No one," he replied nonchalantly as he stood and entered the bathing room, closing the door behind him with a click.

I sat on the sofa alone, letting all the information sink in, the last of my doubts about him floating away like a leaf on an autumn breeze.

CHAPTER NINETEEN

Vukan *loved his parties,* loved the alcohol and drugs, so he decided that we needed another ball to celebrate our wedding. It made me worried though. He seemed to be getting more irritable, more violent and obscene, something I had previously deemed impossible.

The king had a pipe in one hand and a woman's breast in the other. I looked the other way, taking in the guests seated at the table. It had been the first time in a long while, at least that I was aware of, since all the kings had been present together. Our wedding had apparently required their attendance, although I had been too nervous and focused on controlling my magic and emotions to notice who'd been present in the crowd.

There they sat opposite of Lux and myself, each clad in their designated colors. Every king had two colors, one of which was always gray, to represent the unity and fealty to the High Queen, or king now, and the other was up to them. The House Wulfric's chosen color was crimson, which seemed only fitting. Even before the coup, the Wulfrics were in charge of the military. They maintained the navy, since their region was on the eastern coast, as well as a strong cavalry and infantry. Spilling blood had always been a part of them.

It was in stark contrast to the Roh's. They controlled the humid and arid section of the south. Their color was green, perhaps in order to reflect their agricultural contributions or simply the beautiful and lush landscape. The Sosoni House lived in the central region of Racour, which was predominantly grasslands that ran up to the border of Pardus, and the majority of the meat in Racour came from them. They had chosen a light brown, which I had always found atrocious when paired with Racourian Gray.

The other area that shared a border with Pardus was that of House Stallian. They mined the northern hills that were full of precious metals and gems, choosing for themselves a sapphire blue.

Last was the smallest house. The House of Galapos controlled a small series of islands off the southeastern coast. They did not have naval ships like the Wulfrics, instead all their vessels were fishing boats. Almost all seafood came from them. I always thought blue would have suited them best, but instead their color was yellow, most likely inspired by the sun that shimmered on their beloved ocean.

I had met all the Kings when I was younger, although I did not remember much of them. But they were all dead now, except for Dumas Stallian who had taken up sides with the Wulfrics. He was an overweight and balding man who chased money over honor. Then again, honor was what killed the others. Integrity often had a high price with little returns. I doubted the new Kings had any at all, since they were handpicked by the Wulfrics.

On Dumas' left was House Roh's new King, Minsol. He had glasses and looked so nervous that a cough might just cause his frail frame to break. I heard that his two older brothers were killed after refusing to bow to Vukan. On the right was Koodsin Sosoni. He was tall and tanned, his hair long and braided, and his face looked stern. Rumor had it that his sisters were all being held hostage in Wulfric territory, forcing his obedience.

But King Galapos was notably absent.

I had heard that his name was Peten. There were rumors that he had fled and joined a band of pirates, but I doubted that was the truth. More likely than not, he had been killed, and Vukan had written the islands off as more trouble than they were worth.

Minsol refused to make eye contact with anyone throughout the whole dinner, his squeaky voice matching his demeanor. Koodsin never spoke except when a question was asked directly to him. Annoyingly, Dumas talked even if no one was listening, and he stared at my chest periodically. I had to hold Lux's hand to keep him from doing anything. I never would have thought that the day would come that I would do something to protect a Wulfric.

Luckily the meal ended relatively calmly, except for Vukan stabbing a servant who delivered his drink too slowly. It had only been in the hand, so the poor man would live for now. The court was in a sad state when a nonfatal stabbing was considered an uneventful day.

I wished we could just retire for the night, but Vukan insisted that there be dancing, more drinking, and performers in the ballroom. Although not necessarily in that order. The hall was filled with people, many nobles and wealthy merchants who lived in other major cities still present due to the wedding. There were even some children amongst the attendees. I pitied them. Most of their parents would be too drunk to watch over them properly. Yet they looked happy, running around, weaving between the skirts and pillars as they chased each other. I smiled as I watched them. Maybe they weren't so pitiable after all.

They looked well-fed and had grins on their faces. For a moment, I thought how wonderful childhood was, when one was blissfully ignorant, but then Lux's and Egann's stories popped into my mind. Some children never had that privilege.

I gasped and reached out, starting towards a little boy who had fallen some feet away from me on the outskirts of the room. The child cried and clutched his bleeding knee, but muffled his screams, knowing that a drunk parent would likely come to reprimand him rather than console him. Out of my peripheral vision, I saw Lux rushing towards him. The child cowered, fearing the prince, or rather his well fabricated reputation. Kneeling down beside him, Lux looked around, and after checking to make sure no one was near enough to see, wiggled his finger, and a little bird made of flame flew around the child's scraped knee. Lux shifted, to better shield his show of magic from the crowd, although everyone was likely too drunk to notice.

But I saw.

I saw the firebird's wings gently brush against the child's cheeks, drying his tears, yet not singing his soft skin. Lux smiled as the child's eyes grew round in wonder and joy. I couldn't help but also smile. His control of his gift was impressive. Despite all that he had already shared, Lux was surprising me with his kindness. That child could offer him no power, no money, and nothing of worth in return, yet Lux took the time to comfort him. It was a pure act of compassion, and my heart warmed with admiration.

Lux smiled as he watched the boy prance away, yet I could only watch Lux. But suddenly that smile disappeared, his eyes looked worried or maybe even... afraid? I followed his line of sight. The previously happy child was now terrified, his small chubby arm in a harsh grip. Vukan leered over the child, wine drenching his silk clothes.

"I'm s-sor—" the child stuttered.

"You little twit! How dare you? Do you have any idea how expensive these silks are?" Vukan raged.

The poor child didn't have a chance to say anything else before Vukan threw him aside with an impressive amount of force. The small body hit a nearby pillar with a sickening crack. My pulse quickened as I watched in horror as blood pooled around the little child's head. He would never get up.

The atmosphere was cold, and many faces looked shocked and sickened, yet no one dared say anything. I looked around for the parents of this poor child, eventually seeing a woman who had fallen to the floor, with a man whom I could only assume was her husband, covering her mouth in an attempt to muffle her sobs, less they incur more wrath from the king.

Vukan snapped his fingers and some guards came and carried the lifeless body away, scarlet dripping to the floor, and with one glare from the King, the musicians started playing music again. I couldn't believe what had happened, how jubilee had turned to death in such a short time. I looked back to where Lux last was, but he was gone. I whipped my head around, trying to see where he was headed to. I saw his robes just as they disappeared through a side entrance. I quickly weaved through the crowd to follow after him.

Lux dismissed all the guards outside his room, demanding to be left alone. I closed the door behind me, and Lux and I just stood there. I didn't know how to start a conversation about it with him. I waited, every once in a while glancing in his direction. He stood in front of the fire, eyes blank and hands melded to the hearth, dragons nudging them.

I fiddled with my necklace. I wanted to reach out to him, to say something, but I wasn't sure what I could do to help.

After being unable to bear the silence any longer, I finally opened my mouth.

"Lux," I began, "you know it's not your fault, right?"

No reply.

I took a few steps towards him. "I saw what you did right before. When he had scraped himself."

A few more steps. "You aren't your father. You aren't a monster."

He chuckled. "Isn't that what you called me before we got married? A monster?"

I reached out a hand and grabbed his shoulder. "Hey, that was before I knew you."

He shook me off. "Oh yeah? You think you know me now?"

I gently turned him to face me. "I know enough. I know enough that I am happy that I am married to you, and that I get to spend the rest of my life getting to know you better."

The words just came out before my mind really processed them, but they weren't empty words meant to placate him.

His head dropped, shoulders dragging to the floor. "I am not worthy of that. I am a coward."

"Hey, don't say that—"

"Valine, I never stood up to him," he interrupted. "I watched what he did, knowing it was wrong, but not doing anything to stop him. I am as guilty as he is!"

I cupped his face, forcing him to meet my eyes. "Lux, you are not your father, do not bear his sins. And you cannot change the past, only the future. You are strong, and so wonderful to not have become corrupted by him. You are worthy of being loved, Lux."

He pulled my hands off his face. "No, I am not. The things I have done are unforgivable. Egann always talked about The Creator, but I am certain such a deity wants nothing to do with me."

"There is nothing you have done that cannot be forgiven. The Creator loves you, and He is able and willing to forgive."

Lux looked up. "How is that possible?"

I shrugged and offered a hopeful smile. "He is just that loving."

He stared at me, a desire to believe written in his eyes. "How do you know?" His voice was quiet and hopeful.

"A good friend once told me about it, and then I experienced it for myself."

That's all it took for Lux to fall to the floor and weep. I held him as we cried together. After a while, the tears ceased and we sat on the couch.

"Thank you." Lux sniffled.

I rubbed my thumb across his knuckles. "I meant every word."

Lux nodded. "I think you would be a terrible actress, so I know your words were genuine."

I gasped, "You think I am bad at pretending?"

Lux explained, "Of course. Your eyes always bear witness to the truth. Whenever you looked at me, your eyes were full of hatred, even if your words and actions were suggesting otherwise."

I winced, remembering the moments he was referring to. "Sorry. I judged you too harshly."

Lux shook his head. "You have nothing to be sorry for. It's quite the opposite." He squeezed my hands. "You inspire people, Valine. To *do* better. To *be* better." He leaned his forehead against mine. "You inspire me, and I won't stand by and watch anymore."

Tears filled my eyes as he pulled away and knelt onto one knee. He took one of my hands and he placed his other hand over his heart. "Whatever your fate, so shall mine be. Your people will be my people, where you go, so shall I." I was shaking and my whole body warmed as he brought my hand up to his lips and placed a gentle kiss on my knuckles. "Long may she reign."

His words touched my heart and brought tears to my eyes. We slept together in the bed that night, holding each other. We weren't lovers, but we were at the very least friends. Lux had done something Sebastien never could have—never *had* done. The Crown Prince had bent the knee to me, had sworn fealty, had vowed to leave the protection and position as the king's son, for me. However, his oath had been made not only for me, but also for himself, and for the people of Racour. Power and personal pleasure were not more important to him than people's pain. I kissed his forehead before falling asleep.

After our marriage, the guards watching me became fewer, and the ones who shifted through the rotation were all Lux's men or those who had pledged to me. I was relieved to see Falchor and Mordris among those stationed outside our door. Although security had been tightened overall, that seemed to do with Vukan's increasing paranoia and mental instability rather than worry I would escape. He had seemingly become complacent where I was concerned. If Lux was with me, no one questioned us. Perhaps Vukan thought Lux would keep me reined in, take responsibility, or that he had finally broken me. Tamed me.

Thus I had the perfect opportunity.

I asked Lux to do me a favor, and he agreed without so much as a question. He brought me out of the palace to Sanguis Mountain, only Citadel as our guard. I couldn't believe that I hadn't realized that Citadel was Lux's man. I asked them to wait for me at the tree. I was slightly disappointed that Egann was not waiting for me there, when he was aware of so much. Knowing Egann, he wouldn't come even if he knew we were coming. I could imagine his voice. "There was no purpose for me to go there."

It was true that I didn't need him, but I did miss him. I pushed the thought away. There was something I had to do. There was an ancient people that Egann had mentioned offhandedly during one of our training sessions. When I had asked Zasper what she knew, she said she had heard only legends, but if they really existed, they would be invaluable.

CHAPTER TWENTY

*Y**ou're not going to* find them, the ice leopard chided, bounding around in the snow as I laboriously hiked. I kicked the white powder at his face. *Shut it, Dryden.*

He shook his pelt, scattering the flakes. *No need to be rude. I'm simply stating the most likely outcome. The Waodani rarely appear to anyone. They're very seclusive.*

I glared. *I don't appreciate your negativity.*

Dryden shrugged, or at least a big cat's version of one. *I'm not being negative. I'm just being honest.*

I huffed out of both annoyance and exhaustion. *If you were just going to put me down, then why did you come?*

The big cat slowed his pace for me, his familiarity with terrain and superior stamina apparent. *You know it's uncomfortable to be apart from each other. I know you feel the same pang in your heart, the uneasiness and aching.*

I was too busy trying to breathe to reply. I knew what he meant though. Whatever magic or divine power that the bond was made of, it caused a deep seeded feeling of something missing when we were too far apart. It was annoying and comforting at the same time. I looked forward to the day when Dryden would be able to stay with me.

Can't you move any faster? he complained.

Okay, maybe not.

I was about to make a retort when an arrow landed in front of us.

Looking around, there was nothing to see except snow, rocks, and a few shrubs that existed at the high elevation. Except one of the rocks moved. My hands instinctively reached for the knives on my belt.

Dryden swatted a paw at my arm. *Don't bother. They could kill you even if you had twenty blades.*

I kicked his haunch lightly. *Jerk.*

His tail wacked my calf. *Idiot.*

I crossed my arms, and he snickered, whiskers twitching in amusement. Apparently the leopards knew more about the Waodani than we did.

In the short time of our argument, more shrubs and rocks had transformed into people who were now surrounding us. Some had skin so pale it was as white as the snow that they stood upon. Others had tanned from the harsh sun that bore down especially hard upon the mountain tops. Their eyes were striking hues of browns and blacks, while their hair was either black or white with no in-between, braids, feathers, and bones scattered throughout. Their faces were painted in strange markings and designs. These people were so different from me, from the Ebocians and even the pirates that I had met. They were more ancient than any other people in Saego, mere myths to most, if they were in fact the people I was searching for.

Dryden, for once, didn't growl at the newcomers, which was surprising to say the least.

Do you know these people?

Dryden sat down, licking a paw. *Of course. These are the Waodani.*

I rolled my eyes. He was such a know it all.

I can hear you.

I patted his head. *I know.*

His bushy tail hit the back of my calves hard enough to sting.

"Ow!"

He sniggered.

What language do they speak?

Dryden shrugged his big shoulders. *How am I supposed to know?*

I glanced at the people, then back to my companion. *I thought you knew everything.*

Dryden growled, *Very funny. I only know that they don't like to meddle in others' affairs. But they must have recently changed their habits since they have chosen to show themselves to you.*

I turned to the people who had emerged from the snow. *I guess I should be flattered.*

Dryden resumed licking his paw. *You should be. It is a huge honor for the Waodani to appear to someone and not immediately kill them.*

A shiver went down my spine.

I bowed my head in greeting. "Do any of you speak Racourian?"

Silence was my only answer. I peered at each face. After a few minutes, I kneeled in the snow.

What are you doing? Dryden asked.

I'm not really sure. I'm honestly just hoping they don't kill me, I stated.

Dryden snorted, a cloud of warm air emitting from his nostrils. I reached out and drew in the snow.

Dryden looked at the writing. *If they can't speak Racourian, what makes you think they can read it?*

I don't know! But I have to try something.

I looked up at their faces, but they were expressionless.

Maybe you should just let them speak first.

I sighed and rested my hands on my knees. *We might be here forever then.*

After a few minutes of silence and staring, I asked, "So... what's with all the bones?"

What happened to waiting for them to speak first?

I shoved his big shoulder, and he swayed for a moment.

I've never been good at keeping my mouth shut.

Dryden retorted, *I noticed.*

I rolled my eyes and looked around once more. I took note of each person in the circle. The tanned ones held weapons, while the pale ones were empty handed and covered completely except for their faces. One man, who was broad shouldered and had dark blue paint smeared across his tanned face and had the most bones sewn onto his pelts, held a staff tipped on both sides with obsidian points.

He resembled a leader, so I addressed him. "I need you and your people's help."

Nothing.

"My name is Valine Polaris, heir to the throne of Racour. Evil men have taken my kingdom and killed my family. I want to take back what is mine. Tomorrow at twilight there will be a conclave. I would like your people to come."

Again, nothing.

I wasn't sure if they were comprehending what I was saying.

I gestured with my hands and spoke slowly, "I am a Princess," I motioned a crown. "Bad men killed my mother." I made a stabbing gesture. "I need help to kill bad men."

Still nothing.

I sighed. I carefully lifted my hand and drew in a deep breath. The cold greeted me with excitement, like a childhood friend eager to play. I twisted my fingers and exhaled. A weapon, fashioned like a staff with two blades at each end, lay at my feet. It was pure light blue ice. I ripped a strip of my undershirt off and wrapped it around the handle so the wielder would not be burned by the fierce cold. I had made it so that it wouldn't melt even in the summer sun, at least, I hoped that that's what would happen. I hadn't actually tried something like it before. I backed away, leaving the bladed staff in front of the man.

"A gift."

The man simply cocked his head and whistled. A gap was created in the circle behind me.

"Twilight. At the birch cove by the river at the bottom of Sanguis. Conclave. Please come."

I turned and walked through the gap, unsure if they had even understood me. I just had to hope and pray. Dryden followed, shoulders shaking with what I was sure was laughter.

I made sure to arrive first at the birch cove, although I was sure that each group had sent scouts to confirm safety ahead of time. The sun was just about to set, orange and purple hues creating a painted backdrop for our meeting. I had about ten minutes before anyone was likely to show up. Without saying a word, Dryden went off to check for dangers, still upset with me for putting myself at risk by returning to Pardus. Zasper squeezed my hand and went to sit in a tree to pray before the meeting started.

My chest tightened, and I chewed my lips as if I could wear away the worry like a beaver to a tree. So much could go wrong, and so much needed to go just right. I wanted Lux here, but he had to stay behind in case excuses were needed for our absence. And Egann, well, he would show up if he felt like it, and even if he didn't, I was sure he would mysteriously be able to know what happened.

I cracked my knuckles and tried to calm my nerves. I crawled onto a rock a few feet from the river bank, the soft rushing sound helping steady my pulse. The Xian River was too wide and fast flowing to freeze over even when everything else was covered in ice and snow.

It was the tail end of winter, when spring fights to claim its place in the rotation of seasons, most of the snow having melted aside from the small patches taking up camp beneath the safe shadows of the trees. The air was chilled but grew colder as I drew upon my magic. My hands protested as they met the frigid stone face beneath me, only warming slightly as I sat atop them. Lux had offered the advice, mentioning that I relied too heavily upon them for control. I needed to learn how to use my gift with only my mind.

I stilled my body. Ice whispered, chills dancing upon my skin as I blew air from my mouth. A butterfly fluttered in front of my face, the last rays of sun piercing its translucent wings, creating warped images on the ground of the clearing. I smiled and blew out more air, the butterfly flapped its crystal wings faster and higher. It was not a useful trick, but it was beautiful. A crack.

My smile faded and the butterfly fell to the ground, motionless.

The first group had arrived.

My small rebel band was first. There were some new faces that I didn't recognize. Although wary, I trusted my comrades and knew that they would only bring people who could keep quiet, people who would be loyal to our cause. After the purge Vukan made against Yanish's main group, all that remained were a handful of men and women. Most had been scattered throughout the kingdom but had traveled here after I had sent word to them that the time to amass a full fledged army had come.

I greeted Sidian, who updated me on his wife and daughter. Sorin had recently disappointed Korine by expressing her desire to become a seamstress instead of a baker, but a new baby, a girl they named Midia, would provide another opportunity for an heir to their quaint shop.

I also briefly chatted with Laika and Larkan, twins with bright blonde hair and blue eyes, who had been the son and daughter of the loyal chambermaid who had helped sneak me out that tragic night of the coup. Their mother, Lyria, had unfortunately passed away from an illness a few years ago, but they were equally loyal as their mother was. They both had spent the last couple years as a musician and tailor respectively, using both their occupations to learn the secrets of the nobility and any other useful information that they could come across.

Laika informed me that when she performed for a private party in Canton, she overheard a general mention relocating troops to the border of Eboc, and Larkan explained that one of his clients whose tongue flowed loosely during garment fittings let it slip that her husband had to quell a minor uprising of farmers in Roh's region, that more and more people were growing tired of the Wulfrics.

Next, I caught up with Mingi, a blacksmith in a small village in Roh territory. Then Thane, a servant in one of House Stallian's vassal lord's estates who mentioned that Venore had a stench of late that no one could find the source of. Their information wasn't always pertinent, but I was thankful nonetheless.

Lastly, Sidian introduced me to the new faces, Ravi, Nabeel, and Raia, who were foreigners from Percia who had immigrated to Racour under my mother's reign and suffered under Vukan's. I thanked them for their help, and

I promised that when I had time, I would like to hear their stories.

I was still unsure if the Waodani would come.

Spotting my soldiers from the castle, Mordris approached with the two boys. Ferrum and Talom quickly started up a conversation with Laika, whose looks entranced many men. Larkan stood protectively next to his sister, but Ferrum and Talom paid no mind, too infatuated with the pretty girl. Mordris chuckled at the sight of his nephews. They would represent the guards who could not be here, as having a contingent of Vukan's soldiers would raise suspicion and unsettle everyone else. I clasped Mordris' arm and moved onto the next group.

The leopards had come, and a wave of relief swept over me. Dryden and Kalosa walked up and I knelt down, resting my forehead against hers. Dryden had filled me in on the traditional way of greeting amongst the leopards.

"Thank you for coming."

Kalosa's ears twitched. *Do not thank me now. I still have time to change my mind.*

I shrugged. "It still means a lot that you came."

She nodded but said nothing more as she padded away. I stood, brushing the dirt from my knee.

Raucous cheers and jovial laughs alerted me to the arrival of the pirates. Leave it to them to be loud while coming to a secret meeting.

I turned around.

The Pirate Lord smiled, greeting me with a kiss to both cheeks. "I hope you don't expect me to bow just yet, Val. Or should I call you Princess?"

I laughed. "If you called me Princess you'd have to bow. Stick to Val."

Kas grinned. "Reminds you of old times, doesn't it? I miss those days of adventure."

I brushed my hand across his arm. "Stick around long enough and you may retract that statement."

"I highly doubt that," he whispered.

I smiled and patted his shoulder. "Just you wait, Kas."

I walked past him to the tree Zasper still sat in, Dryden at my heels. I leaned against the tree, crossing my arms as my eyes swept across those gathered. "Think they'll come?"

Zasper didn't say anything, simply sitting upon the branch.

I sighed. "Do you think we have any chance of winning this without them? Do we even have a chance *with* them?"

Zasper landed next to me with a soft thud and assessed the strange amalgamation of people and animals. They all, albeit reluctantly, mingled, except for the leopards who were keeping to themselves. Granted no one but myself could communicate with them.

Zasper finally spoke, "I pray this works friend, for everyone who has ever hoped for a better life. I don't know if they will come, or if any of them will agree to fight, but no matter what, I am with you. No matter what, we must try."

I turned to look at my friend. Her eyes were calm, steadfast—like a tree.

I wrapped my arms around her. "From dust, to dust. We will meet again, sister."

Zasper had translated the Ebocian saying for me, and it resonated with me, causing me to adopt it into my own vocabulary. She pulled back. "From dust, to dust. We will meet again."

We parted and turned towards the river.

I looked to the horizon. The sun was gone, and the sky had turned a dark purple.

"Guess they're not coming."

I pulled my hood up. There wasn't any purpose to it, other than I appreciated the dramatic effect it had. I walked to the rock where I had previously sat, the butterfly still on the ground beside it. It was cold enough that it hadn't melted and had yet to be trampled by the hundreds of feet. I stepped onto the rock and scanned my eyes across all those who had come. I waited for the chattering to stop, one hand resting on my dagger belt. The buzz quickly died down.

"Thank you all for coming. I won't waste any time. You all know who I am and have a general idea of why I asked you to come." My voice grew louder as fiery conviction roared to life inside me. "Many of you have been oppressed under the Wulfric regime, others are here because, although they themselves have not experienced the brutality of Vukan, they have compassion on the thousands that have—"

A shout from Kasabian's crew interrupted me, "I'm here cause Captain promised us money!"

I searched but could not find who spoke out. "Whatever your reasons, I thank you for coming."

Whispers swept over the crowd. I wasn't sure how to formulate the question. How was one to ask if they were willing to fight and die, and for what? For me to sit on a throne and wear a shiny crown? For revenge? It may have started that way, but now it was something else.

"Look, I know that what I am about to ask seems insane, which is why I won't think any less of anyone who walks away. But I urge you all to stay. To fight. Against Vukan and his army. He kills at a whim, throws parties while thousands starve, and wants to take over the continent, subjugating millions of people." I paused. I wasn't sure what to say next.

A voice from the back called out, "Why should you be queen? Not everyone knew your mother, but some of us remember. She let people starve too."

I flinched. "I... I know my mother wasn't a good ruler. She was inept and didn't know how to be queen, but she wasn't malicious. She tried. And I am not saying I should rule because I am her daughter. I am saying that I should rule because I care about what happens to my people." I couldn't find the right words to properly articulate my reasoning.

Grumbling and arguing broke out. I tried to talk again, but it was too loud for people to hear me.

"Everybody shut up!"

The clamoring ceased as Mordris shoved his way to the base of the rock. He pointed at me as he spoke, "Princess Valine deserves to rule more than any other person I know. She defended us soldiers against the savage games the king forced us to partake in. She took a whipping meant for my nephews. She has repeatedly put her own life on the line for the sake of others. Princess Valine is my queen, and she should be yours as well."

Mordris fell to one knee, eyes peering up at me. "And I would die for her."

The rebels cheered and some even lowered onto one knee. But the leopards sat stoically, and the pirates whispered among themselves.

I turned towards Kas, who was frowning. An expression I was not used to seeing on him.

"Well?"

Kas rubbed his chin. "I don't know Val. I would pledge myself to you in a minute, but I won't make that promise for my crew. You're asking a lot of them."

"I understand, Kas, but—"

"We may be willing to aid you in your quest."

I whipped my head around looking for the source of the voice as shouts of surprise and confusion emitted from the crowd. Shadow cloaked figures emerged from the forest. Fifty people peeled away from the cover of the foliage, all covered in bones and fur. I fought to keep the shock from my face. The Waodani had actually come. I spotted the broad man from the mountains. The ice staff was not in his hand, but in a much smaller, thinner man who was lean and pale.

The crowd parted to let him through to the rock, the ice staff tapping the ground in front of him. He removed his hood. He was the whitest human I had ever seen, and his eyes were so pale blue that barely any color could be detected, which only furthered the contrast with the crimson paint on his face. For all I knew it could have been blood. He did not look at me, but rather, stared straight ahead, as if looking at something in the distance.

He was blind.

I slid off the boulder. The man was the same height as me, and surprisingly, around the same age. His nose was slightly crooked, as if it had been broken multiple times, and although he was skinny, he was deceptively toned. I began to bow my head, but stopped myself.

The man chuckled. "No need for any of your strange formalities."

I glanced at the man I had met yesterday. "I, uh… I thought…"

The pale man laughed again. "You thought the big one was the leader, didn't you?"

I shuffled my feet. "Well I assumed—"

"You assumed the big burly guy must be the leader of the feared, legendary group of warriors, no?"

He slapped 'the big burly guy' on the back. "This is Leopard's Bane. Well at least, that's the easiest translation."

Dryden intruded into my mind. *Pretentious name.*

I ignored him.

The large man thumped his chest.

I nodded. "My apologies. I meant no offense."

Leopard's Bane said nothing.

The pale man must have sensed my concern. "He's not much of a talker. Leopard clawed his face once and absolutely shredded his tongue."

My eyes widened, and I glanced over at the leopards, who looked indifferent by the declaration.

He probably did something to deserve it, Dryden grumbled.

"Oh don't worry about him. He wasn't much of a talker before. Honestly, I didn't notice that much of a difference." He paused and pointed to his eyes. "I do the talking for him and he does the seeing for me."

The man chuckled again, and reluctant laughter broke out amongst the rebels and pirates.

This meeting was a mess. "What's your name?"

It took the man several seconds to calm himself before he could reply, "I am Raven Bone, Chief of the Waodani." He puffed out his chest—a poor imitation of Leopard's Bane.

I narrowed my eyes. "Not to be rude, I am extremely grateful for you coming, but why are you here if you're not going to take this seriously?"

Raven Bone leaned against the ice staff. "Because you're the most gorgeous thing I've ever seen."

Hoots and hollers bellowed from the pirate crew, and my face turned red.

Sensing my displeasure, he straightened himself up again. "You're no fun."

I bit my cheek to keep my sarcastic reply from ruining this much needed alliance. Raven Bone grinned. I didn't think I'd like whatever he said next.

"Let's fight."

I didn't like it.

CHAPTER TWENTY-ONE

I couldn't believe I was actually doing this. The point of the conclave was to get people to fight *with* me, not *against* me. I already dueled a pirate, and now I had to fight a blind man who looked allergic to the sun.

After my initial shock and indignation, I realized that it might actually work in my favor. If I could show the Waodani and pirates my full abilities, perhaps it would be enough to solidify their confidence in me and guarantee their allegiance. Kasabian had mentioned that it wasn't monetary reasons so much as the odds, that I needed more forces in order for his crew to agree to join me.

A circle about twenty-one feet wide had formed around the boulder with Raven Bone on one side and myself on the other. I stretched my shoulders and focused my mind. At first I had been afraid that I would offend the mysterious leader, but now all I wanted to do was see him land hard on the ground.

A gentle hand rested on my shoulder.

"This isn't necessary."

I turned to Zasper; worry wrinkled her face.

"If I don't, none of them will respect me. The pirates, the Waodani, even the rebels." I grabbed her shoulders, trying my best to convince her. "This could gain us the alliance we need to overthrow Vukan. Have some faith, Zasper."

Zasper grumbled, "I don't like this—"

"Scared little queen?" Raven Bone shouted.

Snickers sounded from the people gathered.

Zasper frowned, lips contorted to the side. "Maybe he could use some humility."

I smirked.

"Alright. Show him."

I pulled her into a hug, but before releasing me, Zasper whispered a warning, "Do not underestimate him."

I nodded and prepared myself to begin the fight, rotating my wrists and rolling my shoulders.

Valine.

What now, Dryden?

Did I ever tell you the Waodani Chief always has magic?

My face blanched. Dryden's timing was impeccable as always. Well, Raven Bone already knew I had magic. He was twirling the very ice staff I had made, but he didn't know I was aware of his abilities. There had to be some advantage in that. I had to focus.

I closed my eyes. Breathe. In and out. I felt the cold manifest into a solid weight in my hand. The gasps signaled my eyes to open. A double edged staff laid in my hand, an exact replica of the one I had gifted the Waodani, except mine wasn't blue. The ice had felt my frustration, resulting in a dark hue that made it appear as a semi-translucent obsidian.

Raven Bone laughed. "This will be fun."

It was risky of me to use so much magic before the fight even began, especially when I had perfectly good non-magical weapons at my disposal. I was betting on the mental warfare aspect, the impact seeing my magic in action could afford, and I would find out soon enough if it had been a risk worth taking.

I began to pace around my half of the circle, Raven Bone's head eerily following me. He was blind yet able to track my movements.

After several minutes, a few men booed. I frowned. One of Kas's men no doubt. I couldn't take it anymore. Raven Bone hadn't taken one step. Fine. If that's how he wanted to play, then so be it. I took a few steps forward.

The corner of his mouth twitched. "Beat me little queen, and the Waodani will fight in your war."

Blood pumping, I lunged at him. My staff came plunging down towards his left shoulder. He easily blocked my hit with his staff, emitting a strange sound of glass colliding with glass. I pulled back and aimed for his right foot, twisting at the last second to swing the opposite end of my staff again at his left side. He parried and managed to land a blow to my right shoulder with the blunt part of his blade. The pirates and Waodani cheered, but Dryden snarled. That was going to leave a bruise.

Dryden spoke in my head, explaining that Raven Bone could feel the vibrations from movement and hear my steps. Maybe if I was fast enough, his senses would be overwhelmed. I sent a barrage of hits at every part of his body. He blocked each one with irritating ease. I grunted and shoved the center of my staff at his nose. Maybe I could break it again. He brought his own staff up, exactly like I thought he would. I gripped his staff with one hand and slammed mine into the back of his knee. His leg buckled underneath him. I brought my foot down on his staff, pinning it to the ground and pointed the tip of my blade at his throat.

"What? No jokes now?"

Raven Bone smiled. My heart skipped a beat and my breath hitched. He spoke so only I could hear. "How about we level the playing field."

Twilight disappeared. Everything disappeared, as I was plunged into darkness.

So he could wield shadows. This was just great.

I couldn't see anything, and I couldn't feel the shape of the staff under my foot anymore. He must have reclaimed his weapon while I stood shocked like an idiot. He could be anywhere, but unlike him, I was not used to being blind. I could not feel nor hear his movements. Instead all my senses were in a frenzy. Jeers and shouts of exclamations and the rushing river rang in my ears, and the smell of dirt and trees and the musk of the leopards filled my nose. Where was he?

Pain exploded in my leg as blood oozed from a long cut on my thigh. I felt *that*. Panic began to make my movements jarred and sloppy. I had to breathe, to think.

"What's the matter little queen? Afraid of the dark?" His laugh alerted me to his presence.

He was right in front of me. I didn't bother trying to hit him. It would have done no good since I would be swinging blindly. Instead, I turned towards the sound of the river.

Laughter followed like a falcon stalking a mouse. "Running from a fight, little queen? Can't say I'm surprised."

We were the same height, so his jests were even more grating. Gritting my teeth, I made my way towards the river. My injured leg slammed into the boulder. I cursed, but that meant I was halfway to the water.

Somehow his darkness became thicker, almost tangible. I tripped. Rather, I was tripped. I heard the whoosh of the staff right before I felt it as Raven Bone slammed the blunt side of the blade onto the same shoulder that was already hurt. I heard a pop and a scream. It was mine. My shoulder was dislocated, arm dangling loosely at my side.

Laughter and a whisper. "I commend you for your willingness to even try to fight, but it's over, little queen."

Dryden snapped. Knowing he was about ready to rip off his head, I shouted, "No Dryden." I spat out the mud that had entered my mouth. "Stay back."

I knew he would obey, so I returned my focus to Raven Bone. I flipped onto my back and kicked blindly. I made contact with something and began to drag myself back towards the river with my one good arm, knees scraping against rocks and twigs, soil gradually turning into mud.

The water was freezing, the cold seeping deep into my bones, but I welcomed it as it numbed my shoulder and thigh. I was able to get to my feet and wade into the river up to my hips. Splashing alerted that Raven Bone had followed me. If he wanted to use magic, I would too.

"You think the water will save you? I know all about your little ice tricks."

His staff was dragging in the water, the current brushing against my body.

During the first half of the fight, I made the mistake of being too aggressive. Raven Bone was great at defense, but his offense was not so developed, which was likely the reason he used his magic. That or he just wanted to show off.

This time I would wait.

I positioned myself down river from him so that I could feel the ripples he made. When the drag created by his staff ceased, I crouched. The water would minimize the force of his blow in case this didn't work, and I was fairly sure it wouldn't. I still couldn't see him. I had to rely on the ice itself. I closed my eyes, as if they were doing anything good for me while open, and reached out. The river was quick to respond to my call. I encased Raven Bone's legs in ice.

He wasn't fazed. "You are turning out to be more fun than I expected!"

If not for my magic I wouldn't have been able to last this long. For a moment, I considered if that was why The Creator had granted me such a gift, knowing I would need it for such a time as this, to rebel against the great evil wearing a crown. My crown.

I honed my attention back on the fight, and I felt the ice break under the crushing weight of his darkness. I flung icicles at him. He hit each one away with the staff. Clink, clink, clink.

I attempted to simply freeze his body, but the strong shadows broke my ice each time I tried to encase him. Any time I flung shards at him, he blocked them with the staff.

The staff.

Raven Bone exclaimed in surprise as his staff melted in his hands. I was slightly sad at having to destroy such a beautiful creation, but I had little time to mourn it. I crept towards him, my own ice weapon firmly in my palm. I swung it at his ribs, sending ice chunks at his back simultaneously. He blocked the barrage with a wall of pure night, and I had to admire his power. But my blade hit him hard in the side, knocking him into the river. I froze the water around him, enclosing him in ice. The darkness disappeared and light flooded my vision.

People had gathered on the bank of the river to watch, torches lighted to illuminate the night. I look down in front of me. There was a murky cloud inside the ice block. I had just enough time to shield my face as the ice shattered.

A soaking wet Raven Bone emerged from the water. He was laughing, of course. I followed suit. I couldn't help myself, laughing as the leader of one of the fiercest tribes of people stood from the water looking like a half drowned cat. His face paint had been washed away by the water.

I raised the staff with my one good arm. "Had enough fun yet?"

Raven Bone coughed up some water and smiled. "That was absolutely delightful."

"I don't know if I could say the same," I grumbled, gesturing to my limp right arm.

Raven Bone walked towards me, and I kept the staff at the ready just in case he wasn't satisfied and wanted more *fun*. He tentatively reached out with his hands and placed them on my shoulder. "This won't be so enjoyable."

I clenched my teeth. "Do it."

He quickly yanked my shoulder back into place as a scream left my throat.

He smiled. "It was smart to lead me into the water where I wouldn't be able to feel your movements."

Shouts and applause greeted us both as we climbed out of the water. Both of us were shivering from the cold, and we accepted the dry, fur cloaks offered.

Turning to face each other, Raven Bone thumped his chest with his fist. "You fought with both your mind and body. You are a worthy opponent. The allegiance of the Waodani is yours."

Cheers erupted from the rebels and soldiers. Raven Bone raised his hand and ran his fingers across my face.

I didn't know what it meant, but I grinned, heart warm despite my dripping wet clothing. "Thank you, Raven Bone." I gestured to his empty hands. "Sorry about the staff."

He laughed as twin shadow blades appeared in his hands. "I didn't like it that much anyways." He twirled the blades faster than ought to be possible.

I frowned. "I hope you didn't take it easy on me."

He chuckled. "Wouldn't dream of it, little queen."

Zasper pushed past the congratulators and felt my shoulder. Warmth radiated from her hands.

I looked at her puzzled, teeth clattering together. "Now you decide to heal me?"

Zasper stated flatly, "War is near. You can't be injured."

She had a strange way of thinking about things, but I couldn't complain at the relief I felt from her healing my shoulder.

After she was done, I raised my voice so that all could hear. "I think that the king will try to kill me next week. That will be our opportunity to escape the castle with Princess Zasper, Prince Lux, and all the loyal soldiers."

Shouts of disdain and curses at the mention of the Crown Prince's name drowned out my words.

I did my best to absolve their opposition. "I vouch for him! He is the one who warned me, who helped me."

Kasabian and Mordris quieted their groups. "If you swear fealty, then you follow orders!" Mordris exclaimed. Ironic, coming from a defected soldier, but I appreciated the assistance nonetheless.

Kasabian shouted, "If you are willing to fight for her, then you should be willing to trust her judgment."

Those grumbling quieted down, and I nodded my thanks. It would take time for them to come to trust Lux like I did, but for now their reluctant tolerance was enough. "We will meet together soon. I'll give the time and location to your respective leaders."

After talking to Kasabian, Sidian, Mordris, Kalosa and Raven Bone, we all agreed and solidified a plan. Everyone began to gather in their groups, the Waodani leaving first, shrouded in Raven Bone's shadows.

I also made to leave, but Kasabian stopped me.

"I have someone who wants to speak to you."

I squeezed the water from my hair. "Make it quick please. I hate being stuck in wet clothes."

Kasabian shouted out a name I hadn't heard before. A young man, well maybe a man, he looked to be in his late teens at the most, walked up to us. He had tight, black curls and was broad but short. He looked like he could crush a melon with his hands.

He gave a deep bow. "Your majesty, it's an honor to meet you."

My eyes widened, and I glanced at Kasabian, shocked by such deep respect from a pirate.

The boy rose. "To the pirates, I am Scylar, but you would know my name of Peten Galapos."

My mouth hung open. "It wasn't a rumor then."

"I was disappointed to hear that while I was gathering supplies at the port, you had graced us with your presence."

I waved my hands. "I'm really not—"

His eyes beamed as he interrupted, "My father told me stories of the queens growing up, and before he gave himself up, he made me promise to find you one day. The divine must have favored us for you to be friends with my very captain!"

Peten was alive and was a pirate.

I held out my hand. "It's a pleasure to finally meet you Peten. I am sorry about your father."

Peten grasped my forearm. "He knew what he was doing."

We released each other's arms. "And your mother?"

He slung an arm around Kasabian, bringing the pirate lord down to his level. "Thanks to this guy, my mother is safe and well taken care of. She runs a little fabric shop in Gwanji."

I looked at Kasabian. "Not so bad for a pirate."

He laughed. "I am more than just my looks, Val. So shallow." I shook my head, and he must have known I was about to say some deprecating retort because he filled in before I could speak. "I don't mean to put words in your mouth, Val, but may I suggest some? Perfection to the point of tears? Or maybe even, the sun and moon may retire for how brightly you shine?"

I jutted my hand out and pinched his lips between my fingers, but I couldn't stop my grin. I turned my face to Peten. "I wonder why Vukan never replaced you?"

Peten scratched his head, uncaring about his captain's predicament. "I think that he underestimates us, that our islands are too insignificant for him, and with the way he has expanded the army in the past few years, it looks like his eyes were locked on bigger lands than ours."

I narrowed my eyes in concentration, releasing Kasabian's lips as he pouted. "That does seem the most logical reasoning."

I was shook out of my thoughts by Zasper, who came to get me to hurry back before our absence was discovered. Lux could only cover for us so long.

Peten bowed once more, placing his hand over his heart. "I promise that the islands are yours to command my queen."

He paused to look at Kasabian, who was rubbing his mouth.

"Oh," he bowed dramatically, voice drawling like an actor in a theater house, "and my ships are yours."

Peten elbowed him.

"Ow! Alright. My ships and men are yours, my queen."

I was excited to return to the castle to tell Lux the good news. The conclave had been a great success, everyone present pledging themselves—even the pirates, who, although entertained by the show, needed a little monetary incentive.

Zasper and I smiled as we walked, having left Dryden with his clan and letting Mordris and the boys go ahead so that we would not be seen arriving together.

CHAPTER TWENTY–TWO

*L*ux *hadn't been privy* to all the information about my assassination. He didn't know the exact day, but today was the most likely. The king had ordered a hunting party to welcome spring, which made no sense since the animals would be skinny and poor quality to eat. Then again Vukan loved killing for the thrill of it, and he would love to destroy me even more. I had been captured twice and now married to his son. There was no humiliation left for him to inflict upon me.

It was time for the kill.

My horse was a beautiful dappled gray gelding, and I hoped he wouldn't be harmed in whatever trap Vukan had planned. I patted his neck, and he responded with a shake of his mane and a deep snort. Hooves softly padded up beside me. Lux looked handsome in his dark red robes, his long hair pinned in a bun at the top of his head. Maybe red wasn't so bad a color after all. His chestnut mare greeted my gelding with a whinny.

"Be careful. Remember you promised not to leave me."

The lack of a joke was worrisome.

I attempted to ease his concern. "Well The Creator has kept me alive this long. I'm sure He didn't put in all that effort just for me to die now."

Lux pressed his lips together. In that moment he resembled Sebastien, always the serious face.

Vukan had decreed that I was allowed no weapons, maybe hoping a wild boar or hungry bear could do his dirty work for him. However, Lux had snuck me two daggers. Those, coupled with my magic, would be more than enough for some wild animals and even a few guards. I just hoped that Vukan didn't know about my magic and would only send a few guards.

The horn sounded like a death's call, and the hunt began.

I gripped the reins and was about to kick the horse's side, but Lux's hand darted out, grasping my own. I turned to see his anxious eyes and furrowed brow.

"I don't expect you to feel the same, but... I love you, my little bird." Before I could reply, he kicked the mare's flank and took off.

I pressed my heels into the gelding's sides, and we trotted into the trees.

It had been relatively quiet since the start of the hunt. Yet my mind was abuzz with a plethora of thoughts of the plan, concern for Zasper and the soldiers, and Lux's last words to me, each taking turns flashing through my head.

A snap grabbed my attention. By luck or divine intervention, I saw the guard aiming a crossbow at me hiding between the trees. My heels hit, and the horse lurched forward just as a crossbolt landed in the tree trunk where I just was. A few shouts signaled at least two more men. The forest was getting thicker, and far too soon it would become impossible to ride. I yanked the reins back, and the horse stopped. I quickly slid off the saddle, running my hand over his forelock. "At least one of us has to survive."

He pushed his head into my palm, and I stepped back and slapped his rear. I didn't wait around to watch him take off as I turned and slipped between the trees. There still wasn't enough foliage to hide, which meant I would easily be spotted even from a distance. Instead I crouched behind one of the larger tree trunks, holding my breath and listening carefully.

Even though I couldn't hide properly, it meant that neither could the guards. I saw two walking in my general direction, swords drawn. Neither of them had a crossbow with them, which meant that the third was somewhere nearby but out of sight. I pulled out the daggers from my riding skirts. One guard was about to pass me, and if he turned just slightly to the left he would see where I was crouched. I sprung before he got the chance. Slicing his neck was easy, but the other guard would have a chance to prepare himself.

I wiped the blood off the blade onto my skirt. He didn't know I had another weapon.

His face changed from anger to shock and then to fear. Ice had formed around his feet and he couldn't move. Before he could yell for back up, I flung a shard of ice at him. It impaled his head, blood splattering as he slumped to the ground.

But I never heard the crossbow.

I only heard the thud and the grunt of pain as the arrow penetrated skin and flesh.

I turned in horror. Egann had an arrow protruding from his chest. His back tore and his cries were muffled as his body absorbed the blows meant for me. My eyes went towards the sound of another arrow being nocked. Ice encapsulated the man before he could finish reloading. He would remain frozen, dead and still.

Egann fell into me, my body dragged down by the weight of his own. I held my dying friend's head on my lap, his eyes still flaming with sparks of compassion. I smiled, my tears falling onto his dark, wrinkled face.

His breath was labored, his voice hoarse. "Don't cry my child," he rasped, "death is not the end, it is simply the beginning. I shall be in the presence of The Creator, and there shall be no more pain." He reached feebly to wipe my face. "And no more tears…"

I smiled down at my teacher, my vision clouded by the water pooled in my eyes. "Egann, why'd you do that? For a wise man you sure are foolish."

He coughed up blood, his lips stained red as he tried to smile. "There is no greater love…" His breathing became more labored. "Than for a man to die for another."

I placed my hand on his cheek, my thumb gently rubbing his face. "I do not deserve your love, Egann."

"And I do not deserve the love of the Creator, yet He sought me out as His son, and so I love you because He loved me first."

An iron grip tightened around my heart, squeezing it. "I hope that I may live as honorably as you, my friend."

He coughed once more, the light dimming in his eyes. "The honor was mine, to see a girl… become a queen, worthy of her title. Do not forget, child, all that I taught you… Look to the heavens and know," his voice was barely audible as he spoke, "you are never alone…"

The light was gone. I leaned over and kissed his forehead and ran my fingers over his eyelids, closing them for the last time. "May The Creator grant you entry," I whispered into the wind.

I couldn't help the guttural sound that escaped me in my grief. Hooves pounded closer, and I raised my hand, prepared to use all the energy I had to freeze as much as I could. Would I be able to cover the whole forest, Vukan and his entourage included? Two horses came into view, one gray and the other brown.

Lux swung down and sprinted to where I held Egann's body.

"He—"

Lux said nothing as he lifted Egann's body, crimson creating dark circles around the entry points, and carried him to the mare. He laid his body as gently as he could on the saddle and snapped the shafts of the arrows off.

He turned his attention to me. "We have to go. I already disposed of two more on my way to you."

I couldn't move, felt weighed down to the ground.

"Valine!"

Lux was in front of me, his hands cupping my face. "We have to go. Now."

I said nothing, my body moving of its own accord. I climbed onto the saddle, and Lux settled in behind me. He guided the horses to a thinner part of the forest, and then we took off in a gallop.

My mind didn't clear until a couple hours later when we stopped by a small creek to rest.

Lux helped me off the horse but didn't let go of my hand. He brought me to the brook and pushed me down softly. Tearing a piece of his robe off and dipping it into the creek, he gently wiped away at the blood that had dried on my face and hands.

"Am I cursed?"

His hands paused their work. "You can't think like that right now. Compartmentalize if you have to. But you can't shut down right now. You have to keep going."

I nodded and stood. After the horses had adequately drank water and rested, we rode again. I did my best to ignore the dark thoughts of doubt and despair that crept in. I had to be strong. I couldn't give up. Too many had died for my weakness to ruin it all. I refused to look at the body on the horse next to us.

Due to the time afforded to us by Lux's warning, I had been able to plan something of my own. All the guards loyal to me had arranged themselves to be stationed at the palace, which was a risk, having only non-pledged guards present for the hunt, but they needed to stay behind to help Zasper and her fellow Ebocians get out. The soldiers weren't enough alone to hold the castle, so we would all meet in the forest near a small village on the outskirts of Pardus. It was close enough to the river that it would make a good rendezvous spot, seeing as the rest of the pirates were still two days out. Only Kasabian's personal ship that we had rode in on was present, the remainder of his ships waiting further down river to avoid suspicion.

Dryden, who would bring his clan, knew the location we were to meet at, and once he was close enough we would be able to communicate mentally. Although they would likely be able to track our scent themselves. Once we all met up, we could finally stage an attack.

We were the first to arrive at the designated spot. Zasper and the soldiers would meet us the next morning, having left later than we escaped. If all went according to plan, the Waodani and leopards would also come sometime the next day.

Lux and I carefully pulled the body off the saddle, laying it reverently on the ground. He waited patiently as I considered how we would give the final farewell. "You knew him too, Lux. We should decide together."

He stared blankly at the sky, unable to look down. "Burning him would be quickest, and it is the Racourian way."

I contemplated for a moment. "No. Ebocians bury their dead. And we have the time anyway."

Lux nodded and we began to dig a hole. Luckily, the spring had already thawed the ground here.

It was twilight by the time we finished.

We placed a pile of stones at the top and covered the rest in budding flowers. We couldn't leave the horses untacked in the event that we needed to make a hasty mount, but we did take off the saddles long enough to brush them down, giving them a momentary reprieve. We tied them within drinking distance of the creek and left a pile of grass and foliage we had collected.

Lux and I sat next to each other. The spring days were warm, but the nights were still cold. A fire was out of the question, since the light would make us too visible. Instead we sat shoulder to shoulder, a blanket Lux had packed wrapped around us.

The waiting was agonizing. It gave me too much opportunity to contrive bad endings to our cause. He dies. She dies. We all die. The unknown, what the enemy was doing while we waited, made me anxious.

The weight on my chest was unbearable, a tight fist gripping my heart, pulling me down like an anchor. "I have been through a lot in my life, my parents and brother dying, losing the only home I ever knew. I have had my heart and bones broken. I have known pain in so many capacities, yet this has been the worst. To see my friends die, for me, for my throne, and I have to go on, live, without them, for them."

Lux wrapped his arm around me, his body heat seeping into my skin.

Tears fell and snot dripped from my nose. "I feel nothing and everything all at once."

I buried my face into his shoulder, and he let me stay there, soaking his shirt.

I continued. "Every time I think I'm better, that I'm over it, that I have left it all in the past, I get hit with it all over again. It's like an ocean wave that gives a bit of reprieve before crashing again. I don't think I'll ever make it to shore. The nightmares, the pain, the depression...

they never quite leave. They come and go as they please, without my consent." I wiped at the snot pouring from my nose.

"I don't have the solution, Little Bird. I have them too, the bad dreams, the internal despair, the pain. Just promise me, that even if one of us reaches the beach, that the other won't be left behind. Let's promise to always hold onto each other, to wait for each other."

I grabbed his hand, fingers interlocking with his. "I'd wait my whole life for you on the shore, and I'd even go back in for you."

He kissed my forehead. "I'll prepare the towels then."

I pinched his arm, and he feigned pain. "Hey, my humor is why you married me."

"Actually, it's because your evil father forced me to," I quipped.

He shrugged and smiled, eyes sparkling with an ember of joy. "I like my version better."

He was almost right though. I may not have chosen to marry him, but I could choose to stay with him. Even after all this was over, I had no intentions of ending our marriage. The son of my enemy actually was a great man, someone who understood me, loved me. His humor was one of the reasons I would stay, his compassion the reason I would wait for him.

"I think..." I paused, realizing the weight of what I was about to say. "I like you."

Lux's eyes widened. "What?"

"I didn't say I loved you," I mumbled, already wishing I could take back the words.

He beamed and pulled me into a tight embrace, seemingly uninterested in the difference between the two words. "Valine, I would travel a thousand miles, learn a thousand languages, wait a thousand years for you."

We held each other for a long while, and eventually we fell asleep in each other's arms.

A strange sensation woke me. I opened my eyes to the sight of two scaly creatures staring down at our faces. Bahm nudged me, and Sol wrapped her body protectively around Lux's head.

Are you trying to replace me?

I sat upright and was pleased to be greeted with the large, furry figure of Dryden. I launched myself at him, and we both tumbled to the ground. Dryden wrapped his big paws around me in what I assumed was his attempt at a hug.

Have we been apart so long that you forgot I could hear you? You didn't need to scream so loud.

I squeezed him tighter in response. *I know you missed me too.*

I finally stood, letting Dryden get up.

He shook the dirt and debris off his pelt. *I miss the snow.*

I smiled. *Good to have you back.*

Lux was also up, his dragons rubbing their bodies along his legs, eerily cat-like. Dryden issued a low growl.

What? Don't tell me you're scared of them.

Dryden flexed his claws. *They're strange.*

I laughed. *Don't worry, I'll protect you from the itty bitty dragons.*

Dryden huffed but put his claws away. Bahm slowly slinked towards Dryden, head cocked, forked tongue darting in and out of his mouth.

How uncouth, Dryden chided.

Be nice, I instructed.

Bahm came to a stop before Dryden; he was only a quarter of the big cat's size. Bahm touched his snout to one of Dryden's paws, and I warned Dryden not to swat the inquisitive dragon away. Dryden argued, but ultimately stayed still. Bahm suddenly darted in between Dryden's legs, rubbing his cobalt scales against the ash colored fur. I held in a laugh at Dryden's obvious disdain at the little dragon.

I think he likes you.

Dryden carefully lifted a paw so as not to injure the smaller animal. *Are you certain I can't eat it?*

I snapped, *No!*

Dryden curled his lip. *Probably tastes terrible anyways.*

I laughed, shaking my head. I looked towards Lux who was now holding Sol in his arms. She definitely seemed the more reserved of the two.

Bahm continued to stay under Dryden, who looked very annoyed. Lux walked towards me, Sol's tongue flicking.

"How'd they find us?"

Lux set her down, but she refused to leave his side. "I told them to follow me, and they likely tracked our scent here. They have an excellent sense of smell."

Dryden flicked his ears. *Nothing compared to us ice leopards.*

I ignored his comment.

The rustling of bushes signaled a large group headed our way. I drew my dagger—the only one I had left—and Lux ran to his horse's saddle and unsheathed a sword. We waited, and I prayed it was our friends and not our foe.

I saw Zasper's ebony skin first, and I dropped my weapon. We ran towards each other and threw ourselves into each other's arms. Words could not express how relieved I was to see her safe and unharmed. Behind her were Mordris, Falchor, the twins and the rest of the soldiers who had slowly come to my side. There were only about fifty.

We were a pitiful number compared to Vukan's vast army, who was surely being recalled from the borders to prepare for our looming battle. If Mordis' information was right, Vukan would be able to acquire about four thousand men. Those stationed at the border would not be able to arrive in time, unbeknownst to them.

There were about twenty or so men left loyal at the palace, but there were a few thousand men stationed close enough to the capitol that could return by tomorrow. Including the pirates, soldiers, and Waodani, as well as a few handful of rebels that hadn't been killed with Yanish's crew, our numbers only came to a little over a thousand. That was including the leopards.

Our chances were pathetically miniscule.

The soldiers had been able to gather enough supplies to last us a couple days. We only needed one. After the rations, weapons, and sleeping materials had been distributed, a few of us gathered to finalize plans.

Mordris thought we should send all of our forces on a direct assault on the castle, but Falchor thought we would be too caged in, the mountains on one side, the castle another, and only one side available for a retreat, one that could easily be cut off with Vukan's superior numbers. He suggested multiple smaller groups that would attack at different locations simultaneously.

Lux suggested sending in a small party through the water tunnels that ended in a cistern on the eastern side of the palace. But if that group got into any trouble, there would be no way to send reinforcements. They could easily be trapped, alone. Sidian suggested a group sneak inside using Raven Bone's magic while Dryden offered to let the leopards take the lead, insisting that the mere sight of the whole clan of ice leopards would cause an immediate surrender. That plan was unanimously shut down, except for Dryden, who just pouted.

In the middle of our discussion, one of Zasper's entourage burst into the tent.

"They're here!"

I looked to Zasper, confused. "Who?"

She smiled apologetically. "I'm sorry I didn't tell you, but I wasn't sure if they could make it in time."

She exited the tent before I could ask what she meant, leaving me no choice but to follow her outside.

My mouth gaped. Outside the tent were rows upon rows of men and women, all varying shades of black skin. I estimated that there were about two to three hundred warriors.

Zasper gestured to her people. "This is an elite fighting force of Eboc. We call them, *Kimya*."

Lux was the one to ask, "What does it mean?"

Zasper grinned proudly. "Silence. You never hear them coming. Unless of course, they want you to."

In all fairness, we hadn't heard their approach. Zasper greeted her people, but one of them stepped forward, a stocky, but muscular woman with a shaved head.

Zasper slipped her arm around the woman's waist as they approached. "This is my sister, Shani. She is the leader of the *Kimya*."

I extended my hand to her, but she pushed it away, instead pulling me in a tight embrace. "*Asante sana, rafiki!*"

I glanced to Zasper, who translated, "She says, 'thank you very much, friend'."

Zasper explained that Shani was better at listening in Racourian than speaking it. I reminded myself that after this was all over, I would have to add becoming fluent in Eboc to my long list of things to do.

We headed back into the tent to resume planning while the *Kimya* sent up camp. Before we could start, the flap of the tent opened once again.

"Oh, what now?" Mordris complained.

Familiar wavy black hair entered. "I can't believe you didn't wait for me." Kasabian choked back fake tears.

It made me think of Lux, my eyes automatically darting to him. They were fairly similar in personality, albeit no one could out flirt Kasabian.

The pirate lord sauntered up to Lux, eyeing him up and down. "So this is your type, Val? I guess he isn't too bad, but I hope you won't regret missing out on all this." Kasabian gestured to himself.

Lux bristled, but he didn't say anything, lips firmly pressed together. I wrapped my arm around Lux's, his body relaxing into mine.

"You are but a candle trying to compete with the sun," I drawled.

Kasabian stumbled back dramatically. "You've mortally wounded me, Val." He clasped his hand over his heart. "I don't think I can ever recover."

"I'm sure you'll manage just fine," I teased.

Zasper interrupted, "We don't have much time. We should get back to the matter at hand."

I let go of Lux's arm, and I could have sworn he looked a little disappointed. Zasper was right though. We had to use what little time we had left wisely.

For the next hour we debated over the best course of action. We hadn't progressed much, and the only thing we could all agree on was that no matter what we did, there would be risk, there would be death.

At one point, when things were getting heated, Lux, in order to relieve the tension, offered jokingly, "What about riding in on an ice horse?"

After that, we decided to take a break to rest and eat. Only Lux and myself remained inside the tent. Dryden had left a while ago to check on the location of the leopards, having left them behind in order to return to me sooner. They were late, as were the Waodani. They also had to travel down a perpetually snowy mountain scape, so perhaps that was what had held them up.

I rubbed the bridge of my nose, sighing. "I don't know what to do. Either way people will die, and I can't accept that."

Lux placed his hand on my shoulder. "You wanted your throne Valine. This is what it means to be queen. You make the decisions, and sometimes the only options you have lead to death."

I shoved his hand away. "I won't accept that! I will not let anyone else die because of me."

Lux slammed his fist on the table, and my body tensed at the display of anger.

"That is not your choice. Everyone here has pledged themselves to you." He pointed towards the men and women outside. "And they are willing to die for you. You do not get to make that choice for them. The decision you get to make is how their lives are utilized for our cause, and if you try to save everyone, more people will perish. Did you really think no one would die? When you were with your comrades, did you really think you could keep them all safe? That is nothing but arrogance and delusion. Every single one of those people then and now knew they could die. But they charged ahead, for you. So make a decision like a queen."

A tear slid down my cheek. I wiped it away with my sleeve as I turned towards the maps we had spread out on the table. I plastered my palms to the wood to steady myself and my resolve.

I took the pencil and pointed to fields southeast of the fortress where the gate was. "We will send two thirds of our forces here, to lure the King's troops out. Kasabian will take his men through the water system to take out the guards inside the walls and open the gate. Then we will have sandwiched Vukan's troops in, which should give us the advantage despite our smaller numbers."

Lux nodded in agreement. He placed his hand over the top of mine. "I am with you no matter what. My sovereign. My wife."

I turned to face him, his expression one of pride. He leaned in and kissed my forehead, his lips soft and warm.

He brushed the hair out of my face. "Now when they come back in, you tell them the plan. You're the one in charge, Your Majesty."

When the others entered, I filled them in. The plans were finalized without any opposition, my voice coated in authority that allowed for no argument. I had planned a battle. I had mapped deaths. For better or for worse, the next day the future of Racour would be decided, as would the fate of the brave souls before me.

CHAPTER TWENTY-THREE

*L*ux had instructed Sol and Bahm to stay behind. They were too small to fight yet, and they could easily be trampled by horse hooves or sliced through by swords. They reluctantly agreed to stay after I told them they had the important job of protecting Zasper in the medic tent. In reality, I still wasn't sure how much they could understand me, but they stayed behind which was what was important.

Although it was a shame to not utilize Zasper's fighting prowess, her skills and magic as a healer were more valuable and in less supply.

She hugged me tightly as we said our goodbyes. "He is with you, *Chui*."

I had forgotten to ask. "What's *Chui* mean?"

Zasper smiled, glancing at Dryden. "Leopard."

I embraced her once more, praying it wouldn't be the last time. I also said farewell to Talom and Ferrum, who would stay back to aid Zasper. A couple of the Kimya were also staying behind to carry the injured back to our medical base. I waved once more, and turned to lead our troops into position.

The sounds of war imminent, snorts of horses, stone sharpening steel, clattering of armor, men saying final prayers before facing a likely death. It was eerie and serene all at the same time, the simultaneous presence of courage and fear.

Eyes gazing across the ranks of men and women before me, our forces were so different from the ones on the other side of the open field. Vukan's soldiers were uniformed and all trained in the same way.

Cavalry. Infantry. Archers.

In contrast, our side was a mixture of Ebocians, fierce warriors armed with bows and staffs, the pirates, who were making their way towards the castle through the aqueduct, the giant ice leopards who had never been seen in these large quantities, the defected soldiers and handful of rebels.

The Waodani had come at last, only arriving after we had begun to set up formation. I had worried they'd changed their minds, that they wouldn't show up after all, but Raven Bone stood next to me, a gnarled wood staff in his hand. A stabbing sensation formed in my heart as I looked at it, reminded of the one Egann used, now protruding from the ground—from a grave—never to be used by its owner again.

I turned away, nose stinging. The rest of the troops gave a wide berth to the Waodani, but they would have to work together if they wanted to win, to not perish. We were all rebels now, our looming battle the symbol of our treason.

The leopards had taken a liking to the three immigrants from Percia, surrounding them in a tight circle. Ravi seemed to particularly be enjoying it, scratching heads and muzzles of the big cats.

To my right stood Dryden, my companion, my protector, and next to him was Lux. Our marriage was forced but our friendship was not. I had not realized everything he had done for me until much later. I was unworthy of such company, of such people to call family. I gathered my strength from them, and soon, we would test all of our strengths.

Get their attention.

Dryden nodded and padded to the edge of the mound we stood on. He roared, and the ragtag army quickly quieted.

I gathered my voice from within.

It was time to address my people.

I wasn't sure what words were proper for such an occasion. I didn't think there were any, but I had read of famous speeches given before battles that had inspired soldiers on to victory.

I didn't think my words would be anything like that.

"Today is the day we have been waiting for. I wish I knew you all by name, for you will never know how honored I am by all of you coming to fight. And I hope you all remember why we are fighting, so that when your arms grow weary you will continue on."

I paused to look at my friends once more. They all smiled at me, and Lux gave me a thumbs up. My chest tightened, and for a moment I saw a lopsided smile and short dark hair. I blinked the vision away as my resolution hardened. Adrenaline started pumping. "We fight for those who cannot fight for themselves! We fight for those who have already paid the price of their dreams with blood, blood heedlessly taken by Vukan! There is no place for such wickedness in Racour!"

As my voice died down, the crowd's cries echoed with passion, and the hope that permeated the air shone brighter than the morning sun that watched us.

I looked upon my castle and upon the valley filled with my people, people who would die for me, die for Racour, die for the hope of a better monarch, one that was better than both Gabrys and Vukan, better than even my mother. I would be that monarch. I would be their servant and ruler, their mother and daughter. I would be their queen. I brushed my fingers through Dryden's fur, and his grumbling purr vibrated into my arm, steadying my erratic heart. I felt a brush against my leg, and I looked down to see Kalosa. She was a leader of her kind, just as I was, and she had gathered the leopards for me, to fight and to die for me all for honor, for the sake of an oath made by our ancestors. So many would die, but it would be so that others may live.

I felt Dryden rub against my hip, and Lux reached over to squeeze my hand. I gazed at those around me.

I smiled, tears blurring my vision, my voice cracking. "I am so fortunate to have such friends in my life..."

The tears clogged my throat, but they nodded, not needing words to understand what I wished to convey.

I cleared my throat, and continued, raising my voice. "There is no greater love than for a man to lay down his life for another, and I assure you, that I love not my kingdom, but the people in it. Know that I love the inhabitants of Racour," I paused, looking at the Waodani, at Shani and her Kimya, at Ravi, Nabeel, and Raia, "Waodani, Ebocians, Manchurs, Indos, and Percians too. We are all creations of The Creator, brothers and sisters, and I will lay down my life for you."

The cheers bounced off the mountains, the cacophony that of a much larger force, and I wondered if the heavens were joining in. I had prayed for hours last night with

Zasper and Lux. Prayed for courage, for strength, for victory. Now I would discover if my pleas had been heard.

I looked to the sky one last time. *Please. I need you.*

And so we began, the culmination of all the sacrifice, the climax of our effort. We marched forward, our motley army, praying for a divine intervention against our more powerful enemy.

We had underestimated how many troops Vukan had been able to muster. Our original guess of four thousand was grossly incorrect. It appeared to be more like seven thousand. Even with Raven Bone, Lux and I's magic, the odds were stacked against us. But there was no turning back.

The battle was upon us.

The arrows came first, sharp projectiles to take out our front lines while the infantry slowly approached. I threw up a shield of ice, arrows protruding on the outskirts where the barrier was weakest. I felt like I could hold a hundred shields for hours, but I knew that was the adrenaline talking and that I would have to pace myself. I melted the barrier, allowing our own archers to hail down arrows in return. We didn't have enough horses for a proper cavalry regiment, but Vukan had over a hundred. They would be the hardest to deal with, so Lux and I would need to focus our energy on them. It would be nice if the fire alone spooked the horses enough for them to buck their riders. I hated the thought of killing the innocent creatures, but war was merciless, a mindless creature who devoured all without distinction.

My ears throbbed with the sounds of pounding hooves, the determined faces of the riders with their weapons drawn growing closer and closer.

For a split second, I questioned myself, my motives, my decisions, but then I saw an arrow pierce the neck of one of Vukan's defected soldiers. I couldn't remember his name, but I knew I would never forget the sight of the blood spraying from his neck, the glossy eyes as he fell to the ground, never to get up. I steeled myself, offered up one final prayer, and prepared to face the onslaught of horses charging at us.

Lux sent a wall of fire towards the oncoming soldiers, the heat radiating in a wave over us. I pitied them as the smell of burning flesh infiltrated my nostrils, but they'd made their choice. Even if they were reluctant to fight for Vukan, they still were a terrible yet necessary casualty. Some fell off their horses, clothing ablaze, others were killed immediately by his blast of raw power. I sent out ice, encapsulating the legs of the horses in order to spare them being cut down or burnt to a crisp. Flashes of fur were the last thing those seated on their horses would see as the leopards tore their throats.

Raven Bone stood behind me, saving his magic for when the fighting became close range. The leopards would be able to smell the enemy while they were blind, and the rest of us would hang back.

The cavalry was demolished swiftly, with few casualties on our side, yet the battle was far from over. The remainder of Vukan's forces marched towards us, footsteps like a drum and armor like a clanging cymbal. I knew Sebastien would be in the formation somewhere, likely near the front of the foot-soldiers, and I prayed that I wouldn't have to be the one to face him, knowing that when it came down to it, I would kill him, even if it broke me to do it.

We used all the arrows we had, but even the ones that made it past shields and armor seemed to only put a dent in their forces. I glanced at Lux whose forehead was shining with sweat, his chest rapidly rising and falling. I worried he had used up too much of his magic too quickly, but he nodded at me and unsheathed his sword. He was still a skilled swordsman in his own right. He would be fine. He would have to be.

As Vukan's men drew nearer, a sudden chant filled the air. The Kimya had started up a war cry, and although I could not understand the words, I felt energy surge within me. The Creator had brought so many of us from different places together, for such a moment as this one. I inhaled once, twice, three times.

The sounds of men and women throwing themselves into battle, the clashing of metal, the screams of agony as precious life was snuffed out, the metallic smell of blood that permeated the air. War was never pretty, never pleasant, no matter how righteous the cause.

I threw up a wall of ice, doing my best to create an obstacle, even a temporary one. We forced the few enemy men on our side of the barrier back up against it, cutting them down with brutal efficiency, but more were pouring in from the sides. I released the ice, and the ground became soaked in a mixture of crimson water. Ranks upon ranks descended on us. I watched as one after another fell under a sharp blade. Death surrounded us all.

I prayed Kasabian and his men had made it through safely, and that they would be able to join us quickly. I did my best to ignore the bodies of the fallen, but a gray pelt caught my attention.

Dryden!

I sprinted towards it and flipped the body over. A selfish sigh of relief escaped my chest. The leopard was not my companion.

Dryden must have gotten further away, for when he spoke his voice was quiet. *I'm fine. Focus.*

I reluctantly left the big cat's body, returning my attention to the fighting. I had been staying relatively to the back with Lux, so we could have a better vantage point to discern where and how to use our magic. But we were both tiring, so we would have to use our remaining reserves carefully.

Lux looked at me with such love, affection, and pride that Sebastien and even Kasabian had never shown me. "I'd kiss you, but I think that will have to wait."

I smiled, the looming threat of death causing words I would have never otherwise spoken to come out. "It will give us something to look forward to after we win."

Lux's eyes danced in delight, and we charged into the fray.

I lost track of time, lost track of the men that fell before me. I had lost sight of Lux too, but when I finally did take a moment to look up, I saw that we had gotten closer to the castle walls. I could even see a figure, dressed in royal robes and gilded crown, watching from the top of the parapet. Of course he would be hiding behind his walls. Coward.

I gripped my sword tighter and continued making a bloody path to those stone barriers. As I slashed at bodies, my mind emptied as my muscles reacted according to my training. But a cruel pair of eyes and sneering smile broke my lethal trance. Hagan shoved one of his fellow soldiers to the ground, causing the poor man's arm to crack, the bone jutting through the skin.

"Today I will kill you," he promised.

I rotated my wrist, blade reflecting the sun in the few spots it wasn't covered in blood. "I sentence you to death," I proclaimed, readying my sword.

He charged, his anger once more leaving no room for strategic thinking. Hagan brought his sword down at my neck, a kill strike, but I lifted a hand, ice encapsulating his entire arm. He stumbled and fell, the sudden additional weight throwing him off balance. I took the opportunity to grab his free hand and twist his arm behind him. I let my blade rest against the tender skin of his neck.

"May The Creator deal with you accordingly," I whispered before slicing his throat. Warm blood coated my hands as his body slumped at my feet.

Out of the corner of my eye, I thought I saw some of Vukan's men running away, weapons cast aside as they made for Pardus less than a mile away. But I couldn't confirm it, instead my attention was solely on reaching the castle, on reaching the cause of my suffering. I tightened my grip on the hilt of my sword, now slick from blood. My whole body was covered in it, and I wouldn't have been able to tell if I was bleeding or not. My mind emptied as I thrust my blade into yet another man, his body crumpling at my feet.

Suddenly, night enveloped us, shadows blocking out the sun and obscuring vision like a blizzard. The snarls of leopards and the screams of men emitted from the darkness. I took the opportunity to push forward until I collided with hard stone. I wasn't sure if I imagined it or not, perhaps I had just adjusted to the sounds of death, but I thought it had gotten a bit quieter as I finally reached the entrance. The shadows evaporated, revealing the open gate and a scarlet stained, yet smiling Kasabian standing in the opening. I stumbled, using my sword to prop myself.

"You're always late." I got out through labored breaths.

Kasabian shrugged nonchalantly. "I knew you could do it."

I wanted to laugh, but there was something more serious that needed attending to. "Where is he?"

Kasabian looked nervous. "I'm not sure. We didn't see him."

"What? He was just on the top of the parapet!"

I ran past Kasabian and charged up the stairs of the wall. There were a few bodies strewn around, arrows protruding from their flesh. But there was no Vukan.

Dryden's voice unexpectedly burst into my mind. *He's over here! You better come quickly or your mate is going to roast him.*

I leaned over the turret and gawked at the sight beneath me. I rushed back down and out of the gate, sprinting around the corner, and there they were.

"Lux, stop!"

I ran to him and grabbed his arm. "Don't do this. Don't go down to his level."

Vukan writhed in pain as his fingers and hair slowly burned. Had it not been such a gruesome scene, I might have been impressed with Lux's control of his power. But I couldn't let him continue, couldn't let himself become like his father.

I grabbed Lux's chin and forced him to look into my eyes. His own were full of confliction, of grief and rage.

"Lux, please. Hate and revenge are an endless cycle. If you kill him like this..." I glanced to Vukan's twisting body, his screams echoing. I placed my hand on his face. "Light is the only thing that can drive out the darkness." I brought his hand to my chest, pressing it against my heart. "Love overcomes hate."

Lux closed his eyes and the screams lessened ever so slightly. I kept my gaze fixed on Lux as I sent a wave of ice to cool Vukan. His screams turned into groans and whimpers.

We had won the battle, but Lux looked defeated.

He peered at me. "Do you forgive him?"

I nodded. "Yes."

His voice cracked, anguish soaking his words. "How can you do that?"

"If you don't forgive him, you'll be forever haunted by him, turned bitter. Forgiveness is the key to unlocking your own chains, those forged by hurt and anger."

"So you are going to pardon him? Exile? Life imprisonment?" Lux questioned.

"No. Forgiveness does not replace consequences, but the punishment will be carried out in the name of justice, not of revenge."

I had never seen him look so despondent. Lux nodded but said nothing, and I hugged him, bringing him against my chest, strands of his hair having fallen out, tickling my nose.

The sound of someone approaching broke us apart. Falchor and Mordris looked down at the pitiful excuse of a man on the ground. I was glad both men had survived, but such sentiments, such celebration, would have to wait until later.

Vukan's hair was almost completely gone, only burnt stubs left, and he had major burns on his hands. "Falchor, take him to the dungeon," I instructed.

He saluted and called over a couple soldiers. They picked Vukan up, causing him to cry out in pain.

"And the Legate?" I asked Mordris.

He pointed to a circle of our men, who surrounded a group of Vukan's soldiers, all sitting on the damp grass, weapons piled nearby.

"Once the pale one used his shadows, it convinced the remaining men to surrender. The Legate amongst them."

Raven Bone would not have appreciated Mordris referring to him as such, so for Mordris' sake I would keep it a secret. I nodded. "Put them all in the dungeon. We will decide their fates later. First we need to secure the castle, and then we need to prepare, in case Gabrys and his men decide they want to fight upon their arrival."

I looked around at the carnage, my stomach twisting at the sight of the multitude of bodies. *Please let them give up peacefully. I can't take any more.*

Shani had gone back to retrieve Zasper and the others who had remained at our base as soon as the shadows lifted. The two princesses now picked through the bloodied field, attempting to locate survivors, healing people from both sides.

After the palace was secured, the Waodani left immediately, wanting to bury their slain brethren according to their customs. I thanked Raven Bone for his help, and he promised to return for my coronation. Then I gave instructions to the soldiers, commanding them to look after the injured, bury the dead, and station sentries to watch for Gabrys. Vukan and Sebastien were also to be guarded at all times.

The adrenaline completely subsided, and exhaustion crashed into me.

I laced my fingers with Lux's, who had remained eerily quiet, and led my husband home.

He hadn't spoken since I stopped him from giving into his need for vengeance. We were both sticky from the crimson liquid that coated us. We entered our room, Sol and Bahm, having beaten us to it, were already waiting on the hearth.

I gently ordered, "Strip down to your undergarments."

I waited to make sure he complied and went to the bathing room. I found a cloth and dipped it in water. I brought it back out and began to wipe Lux's face, arms, and chest. Blood, dirt, sweat, and ash stained the rag, and Lux sat still, watching my hands. After I was done, I brought him a clean shirt and helped dress him. I tucked him into the bed and kissed his forehead and turned to leave.

He grabbed my hand. "Stay. Please."

I didn't deny his request and crawled next to him. I leaned my upper body against the wall, and Lux put his head in my lap. I brushed my fingers through his matted hair while Lux wept. I just sat there, his head in my lap, as he mourned.

Late into the night we had visitors, someone inquiring on what to do with so and so, updates on Gabrys' movements, or whatever other questions or information was relevant to staking claim to a kingdom. At some point, I drifted off to sleep, curled next to my husband.

CHAPTER TWENTY-FOUR

P*ounding on the door* woke me from my deep slumber. My head was aching and my throat was parched, my stomach rumbling as I stood. Lux slowly blinked his eyes open, grumbling about how early it was. He was adorably grumpy in the mornings. I opened the door, Mordris and Talom standing in the entryway.

"What's—"

Talom cut me off, "Gabrys and the border troops have arrived at the gates!"

I grabbed my sword from where I had discarded it the previous night, blood still crusted on the blade. I gathered my leather vest, ignoring the atrocious smell, and slipped it over the clean, loose pants and shirt I had put on the night before.

I made the same walk up the castle wall steps, my sore body protesting, and came to a stop atop the turrets. Thousands of soldiers were standing outside the palace gate, with Gabrys sitting atop a black horse at the very front. As soon as we made eye contact, Gabrys unsheathed his sword. I was still spent from yesterday, but I dredged up what magic I had left, prepared to use it all to freeze Gabrys and as many of his men as I could. But to my surprise, he ceremoniously dropped his weapon, dismounted, and fell to his knees. The rows of men behind did the same.

The only sound was their knees hitting the ground until one man amidst the crowd shouted, "Long live the queen!"

The collective shouts that followed were louder than a thunderstorm. I was relieved, my grip on my own weapon loosening, the magic subsiding.

Until we had a chance to discuss and subsequently meet the members of the surrendered army, the lowest ranking men were stripped of their positions and weapons, but they were allowed to sleep in the guest rooms or return to their homes if they so desired, except for the high ranking officers and Gabrys, who were chained and put into cells. The fate of the Wulfrics would be decided today. Before that occurred, I wanted to meet with someone first.

Two men of the same blood, yet they were entirely different at their cores. One was now my husband, but one had been my friend, something more actually. Even though he betrayed me, I still wanted to see him once more.

Seeing him now, I wanted to make excuses. It was his neglectful upbringing or maybe the inherent cruelness of being a soldier and seeing death and the brutality of humans. No. There were plenty of people who suffered the same and were still tender and kind alongside their brokenness. Egann, Lux, and even myself were prime examples. There was no good reason for the betrayal, for the twisted delusion of subjugating people into peace.

Sebastien sat on the cot of his cell, staring blankly at the wall. Even imprisoned, he still kept his perfect posture. I leaned my hands against the cold bars, unsure how to start the conversation.

"I'm glad you're alive."

Sebastien refused to look at me. "I won't be for much longer."

I sighed. "I'm not going to execute you."

He scoffed, "Just my father and uncle?"

My fingers clenched the bars. "They will be dealt with according to their crimes."

Sebastien finally looked at me, poison in his eyes. "I'm sure your husband will be spared. I'm not surprised he would sleep his way to safety."

"Don't you malign him," I hissed.

"You seemed so in love with me not too long ago, and yet you're already with another man," he spat.

I was taken aback by his words. "You were the one who betrayed me! *You* were the one who chose your vile family." I paused, seething, "Don't you dare make yourself the victim." I inhaled a deep breath, forcing my nerves to settle. "Lux is more of a man than you ever were, and don't you dare disrespect my husband or you will share the fate of your father and uncle."

I walked away, a small part of me hoping that he would say something, call out to me, want to be friends, apologize, but silence was his only goodbye.

As I stalked through the prison, a raspy voice called out, "Wait, please."

I stopped, searching for the owner of the voice.

Gabrys looked nothing like the quiet, yet proud commander I had always seen him as. His beard had grown longer and his clothes were torn. He stared at me, face haggard and eyes sunken. "I'm sorry. I loved your mother. Ariella was supposed to live. I never wanted this to happen. My brother made me... it was his fault."

I glared down at him, all sense of pity leaving me. "No one made you do anything. You made your choices, and now you can die with the consequences."

I left him, not deigning to listen to his poor attempts to justify himself. Every man made his own choices and had to live and die by them.

Four kings were present in the throne room. Lux stood on one side of my seat, Dryden on the other. Zasper, Shani, and Kasabian stood at the bottom of the dais, along with Peten, Dumas, Koodsin, and Minsol. The three kings present at my wedding didn't get the chance to return to their respective territories. All the more convenient, since they wouldn't need to travel for my official coronation the following day.

We had gathered to discuss what to do with the soldiers that had surrendered and what punishment should be handed to the Wulfrics.

Dumas offered his opinion first. "We should execute them all, Your Highness."

Leave it to Dumas to wish to discard whoever didn't benefit him.

Dryden growled, and Zasper corrected, "I may be misinformed, since I am a foreigner, but I do believe it's 'Your Majesty', King Stallian."

I couldn't help but smile at my friend.

Dumas wiped the sweat off of his forehead. "Ah, yes. But my suggestion is the most beneficial to our queen. She must show herself strong and capable."

I glared at him. "I do believe I have already shown myself to be both of those things."

Dumas opened his mouth to speak, but Peten interjected first, "I think that the Legate, Commander, and previous King should all be killed, and those loyal to the Wulfrics exiled, but the low-ranking soldiers should be allowed to prove their loyalty to the queen."

I nodded in contemplation, but I still felt a pang in my heart at the thought of executing Sebastien.

Lux put his hand on my shoulder comfortingly. "I think that Gabrys and Vukan should be executed, but Sebastien should be exiled." I wondered if those words came easy to him. I doubted it.

Koodsin spoke, and it was the first time I remembered hearing him speak more than one word at a time. "The Legate would be a potential threat. He could instigate another coup."

Minsol added, his voice soft and indecisive, "I agree with King Sosoni. We shouldn't let him go."

Kasabian offered his opinion. "I don't care what happens with the Legate or Commander, but Vukan needs to be done away with permanently. The soldiers should be pardoned."

As per usual, someone always disagreed with someone else, and our conversation began to drag on. I was the queen now, the decision ultimately mine.

I didn't make eye contact with anyone as I gave my decree. "Tomorrow, before my coronation, Vukan and Gabrys Wulfric, the usurpers and murderers of the late High Queen Ariella Polaris, will be hanged publicly from the gallows. Sebastien Wulfric will be exiled, will no longer be a citizen of Racour, but he will not be harmed unless he returns. If he re-enters into the borders of Racour, he will forfeit his life. The high ranking officials and military members who had any part in the coup will be executed as well as Vukan's personal squadron, and the rest of the soldiers will be given a full pardon, as well as allowed the opportunity to remain members of the Queen's Royal Army."

I paused, taking a moment to look at Kasabian. I had another promise to keep. "All the pirates under Lord Kasabian shall become members of the navy or a new guild of merchant vessels under the ministry of the royal palace. They may choose which position." Kasabian bowed in thanks, but I wasn't done. "And let the decree be spread throughout the nation, that the territory once held by the Wulfrics is now under the reign of Kasabian Armani. He is the new sixth ruler of Racour. Long live the king."

Kasabian looked at me with surprise, and I could have sworn there were tears in his eyes. Everyone in the room, except King Dumas, cheered enthusiastically for the new king.

As soon as business was finished, Lux and I made a hasty exit. When we had returned to our rooms, I sat next to Lux on the bed.

I took his hand. "I'm sorry for not telling you about the Wulfric land being granted to Kasabian."

Lux shook his head. "I'm not a Wulfric anyways." He paused to look at me, eyes staring deep into my soul. "I'm a Polaris."

My heart leapt in my chest. "Thanks for not dying."

Lux joked back, "I told you before the battle that I wanted to kiss you. Nothing was going to stop me from fulfilling that wish."

I leaned over and kissed his cheek. "That will have to do for now."

Lux's ears burned red, and his hand went to the spot on his face where my lips had just been. "You're worth the wait."

We laid down next to each other, wrapping our arms around each other.

I nuzzled my head into his shoulder. "Are you okay?"

"Okay? I'm great? Why do you ask? It's not like the only father I ever had was a psychotic man who reveled in violence and is about to be executed."

I felt something wet land on my hair. I turned my head to see his face. Tears were streaming down his cheeks.

I reached up and wiped them tenderly. "I'm so sorry Lux."

His voice croaked. "There is nothing to be sorry about. It's not your fault my father is a monster."

I squeezed him tightly. "Still... he is your father, and even if you can't mourn him, you can mourn the father you wished you had."

Lux didn't reply, and we just lay there, letting ourselves feel what we needed to, to work through the pain.

"I'm here, Lux. I'm waiting on the shore."

The next morning was bustling with commotion, preparations for some peoples' ending and others' beginning. A couple servants whom I hadn't met before helped dress me in royal attire, although I would need to change into a different set of garments for the coronation. The black robes with gold trim were beautifully layered one on top of another. One girl tied a sash around my waist while the other placed pins delicately into my hair. *The larger the pin the more prestigious the person.* A smile crept onto my lips as my mother's words randomly popped into my head.

Would she have been proud?

I squashed the question. There was no use in such inquisitions. I exhaled and turned, guards opening the door for me. When I walked out of the room, Lux was waiting in the corridor, chatting with Zasper. Lux looked resplendent in his purple and gray robes—the Polaris colors. My heart filled with warmth and gratitude towards my husband. Zasper was dressed in her traditional clothing of Eboc, the bright orange patterns danced across the brown and yellow fabrics. Her hair was in small braids, tiny gold rings and beads intertwined. I felt a bump against my leg.

Dryden looked up at me, turquoise eyes luminescent in the light of the torches. *What's there to look at? Human clothes always look the same to me.*

I laughed aloud, startling those around us, forgetting that they couldn't hear him. I smiled. *If you want more attention just ask for it.*

Dryden's ears flicked and his tail twitched. I gave in and rubbed his head. A purr reverberated through his body.

A crash sounded, and we all jumped, Falchor and Citadel unsheathing their swords. We looked at the origin of the sound. A decorative vase had crashed to the floor, shattered into pieces, an apologetic Kasabian smiling sheepishly.

"Sorry?" he offered.

"King Armani, I do believe that you will be paying extra in taxes this upcoming tributary season," I scolded halfheartedly.

Kasabian pouted, "I see friendship means nothing now that you're queen."

I rolled my eyes. "Let's go, or we will be late."

We rushed down the hall and staircase to the carriages waiting outside. We rode in groups of four, with a large retinue of guards on horseback surrounding us.

The city was eerily quiet, although there were a few premature coronation decorations already hanging from some shops and stalls. Our entourage came to a stop in the city center, a circular area with a well in the middle. Although it was rarely used for water since the aqueducts had been made a century ago, it was a popular spot for people to congregate.

Hundreds of people had gathered around the gallows that had been temporarily set up in the center. A group of ten soldiers surrounded two caged wagons that housed several people inside each, one of which held Vukan's black clad squad. Some of the citizens nearby hurled rotten food and insults at them, the guards doing little to dissuade the people to stop. I looked at each one of the men inside. By my word their deaths would be carried out, but I steeled myself, knowing that their own decisions had brought them to this point.

Lux got out first, holding out a hand to help me down. I took it gladly, appreciative of the warmth and steadiness of it.

"Thank you," I said as I stepped down.

Lux just nodded in response. I couldn't imagine how difficult this all was for him, and I didn't expect him to say anything. With my guards and friends at my side, I walked up the steps of the platform. When I was younger such stages were used during festivals to showcase theater, dances, and musical performances. This was nothing like that, but maybe one day it could be used for those purposes once again.

I looked out over the crowd, thankful that the people had left their children at home. No child should see something so brutal, even if it was proper justice being carried out. I nodded to the soldiers at the wagon, and they opened the first cage. They led the squad of men up the platform and stationed each one next to a noose. One by one the rope was placed around their necks. These were Vukan's crew of kidnappers who had stolen women across the country for the king's sick pleasure. Any remaining pity left me as I recalled the crimes that brought them to this moment.

They weren't even worth words, and I signaled for the lever to be pulled. The men fell as the wood beneath them vanished. Half of them died immediately, the others wriggling, unable to remove their necklaces of death since their arms were tied behind them. I turned my eyes away, unable to relish in their slow suffocation.

Finally, the last man took his final breath. No. Man was too kind a word for him. Monster was better suited for such revolting creatures.

"Bring out the rest," I commanded, praying what little food I had eaten this morning would stay in my stomach.

As some soldiers removed the dangling bodies, the others unlocked the metal crate and dragged the remaining prisoners out and onto the gallows.

As nooses were placed around their necks, one man, who had been a general under my mother's reign but had joined hands with Vukan, soiled his pants. Another, some noble who had helped traffic women for the king, vomited, the repugnant semi-liquid running down his face and clothes. Gabrys looked sad but resigned to his fate, but Vukan seethed, indignant rage roiling in his eyes as he looked at me with loathing.

He had been bested by me, the daughter of his sick obsession who he had tried to break again and again. He began to curse me, but a guard tied a cloth around his mouth, silencing his vile words. Vukan looked pathetic with no outer remnants of royalty. Hair almost burnt to the scalp in some places and hands covered in ugly, red oozing burns that left untreated and open to the elements would fester and possibly kill the host, but he didn't need to worry about such things. I would execute him before the infection had a chance.

I cleared my throat and spoke loud enough to drown out their cries. "Citizens of Racour, today we execute justice, end tyranny, and begin a new era. These men are all charged with treason against the High Queen and the murder of thousands of innocents. They will pay for such crimes with their lives."

I flicked my hand, unwilling to draw it out, and the floor beneath the men was pulled out from under them. A few died immediately with a snap, but the innate desire for air, to breathe, caused the rest to writhe. I couldn't bear to watch, or I would start to imagine Sokah's body hanging there instead.

Before leaving, I addressed the crowd once more. "This is the end of the punishment. There shall be no retaliation against anyone else. All soldiers have been offered clemency. Any violent action taken against them will be deemed treason. It's time to heal, time to rebuild what remains."

I walked back down the platform and got back into the carriage, the applause of the people and shouts of "Long may she reign" roaring a farewell. However, the ride back was somber, not celebratory.

While the execution was taking place, I had ordered for Mordris to arrange for Sebastien's exile. He would have been taken to the border, with nothing but the clothes he was wearing and a week's worth of supplies. I was almost certain that Sebastien would not be grateful for it.

As soon as we arrived back, I was whisked away for the coronation. The servant girls who had so painstakingly prepared me once this morning were now helping me change into lavender and ash colored robes. They once more rearranged my hair, moving the pins around so that a crown could still be placed on my head. Once they were finished, I instructed them to leave. I needed a few moments alone.

The sound of the door opening annoyed me. I just wanted some peace and quiet, which would be a rarity in my future. I turned around, exasperated, but I stopped the harsh words that were about to come out.

Lux stood in front of me holding flowers.

He kneeled down and handed me the bouquet. His eyes burned with passion, and his words were coated in sincerity. "I'd give you the very heart in my chest if I could, I'd burn down your enemies with a single word, and I'd throw myself in front of any danger to protect you."

He paused, brushing my robes away. He leaned down and kissed each of my feet. I sucked in a breath and clutched my chest, eyes welling with water at his declaration.

He looked up again. "I love you, Valine Polaris. I love you not only as my queen, but also as my wife. Even if you weren't queen I would have chosen you, my Little Bird. I will work every single day of my life to earn your heart, and I will do everything to protect it. I am thankful to The Creator for granting me such a woman. I am honored to be by your side."

The wet splotches that appeared on my garments made me realize I was crying, and the pastel purple turned dark where my tears hit.

I grabbed his hand and pulled it to my chest. "Lux, you are a gift from the Creator. Because of you, I am not afraid to go on, to live." I leaned my forehead against his. "You are a salve to my wounds, and I cannot imagine living the rest of my life without you."

Our lips pressed together, warm and soft, and I wrapped my arms around his neck, fingers brushing along his skin. His hand grabbed the back of my head, careful to avoid messing up my hair. My body flushed with heat and my skin tingled as our mouths danced together.

"Your Majesty, it's time."

We broke away and gasped for breath.

Lux stood, offering his hand. "My queen."

I smiled, cheeks hot, and took his hand.

As we walked out the door, I inquired, "Why did you call me that?"

"Call you what?"

"Little bird," I reminded him.

He paused, turned me to face him, and brushed a stray hair out of my face. "Because you were like a beautiful bird, locked in a cage." He kissed my forehead. "But now you're free, and it's so much better seeing you fly."

Lux smiled brightly, and I vowed to make him smile more in the future.

As we approached the throne room, the noise grew. The hall was loud and boisterous, filled with nobles, friends, allies, and subjects all having gathered for the coronation.

A guard announced our entrance, and the large wooden doors creaked open. I was pleased to see that Kalosa and Raven Bone had attended. They stood near the dais along with the others. Shani and Zasper stood on the left next to the leopard and Waodani leaders, and the *Kimya* stood behind their princesses. The men who were previously pirates stood in two groups. Half were gathered behind Mordris, the new Commander, along with the new Legate, Citadel, and the other half were behind King Kasabian, whose territory would no longer be used for the military but would instead be used for commerce and trading ships. The military would now be trained and well watched over near Pardus, which also meant building for their new center would commence as soon as funds were allocated. The navy would be shifted to King Peten's jurisdiction.

The beating of drums quieted the people, silence slowly creeping over the crowd. Lux and I strode forward towards the throne. One of the servants had discovered the old Polaris throne, discarded and in poor condition in a cellar storage room, but there had been just enough time to repair it. Dryden stood on the left of the throne, the spitting image of the ice leopard figure at the top of the intricate chair.

Can't you walk any faster?

I did my best to not stick out my tongue at him. That wasn't the image I wanted to portray as a new sovereign.

Once we reached the dais steps, we stopped. Lux bowed, allowing me to walk up them alone. Most of my focus was on not tripping on my long robes. Once I sat, relieved as to not have made a fool of myself, I waved Lux up. He bowed once more before joining me on the dais, standing on the right of the throne.

A servant brought out the crown on a plush cushion, coming to a stop at the bottom of the steps. The five kings stepped forward and arranged themselves from youngest to eldest. One by one they passed the crown up. Unfortunately, Dumas was the oldest of the five, so he was the one to place the crown on my head. I had wanted to depose him immediately, but there had already been too much change for the country. I needed stability in my reign, and I already had made Kasabian, a foreigner, king of the once Wulfric territory. If I dismissed Dumas, the nobles and perhaps even some of the people would be displeased. I was too exhausted to deal with him now, my body yearning for rest. After I had some peace and time to recuperate, then I could handle him. Until then, I steeled myself as the portly man lumbered forward, his large hands placing the crown on my head.

"Congratulations, my queen."

I said nothing, afraid my disdain for him would leak into my voice.

As soon as Dumas returned to his place, Dryden roared, and shouts of "Long live the queen" resonated in the hall.

I had done it.

I was queen.

CHAPTER TWENTY-FIVE

I *woke up nestled* against Lux. We still hadn't consummated our marriage, as I was not ready, but we had decided to continue to share the same bed.

Lux's eyes slowly blinked open. "Good morning, Little Bird."

I was still exhausted both emotionally and physically from the previous day, and my only desire was to spend the whole day in bed gorging on sweets from the kitchens. Sadly, our duties forced us from our bed.

I dressed myself, choosing an intricately patterned purple dress with white flowers embroidered throughout. I had acquired a new set of clothes, apparently a group of seamstresses in Pardus had wanted to celebrate my coronation with an impressively quickly made new wardrobe. Of course, I made sure to pay them handsomely, despite their refusal of compensation. I grabbed a random gold pin with pink blossoms and put my hair up.

"I'll meet you in the throne room after I meet with Mordris." I told Lux as I walked out the door.

I almost ran into King Koodsin, who apparently was waiting for me outside our new royal rooms. His hair was in his usual braid, but he wore a sleeveless tunic and simple pants. It was strangely casual for palace attire.

"What can I do for you, King Koodsin?"

His voice was deep as he spoke, "Thank you for finding my sisters." His pitch lowered even more. "Watch out for Dumas."

He gave me no chance to reply before walking away and disappearing around the corner. Before their executions, Vukan's squadron of woman stealers had been interrogated into revealing the location of King Koodsin's hostage sisters. They were kept in the basement of one of the storage buildings on the palace grounds, having never been allowed outside in nearly seven years, their only interaction with people was the guards who brought them food and the maids who occasionally came to empty their chamber pots and clean their clothes. Fortunately, they had never suffered a sexual assault, yet I knew their mental torment must have been great. Now reunited with their family, hopefully they would be able to heal and overcome their ordeal.

The other women Vukan's black squadron had captured for him were not so fortunate, most being killed as soon as he "grew bored" of them. A few had been sent to brothels across the country, and it would be one of my first orders of business to investigate the matter and locate the missing women. As far as the warning, I had no time to ponder the strange message that was so vague it would have made Egann proud, as I was late for my meeting with the new Commander.

I apologized as I entered the military office. Falchor, Mordris, and Citadel all waited, standing around a table. In front of Falchor was a plate covered by a cloth, a sweet aroma filling the room.

Falchor jested, "I'm glad you weren't any later, Your Majesty. I'm not sure how much longer Mordris could resist." He pulled the cloth off, revealing a heaping pile of pastries.

I grinned, hands clapping together. "Your wife's special tarts! I can't believe you remembered." I grabbed one and shoved it in my mouth, blackberries and sugar glaze coating my tongue, and motioned with my other hand for the others to do the same.

"These superseded my expectations, Falchor," I mumbled through another mouthful. "Should I make your wife the official baker of the palace?" It wasn't completely a joke.

Falchor beamed with pride. "I told Your Majesty they were amazing. I will pass on your kind words, but I think she is likely to decline your offer. She would hate to not be able to spend as much time with Draque, even if it was for the purpose of serving Your Majesty."

I sighed, savoring the flavor of the last bite. "That's unfortunate for me, but I understand."

After we finished our breakfast, we got to work.

Citadel gave an update on the number of current soldiers, and Mordris suggested on where to station them. With my coronation there had also been a cease to the war with Indo, a signed declaration already sent on its way to the island country, so there was no longer a need to send so many troops to the south. Falchor, who was now in charge of the Royal Guards—a new sect of soldiers that were chosen by the three men to protect me specifically—suggested that their pay be slightly above the rest of the guards, since technically they would be more skilled than an average soldier. Also their position was inherently more dangerous, since assassins were a common threat to any monarch. I agreed to it, and we moved on to the next topic.

I was starting to make a habit of being late to everything. I hoped that it was a common trait of rulers, whose schedules were packed with responsibilities and meetings.

I ran, which was definitely undignified, but I had to get to the throne room. Commoners were coming to the palace to share their grievances or congratulations to their new sovereign.

I slowed down as I reached the doors, attempting to calm my breathing. I nodded, chest still heaving, and the guards opened the doors. I made my way to the dais, past an already long line of people waiting to address me. Dryden was sitting behind the throne, his head visible from one side, his tail peeking out from the other.

Getting lazy already Dryden? I quipped.

Dryden's lip twitched, revealing a large canine. *Says the one who is late.*

I let myself smile before I turned and sat. I lifted my chin, attempting to appear as regal as possible. I finally spotted Lux who was talking with Citadel, but I didn't have time to wait for him as the line had grown longer since I had entered.

It was well into the afternoon by the time the last person was finished, and my shoulders were aching from sitting as straight as a pane of glass. I was grateful that so many had shown up for me, trusting me with their problems and offering words of encouragement. I was about to dismiss the court when someone walked through the doors.

The woman was dressed in a flowing black dress, its hem shredded. Her skin was milky white, similar to Raven Bone's, her hair was pitch black, as if completely absent of light and color, her eyes swallowed, and her cheeks sunken in as if she hadn't eaten in months.

She spoke through cracked lips, "The queen is dead, the queen is dead." It was a silky and smooth chant, like a siren bewitching her prey.

I chided, "I am not sure what the meaning of this is. I am very much alive and well." I motioned to myself.

Dryden crouched and growled, the woman cocking her head at him. She smiled; her teeth were silver. Pure, shining sharp shards.

"A darkness is coming... The young queen will wander in the wilderness," she sang.

I was unnerved by her, but couldn't let it show. I rolled my eyes and leaned back on my throne. "Trust me, I've done my fair share of walking through the woods, and I don't plan on doing it again anytime soon."

The strange woman crouched down and traced something on the floor with her finger, her creepy chant echoing in the hall. "The seas will anger, and the earth will shake. The beasts shall disappear, and the skies will open. Then..." she looked up at me with tears in her eyes. "The little queen will be swallowed by darkness."

Bloody drawings were left behind on the floor.

I stood from my throne, fear pounding in my chest, chills jumping along my skin. "Who are you? Why have you come here?"

The woman stood, her knee cracking. "My name is..." She laughed. "I don't recall."

"You better answer me," I growled.

"Confusion," she smiled, her eerie teeth glistening. "I like that." She bowed low, her back making snapping sounds. "Confusion I am."

Suddenly, a man with the same pale skin and black hair, but lacking the emaciated look, appeared by Confusion's side.

I glared. "And who are you?"

He grinned. His teeth were black obsidian points. What was with these freaks?

"I am whoever you wish me to be," he replied, voice deep and soft.

The man moved faster than I could have believed possible. He stood behind me, in between me and my throne. Dryden snarled and the magic in my blood flared. The man stroked my arm, a chill spreading throughout my body.

"Oh little queen, my twin came to warn you," he whispered in my ear.

I let ice slowly creep towards him, and I turned my head slightly, trying to keep his attention on me. "And why did you come?"

He pressed a kiss to my temple before I was able to do anything, and just as quickly as he had come to me he had left—returning to his sister's side. My skin crawled and irritation boiled in my blood. Confusion traced some invisible signs in the air, and her brother patted her head.

He smiled and licked his teeth. "I am here to stop her."

Confusion gasped, her mouth opened to scream, but no sound came out. Before she hit the floor, her brother caught her. He adjusted her small, bony, unconscious body in his arms and winked. I sent ice to his feet, to bind him where he stood, but he was unnaturally quick and was gone before my ice even touched him.

They simply vanished.

Bumps spread along my arms as a voice whispered, "Noctis."

I whipped my head around, but no one was there. Dryden's fur stood erect, a growl still rumbling in his chest.

What was that? Who was that? I asked, panicked.

Dryden snarled, *I don't know. But if I see him again, I will rip his throat out.*

I collapsed into my seat. *He could have killed me. He moved so fast Dryden. I could have been killed, and no one would have been able to stop it.*

Dryden whimpered and leapt onto the arm of my throne, balancing his large body. I wrapped my arms around his neck and he purred, the vibrations soothing my unsettled nerves.

Dryden, I don't know what to do. I just got my kingdom back. I can't deal with another crisis.

I left to look for Lux, Dryden in tow as he was afraid the strange man would return.

But I couldn't find my husband.

I had searched the entire palace, inquired after him, but no one had seen him since the afternoon. I sent Dryden off to check outside, hoping his keen sense of smell could find Lux. Eventually one of the many guards I questioned told me that I should ask King Stallian, having seen him and Lux together a little over an hour ago. Nerves wracked my stomach.

I had a terrible feeling.

I thrust open the door to the noble's office, the force causing papers to go flying. Dumas was there, along with some lords who had pledged their fealty to me the previous day, most likely to maintain their power rather than out of a sense of loyalty.

A man clothed in elaborate robes and jewelry stepped forward, giving a shallow bow. "Your Majesty."

The room followed suit with bows and murmurs.

I recognized him. He was the youngest man in the room with red hair and a pointed nose. He was a scrawny thing, all limbs, and his smile was forced. Harmon Fernal, a vassal under House Stallian. If I remembered correctly, his territory lay the furthest north. His eyes were as cold as his lands.

I nodded, eyes narrowed. "Lord Harmon."

"To what do we owe the pleasure of your royal Majesty's company?"

Ice hummed in my veins. "Where is Lux?"

Glances were exchanged around the room. No one spoke.

"Answer me!"

Ice shards flew across the room, though none hit any of the men. Nobles shouted and ducked.

Tavian, another vassal under Dumas, was the only one who spoke, "We gave him to..." He chose his words carefully. "A man."

"You gave Lux away?"

The windows shattered.

Ice exploded around me, chunks flying and impaling the wall. The lords trembled in fear, one even fainting from shock.

But Dumas just smiled. "Of course, Your Majesty. He is a Wulfric, the son of our enemy. The man who came for him was quite intimidating, making all sorts of threats. We couldn't possibly risk the lives of such righteous and loyal subjects for a traitor."

I jabbed my finger at his chest. "He is my consort."

Dumas placed his palms up. "Please, Your Grace, everyone knows your marriage was forced, and that Vukan planned to have you killed soon after your wedding. We figured you would be thankful to be rid of the offspring of the man who killed your mother."

Ice crawled up the walls and crept along the floor, the men in the room shifting while keeping an eye as the ice snaked towards them. I was never very good at controlling myself. Even Dumas began to finally look worried. I stepped towards him until our noses almost touched.

"You better hope I find him unharmed, or you will be the one guilty of treason. You know how I deal with traitors."

He had gone pale, which I hadn't thought possible for such a pasty man to become any whiter. I turned on my heel, letting the ice melt from where it had encrusted his legs, and ordered my guards to take him to the very cell that Vukan had been held in.

The nobles tried to voice opposition to my decision, but the ice daggers I formed in my hands was enough to silence them. What I must look like to them, my hair a mess, with the wrath of a thousand suns in my eyes. I would be their retribution, their reckoning, if my husband was not returned safely to me. I slammed the doors shut behind me.

They had all been House Stallian's vassals. Only Stallian had all male lords, the other houses having a mixture of men and women lords. I had been a fool not to notice sooner.

CHAPTER TWENTY-SIX

VALINE

The **dragons made a** strange whining sound. Sol sat, refusing to look anywhere except the door. Bahm kept pacing around the room, tongue flicking, as if in search of something.

Someone.

It was already dark out, so I had to stay put for the night. In the morning, I would leave to search for Lux. Dryden, Citadel, and a few other hand picked guards would leave with me. We had to move quickly, so a larger group was out of the question. Kasabian would remain here, acting as my regent. Zasper decided to also accompany me, against the wishes of her sister. Shani and the *Kimya* would be without their second eldest princess for a while longer, returning to Eboc alone.

I was also acting against the wishes of my nobles and advisors. Mordris and Falchor begged me not to go. The former were worried about the stability of the kingdom, the latter about my safety. I ignored them all. I was going to get him back. I had made a promise. I wouldn't leave him. I wouldn't forsake him. I had worked so hard to become queen, trained to become stronger, and if I couldn't even keep my husband safe, what kind of ruler, what kind of person, was I?

I fell asleep curled into Dryden's warm pelt. I could have sworn I felt scales against my legs.

LUX

I woke up, head pounding. The last thing I remembered was standing in the throne hall. I'd been watching Valine speak with her people when someone had grabbed my attention. King Stallian was whispering with a cloaked figure behind a pillar in the corner. I didn't trust him. He was too snake-like. I didn't believe he would serve my wife faithfully, so I moved closer to them.

As soon as I got close though, they made to leave, slipping out the doors, easily avoiding suspicion from the guards who were more focused on those coming in than going out. I'd followed them to a dark room. Then something collided with my head, and the rest was unknown to me.

Nothing was covering my head, but it was still pitch black. I brought my hand up and tried to summon fire for light. But nothing happened. I tried again. Nothing. Panic swelled in my chest. What was happening? Where was I?

A voice suddenly emitted from the darkness. "Oh, the little wolf. Not so fierce now, are we?" The voice was slick and low.

"Who are you?" I asked.

The eerie voice responded, "I am the darkness, or more specifically the thing that hides in it."

There was a sound of clanking against metal. That's when I realized I was in some sort of cell.

The thing continued. "I am your nightmares, your fears, your darkest doubts." The screech of metal on metal made my skin crawl. "Separate the wolf from its pack, and it's easily killed," it whispered.

I whipped my head towards the direction the sound came from. "What do you want?" I snapped.

Wet hands grabbed my chin, and the smell of something metallic stung my nose. "I want you to give up, to give in. Like your father."

I tried to wriggle out of its grasp, my hands clawing at its own, but it was to no avail. "I'm nothing like my father," I said through gritted teeth.

"We shall see about that."

Finally, the creature released me.

I wiped at the sticky liquid it had smeared on my face.

The creature spoke, but it sounded as if it was whispering directly into my ear, "It was your own people who gave you up to us."

I refused to believe it. "No. Valine would never allow that."

The creature hissed, "Yet here you are. Poor little pup with no pack."

It's voice seemed further away now. "The lone wolf dies. No one is coming for you, little pup."

I covered my ears with my hands. I didn't want to hear the thing's words anymore. Valine promised she would stay with me. She was an honorable person who always kept her word, so she would come for me. I had to believe that.

A wicked laugh echoed. "Foolish boy, I don't even need to speak aloud. I can speak into your mind."

My hands dropped in defeat.

You can't keep me out. The darkness permeates everything.

The creature laughed maniacally in my head.

I prayed to The Creator. *Help me.*

Immediately the creature's voice stopped.

Silence.

Thank you.

ACKNOWLEDGEMENTS

I am still amazed that this book has finally come to fruition. I couldn't have done it without the support and help of so many.

Firstly, to my husband, Minje. Without your kind words, shoulder massages, and hugs when I cried, I wouldn't have been able to complete this book. Next to my wonderful parents, who support through actions and words and never once questioned my ability to publish this story. I am truly blessed to have such a supportive and compassionate family.

Then there is BookTok, an unexpected haven and community. In particular, Megan, Ester, Ruth, Ashley, and River, a wonderful group of women who encouraged me and offered wonderful advice, along with the occasional meme and gif. A thanks to Alexis who was willing to beta read a stranger's book off of a DM. There are so many more who I have discovered and created relationships with on the platform. Additionally, to all the ARC readers who gave me a chance and their precious time.

Lastly, to Jesus, my best friend and the only king to whom I bow. I am only here because of you and all the people you have brought alongside me.

To my readers, may you never give up and know in your heart that there is always light waiting, and you are never alone.